Pouraka

Dianne Lynn Gardner

Copyright © 2015 Dianne Lynn Gardner
All rights reserved.
ISBN: 069247613X
ISBN-13: 978-0692476130
LCCN 2015910585

All characters are fictitious and any resemblance to
any place
or person purely coincidental.
More works by the author as well as video and audio
are listed on the author's website.
http://gardnersart.com

"The sea is a cradle of mystery."

So begins the prose set to a haunting melody in Pouraka's book trailer. "Entities shielding one another, caring for one another, so that those things which are sacred are not violated by strangers."

Mankind's science has unraveled obscurities in our world, traveling through outer space as easily as he explores molecules. Yet the ocean remains vague, a pounding mass whose greatness has been unexplored in comparison.

Creatures similar to the human species, mammals that give birth to young and grow hair, live in the deepest abyss of the sea. Yet we treat them as strangers, aliens that we know little about and in many respects, treat as lesser than ourselves. Abuse even.

They congregate as colonies, in schools and pods caring for one another, defending each other. Studies show that they speak to each other and surely in the case of spinner dolphins, they dance with each other. Their delight is in freedom and I can't help but wonder if the very essence of their being intimidates mankind.

If mermaids and mermen did live in the deepest waters, what would they think about men? Having lived side by side with dolphins, orcas, gray whales, and the multitude of species that call the reefs their home, the currents their roads, the ocean floor their cradle, how would they view the intrusion of humans?

I grew up by the Pacific Ocean. I'm certain that when one falls in love with the sea, it will always beckon you no matter how far from a body of water you live. I think that when you breathe that salty air in long enough it becomes a part of you. I well understand the sailors' dilemma. How a man can spend months on a creaky boat bouncing on swells that rise well overhead, suffering through the blast of a storm or enduring days of blazing heat with nothing but water to mirror the sun's rays. Still they set out again and again because they had a taste in their mouth that was insatiable. It's little wonder that in those endless days of sailing, stories of mermaids would take form. Half human, half sea creature

Indeed. A link between two worlds. Such is the story of Pouraka. Pouraka is not only a romance that accentuates the natural and unyielding love sea mammals have for one another, but it also speaks of the everlasting battle between the meek and the strong, the powerful and the powerless.

I dedicate Pouraka to all the brave souls who are working to keep the sea clean, pure and safe for its inhabitants, and who have dedicated their lives to free the sea mammals that are needlessly in captivity.

Pouraka (Pou-ra-ka)

Maori for *Cradle*

Pouraka

Contents

1. The Threat — 10
2. Exodus — 13
3. Cora — 17
4. Barnacle Bay — 24
5. Amity — 31
6. The Good People — 35
7. Division — 39
8. Collision — 43
9. Impact — 46
10. Ko — 61
11. Pouraka's Magic — 63
12. The Cradle — 68
13. Merchants — 85
14. Tas — 100
15 Riggers — 108
16. What's this about Mermaids? — 115
17. Confrontation — 129
18. Mourning — 136
19. Moonlight — 141
20. Distress Call — 143

21. The Fisherman's Daughter _____ 151
22. Knots _____ 162
23. Pouraka Compromised _____ 166
24. Disappointment _____ 174
25. Distant shores _____ 180
26. Rainbow Coral _____ 189
27. Beth _____ 194
28. South Shores _____ 205
29. Aquatic Specimens _____ 208
30. Lady Rigger _____ 215
31. The Holding Tank _____ 226
32. Change for the Better _____ 237
33. They Answered _____ 245
34. The Foreman _____ 261
35 Pipeline _____ 273
36. Sea Rose _____ 279
37. Intervention _____ 283
38. The Dolphins _____ 292
39. Buried Treasure _____ 300
40. Come home _____ 312
41. Cleansed _____ 318
Epilogue _____ 327

Pouraka

1. The Threat

All life comes to the same end, whether on land or in the sea. Tas could accept that. Death did not disturb him, for a mer's passing was graceful, as is the swaying of the ocean under a summer moon. If his mother had died naturally, he would have taken comfort in knowing she was fulfilling the final cycle of life.

But she didn't die naturally.

Because of that, grief would adhere to him as mussels to the pilings under the pier; skeletons of forgotten shapes crusting over remnants of a once-living creature.

Tas will never forget.

"Come on," his brother said softly, leading him away from their mother's grave. "Mom wouldn't want us to mourn so long."

Tas let his gaze settle one last time on the sandy mound. Ripples of sunlight filtered through the water in the shapes of dancers that seemed to beckon the fallen mermaid to return. Or were they his own hopes, visualizing her as a hapless phantom putting an end to his nightmare? Soon her body would be consumed by living organisms, transformed into clams, sea snails and sea stars. Rainbow coral would grow over her, and colorful fish would hide in its branches.

Tama patted him on the back. "Life goes on. There's work to do."

Though Tas swam from his mother's grave that day, the darkness of death went with him.

The work was seasonal. This time of year, storms in the west uprooted masses of kelp and pushed it toward the coastal waters. Should it be allowed to congregate, the vegetation would suck oxygen from the fragile aquatic life in the cove. The merclan took it upon itself to disperse the floating heap. Some of the broad leaves would be woven into baskets by the mermaids, some used for food, and some scattered to open waters where it would drift again out to sea.

The weeds were heavy and difficult to maneuver. If the mermen weren't careful, they could easily be tangled in the long gangly branches and drown. Unknotting the kelp was an art taught by the elders and handed down to the next generations. Because of the mermen's skills, rarely did causalities occur. Still haunted by the horror of what had happened to his mother, Tas worked attentively yet kept a keen eye out for intruders. A raid on the mermen during a kelp harvest would be a catastrophe.

"Pull harder, Tas!" Red, a young and ambitious merman called out. Red's head bobbed above the surface, his brilliant hair bright against the blue water. He yanked a long string of kelp taut, jerking the end that slithered through Tas' hand. Tas tugged in the opposite direction and the mass fell free.

"Look out, Tas! Dive!"

Tas bolted. Red disappeared with a splash followed by a dark shape hitting the water after him. A harpoon whistled by Tas' ear. He dropped into the seaweed as other harpoons sped by.

"I'm hit!" Tama's mer-utterance rumbled in the water. Tas pushed through the kelp in search of his brother, and when he saw him tangled and bleeding he raced to his side. A harpoon protruded from Tama's flank, buried deep in his flesh. The rope that was attached to the projectile tightened and yanked Tama through the weeds. Above them a propeller agitated the waters and beyond that he could see the hull of a boat. Tas grabbed onto Tama, adding his weight to slow the drag, hoping it would give him more time to remove the harpoon.

"Flee, Tas. Get out of here!" Tama protested but Tas wouldn't do any such thing. He wrenched at the spearhead; the triangular barb cut more flesh on its way out than it had when it penetrated, but at least Tama was free. Blood gushed from the wound and Tas guided Tama's hand to press against it.

"Hold that wound closed as best you can while I swim you out of here."

Tas dropped the weapon into the kelp and pulled Tama away, under the seaweed toward the other mers that had escaped the attack. He carried Tama through the currents into the darker waters toward their home.

2. Exodus

"To stay here another season will bring untimely deaths to all of us." Tas spoke slowly even though his pulse raced, certain his father would be less likely to agree if he sounded too anxious. "We have to leave these waters. There are ships everywhere. Men are killing us. One by one they're picking us off." He took a quick look at the nest of seaweed where his brother lay. Tama was recovering; color had returned to his face. "Those of us that don't perish by harpoons will be poisoned. How long can we hide? We can't even surface for air without fighting through the black slime from the ships and the fear of being seen."

"Where would we go, son?"

"North."

Tas' father nodded. The chief's caudal fin curled along the upper shelf of the blue reef. Slow to move, Henning's age and stress had taken a toll. He stayed near the surface, as did many of the other aging mers, where the journey for air was not as laborious. "There are heavy currents north of here with strong waters and many storms." He scrutinized the congregation of families lingering in the crevices of the rocky atoll. They were listening intently to the chief. His word was law. The old merman squinted at his eldest son, his eyes resting on the wound that was now wrapped tightly in kelp, an ugly reminder of what might lie ahead for all of them. "Some of us are capable of the journey. Some of us aren't. I trust your judgment, Tas. If that's what you propose then I will tell everyone to follow. But I will stay behind."

"You can't stay behind." Tas' aunt protested, shooting daggers with her eyes at Tas. "He's old, Tas. It's our duty to stay with your father and take care of him."

Henning held his hand up as a sign for silence. "No Isa, we can't risk the well-being of our people for the sake of one old mer. Tas, tell us all so we'll know your reasoning. Why north?"

It was as horrible a thought for Tas to leave his father behind as it must be for Isa. But the mermaids, the children and even his brother now needed safer shores. "Dolphins. I've seen them and they've seen me. I heard their voices."

"What did you hear? Was it as the legends tell? Did they hover and wait for your attention?" his father asked.

"I saw dancing dolphins from the north. And yes, they did hover over me. Even Mother mentioned seeing them. She said they were trying to steer her away from the coral reef. Maybe they'd have saved her life if she had heeded their warning."

Henning covered his eyes. "Don't talk of what might have been. I still mourn her passing."

"I'm sorry." Tas sunk back against the rock, surveying the pitiful scene before him.

The clan, which had once thrived peacefully along the southern coast of Talbatha Island, was now only a remnant barely large enough to form a school. Sameri had been their clan's home, a grand and beautiful cavern where hundreds of magical pools gave both healing and life to the mers.

But the cavern, located at the tip of the island, had been discovered and invaded by men and turned into a tourist attraction, luring so many visitors that the merpeople couldn't hide any longer and were forced to leave. They divided their number into thirds hoping to find a home elsewhere. Sadly, Tas' clan failed to discover a another magical pool that would sustain them. His family was dying more rapidly than babies were being born. If they didn't migrate to enchanted waters capable of giving them oxygen they needed, they all would perish.

"I've seen them too." Bella, a young mermaid joined the conversation. "Some of us should swim along the coast and explore. It could be there are other mers farther north."

"It's possible." Red agreed.

"I think we should all leave, not only a few of us. There's no time for scouting." Tas found it hard to quiet his angst. Even his father's closed eyes would not still his heart. "Today men attacked. They know we're here. They want to hunt every last one of us down. Look!"

He pointed at Tama. "Is that what we want for our children? We can carry you, father. I'm sure if we school together we'll generate enough strength for even the weakest mer to make it to the quiet waters of the northern bay. If the legends are true, the dolphins will come and help. We have to try."

"There's a chance we will happen upon spring waters," someone suggested. Confirmations and chatter continued to ripple through the cave until Tas' father opened his eyes again.

"Very well, we'll travel as one body."

3. Cora

Reflections flickered on the walls of the great sea cavern Pouraka, magnifying the light that trickled from the narrow opening above. Cora slid into the spring-fed pool. As soon as the magic touched her skin her flesh glistened, her pores separated into scales and her legs fused into a fin, a transformation she'd experienced many times before. "Ko you'd better wait for me!"

"Hurry, Cora!" Peara summoned.

"You spend too much time on shore, Cora. We've been waiting for you all morning." Ko, her brother, hovered in the water below Pouraka's magic pools. "The plankton isn't going to linger and wait for us, you know. The current only shifts this way during a southern storm."

"I know." Cora picked up her basket and slid across the smooth boulder into the sea.

"Are you ready, yet? Let's go!" Radcliff, Cora's impatient cousin circled ahead of them.

Only a short time ago Pouraka mers had no need for the plankton that shifted with the tide. Food had been plentiful on the northwestern shore of Talbatha Island, but pollution from live on shore had inched its way along the coast, and what sea life survived was forced into deeper waters. Though Cora and her family still foraged along the reef, plankton was a staple they now depended upon.

"Stay close to me this time." Ko took Peara's hand. "Radcliff says the waters ahead are rough."

Cora snickered. "You doubt a mermaid's ability to swim in turbulence?"

Her cousin stared at her, his tail fins swirled with arrogance. "I have reason to question everything you do. You've fallen behind more than once."

Cora rolled her eyes.

The waters grew rough more quickly than Cora had expected. As soon as they were beyond the pier, the ocean hurled them about. Clusters of moon jellies floated in the swells but Cora had a difficult time gathering the transparent morsels. The day was windy above the surface; she could tell by the surges and white caps that splashed, and the sunlight bouncing around in quivering shapes leaving spots in her eyes which made gathering the plankton even harder. She eyed Kaile sweeping his tail from side to side, generating his own current that forced the plankton into his basket.

"What? It works!" he said when he caught the mermaids laughing at him.

"It's genius!" Cora said.

"Cora, wait!" Ko had been far ahead of the mermaids and Kaile, but he now swam toward her, his voice bearing urgency. "Stay close together. There are strangers ahead. Radcliff asked us to fall behind until he can identify who they are."

"Strangers? What do you mean, strangers? What kind of strangers? Mers?"

Though the agitated waters were now murky, Cora saw her cousin and his friends conversing with a small group merpeople. Several of the foreign mers were bundled in kelp, their mats carried by others. Few mermen were among them.

Kindermers held tightly to their mothers and peeked out from behind their mothers' fins. Radcliff gestured and pointed west as though disturbed with the dialogue. The leader of the school of strangers nodded north, toward Pouraka.

Cora watched with great interest. Most of the foreigners were underfed and pale, but the leader was strong and handsome; his long brown hair flowed gracefully, and he moved with determination.

"Stay here," Ko ordered. He left Cora and swam to Radcliff.

Cora hated being left out of things and smiled when Kaile signaled that he was going to follow Ko. Together the two drifted forward unnoticed until they were close enough to hear the conversation.

"We can't let you come to Pouraka if you're diseased. It's my duty to protect my people." Radcliff had his arms folded across his chest. "I'm sorry, but coming any farther north is forbidden."

"We're not diseased," the leader pleaded, his demeanor humble if not needy. "Wounded, thin and weak from the journey, yes, but we bring no plague. We only ask for a safe place, some shelter. Healing waters for our injured if you have them. Temporarily, if you insist."

Before Radcliff answered he spotted Cora and waved her away. "Why did you disobey me, Cora? Get back for your own safety. Kaile, don't come so close! These mers could be infected."

Cora was not about to obey her cousin. He held no clout over her. She opened her mouth to argue but Ko spoke before she could say anything. "You're misunderstanding the situation, Radcliff. Let them speak. Perhaps Pouraka would be a pool of healing for these people. Let me talk to them."

Radcliff's eyes flamed with fury, but Ko held the same leadership position as he. The two would have to settle any seniority dispute with the elders should this dialogue not be resolved quickly. To do that, everyone would have to go to Pouraka.

"Very well, Ko. Satisfy your curiosity."

The young chief of the foreign clan moved forward and addressed Ko. "My name is Tas. My father's name is Henning." He nodded toward one of the bundles on which an old merman rested. The aging mer's eyes were barely open, his gray hair tucked under the leaves of his wrap. "It's been a long and slow journey for our elderly and the wounded. Having no fresh spring water we must surface daily to breathe. That has made our travels even harder. We come from the southern shores."

"Why? Why did you leave the safety of your homes to make such a long and treacherous journey when none of you are fit for travel?" Radcliff's voice was sharp and angry.

Where was his compassion? Cora wanted to slap him for being so heartless.

Ko gripped her arm.

Tas continued. "Men invaded our home and destroyed it. Our people divided into schools, travelling in opposite directions hoping we'd have a better chance for survival in smaller numbers. During the summer my clan took shelter in the secret crevices of a sunken island, but recently we were attacked by men. My brother Tama is not ill, he was wounded, having been hit by a harpoon. Divers would soon have found our hiding place and would have killed all of us. Please. We only ask for a bit of your time and a safe place to recuperate. Nothing more. When we're strong, we'll continue our journey."

Cora's heart went out to the brother, and to the feeble elder laying on his bed of kelp. He looked as though he would melt away at the slightest shift in current.

"Radcliff!" Cora pulled her arms out of Ko's grasp and bolted forward. "If that were Ko lying invalid, or Kaile wounded and suffering on that mat, wouldn't you expect fair treatment from your species?"

"Cora it's not your place..." Ko began but Cora ignored his warning.

"Don't try to stop me, Ko. I'm speaking the truth and you, Radcliff, need to hear what I have to say. Regardless of tradition we can't turn these mers away. We have something to offer these people, so let's bring them home with us and take care of them. If they happen to be sick, which I suspect they aren't, Pouraka has more than enough magic to heal them. Sick or not, these people need nourishment. Look at them. They're starving!"

She met Radcliff's glare with her own rage. "Yes. You heard correctly. Bring them to Pouraka! These are merpeople, Radcliff. It's not like they're humans. It's appropriate to let them into our waters."

Cora had dealt with her cousin's temper before. How he felt about her was of no concern, not in comparison to the state of these weary travelers. Ko moved between Radcliff and Cora.

"She's right, Radcliff. Let's give these people a chance." With that he waved the pathetic school of mers north and Kaile appointed himself the lead.

"Follow me!" Kaile swam with much more energy than any of the foreigners could match, but he circled back around and took the hands of two kindermers. Cora studied the failing chief wrapped in seaweed on a travois as he passed by. She perceived Henning as older than he really was. Perhaps his lack of health had been from the weight of too many troubles. The old man's eyes were barely opened, but she touched his hand and gave him a smile. His wrinkled lips twisted upward in an attempt to return the greeting. Whether he would live much longer was hard to say, but at least in Pouraka he'd have a place to pass to the Quieter World in peace.

Tama thanked both Ko and Cora and held out his hand as an offering. He was a strong man, bronzed skin and arms the size of Ko's. His thick auburn hair had been braided with seaweed and coral ties. There was strength in his handshake and in that he reminded Cora of her brother. Perhaps he and Ko would be friends someday.

Tas held his hand out to Radcliff but was met with a scowl and a refusal.

"He'll get over it." Ko said as his cousin swam away.

"I'm sorry we brought ill feelings," Tas said.

"Only Radcliff has ill feelings. Not all of Pouraka resents helping those in need."

"Thank you. You've saved our lives. I don't know how to express my gratitude."

Tas turned to Cora.

"You are a courageous mermaid with a kind and compassionate heart. Thank you for speaking on our behalf. I hope I can repay you someday."

"All I did was help a group of mers who were near death. Pouraka will be a refuge for your people."

"I hope." he replied.

4. Barnacle Bay

Even though her heels burned in the sand, Cora had given little heed to Beth's suggestion that she wear shoes. Beth had even offered her a pair of leather sandals with bright blue beads and braid work on the straps. But Cora wouldn't take them. The only places Cora ever went in human form was to Beth's house, and to the pier, and maybe to the little convenience store on the corner of Beth's alley, where she would wait and smile until Mr. Cohen gave her a burrito.

Bringing a pair of sandals back to Pouraka would cause problems. Most of the mermen frowned upon human litter in the cavern. Ko said it would leave a trail, and that people would become curious and eventually invade Pouraka. Ko said it was bad enough that everyone in Barnacle Bay knew Cora was a mermaid and that they knew merfolk lived up and down the coast. He told her she shouldn't be going to town so frequently, and that people would start asking questions.

Cora didn't believe her brother. Nothing that Beth did or said gave any indication she or her friends wanted to harm merpeople. The citizens of Barnacle Bay were respectful. No one, not even Beth, or Jamie or Leni, who owned the biggest fishing boats along the bay, ever followed a mermaid to Pouraka. No one cared where the mers lived. No one asked any questions except Beth's younger sister Sasha, who was so young that the child could be satisfied with simple answers.

Beth was on the beach that morning lying in the sun on her brightly colored towel. She was easy to spot from the top of the hill above Pouraka. The colors of the terrycloth under Beth burned Cora's eyes if she looked at it directly. Cora was used to Pouraka's turquoise pools and red coral, but filters in the sea kept pigments from appearing too brilliant and were never as painful to look at as the intense colors in man's world.

She squinted and focused instead on her feet and the sandy trail that meandered down the hill. The sooner she reached her friend the better. Beth probably would have an extra pair of sunglasses she could borrow.

"Good morning, Cora!" Beth jumped up and brushed the sand off her shorts. "You're up bright and early."

It had been awhile since Cora spoke in human tongue. Most mers were taught from their youth how to converse above water but they didn't use it often. English had been taught as an alternate language in case anyone found themselves land ridden in a storm, which seldom happened. Pouraka mers used the tongue mostly for their own pleasure while sun bathing on the rocks, or in this case, visiting humans in Barnacle Bay.

"A bit too bright, I think!"

Beth laughed and dug into a straw beach bag. "You're lucky I keep these around in case you happen by." She pulled out a pair of dark lensed glasses and handed them to Cora, who immediately put them on. "What's up? I haven't seen you in forever!"

"I don't know." As excited as Cora was to tell Beth what had happened since she saw her last, Cora was suddenly tongue tied. "Everything, I guess."

"Everything? Well I have a couple of hours before work. Sit down and tell me what everything is!"

Cora laughed nervously. "It's hard to tell you the kind of stuff that goes on down there."

"Under water? Well, I will remain completely open, Cora. I find your life amazing and all your secrets are safe with me. I love being your friend!"

The tone of Beth's voice assured Cora her friend meant every word. Beth was always sincere. Cora wasn't as close to anyone, mermaid or family member or any other being as she was to Beth. Cora trusted her brother Ko, but talking to him about important matters, matters of the heart, was impossible. He never had the time, or the patience to listen to her hopes and dreams. If she ever did get the chance to confide in him, he either disagreed or brushed her off as being silly. Cora cherished every moment she spent with Beth.

She sat next to her friend on the towel and drew a deep breath. The day was warm and pleasing and a slight breeze carried the call of gulls and salty spray from the breakers. Cora listened to the gentle roll of the waves for a moment, a sound that mesmerized her. The ocean breakers had a completely different voice on land than underwater.

"Things have changed. We've been visited by mers from the south. This new clan has had a really rough time."

"Really?" Beth seemed surprised. "There are merpeople in other parts of the ocean that you didn't know about?"

"Yes. I had no idea they existed. I thought we were the only ones in the world, even though our legends tell otherwise. It was fun to meet them and learn about them. They're different."

"How so? Do they look different?"

"Somewhat. They're thinner than we are. They're lighter in color, with much more blue in their scales but that could be from the environment they lived in. Over time their color may change. The biggest difference is in their temperament. They're more timid, and the mermen seem angry. Their manners are unlike ours."

"In what way?"

"For one, they don't have the same traditions. They don't have a dolphin pod that watches over them like we do. Maybe that's why they're fainthearted. They seem anxious about humans. I don't think they've ever dropped their scales before, which is something I wanted to talk to you about."

Beth waited, her blue eyes glistening.

"I wanted to know if I could bring someone with me next time I visit Barnacle Bay."

"Who? Kaile? You know I enjoy seeing Kaile."

"No, someone new."

"You have a new friend? From the new clan?"

"I do."

Beth's smile grew wider. "Tell me about him, Cora. Is he your boyfriend?"

Cora didn't know how Tas felt about her, so how could she answer? "I wish. Maybe. Maybe someday. He looks at me in a way that tells me he's interested in me. He comes to visit me more than any other merman ever did. He always says nice things to me. He's very polite."

"And you like him."

"My heart beats wildly when he's around! That's just between you and me, though. I'd die if Ko found out how I felt. Or Kaile. Kaile would for sure tease both of us and embarrass me."

"Kaile can be a rascal, that's for sure." Beth laughed. "I hope it works out for you, Cora. You deserve a special person in your life. As far as bringing him here I hope you do. I would love to meet him."

"He's shy, Beth. He doesn't like people very much and I wanted him to meet you. Maybe we could introduce him to your dad. I want him to see that there are good humans in this world."

"Why doesn't he like humans?"

"His clan had to run from them. His brother was harpooned. Other things happened in his life that he doesn't talk about. The trip was too hard on his father and the poor merman died recently."

"I'm sorry."

Beth was quiet for a long time. They both looked out over the ocean. Cora pressed the large sunglasses further up her nose. When Beth spoke it was in a whisper. "If only people could learn to be more kind so that sea creatures wouldn't have to struggle so. Cora, I would love to meet your friend. What's his name?"

"Tas."

"I'll tell Pops about Tas and his clan. My dad is pretty good at patrolling these waters, you know. We don't get harpoon fishermen up here and that's because of Pops and Benson. When you bring Tas, you should bring Kaile with you too."

"Why Kaile?"

"He's always so happy. I think if Tas saw another merman with us, he'd feel more comfortable. Besides, I haven't seen Kaile in a long time. I miss him."

Cora smiled. "Okay."

"Take your time."

"What do you mean?"

"Don't spring this on Tas too soon. If he recently lost his father, and is still recovering from trauma, it might not be a good time to bring him up here. Introduce him to Barnacle Bay slowly."

Cora had planned to go back to Pouraka that very day and get Tas. The weather was perfect for a picnic on the beach. Cora studied Beth's smile without responding.

"Cora. Don't rush him. Wait for the right time. You'll know when."

5. Amity

The sun was already low in the sky when Cora climbed down the slate staircase into the cavern. As she wrapped her bare toes around the mossy rock, Cora pondered Beth's advice. Maybe she was being impatient. Maybe she should wait to tell Tas about stepping into the magic pools. She very well could ruin their budding relationship by being impulsive. Tas was extraordinary. And cautious. Cora hoped their friendship would last for a very long time.

Several mermaids were talking near the mouth of a cave when Cora entered Pouraka. The mermen were feasting on clams in another adjacent hollow but their voices quieted as daylight dimmed. Soon everyone would find their shelf or crevice in which to sleep. Cora was ready to bed down as well. It had been a long day.

Cora descended the stairs and slipped quietly into the Cradle. Changing into human form and back again wasn't unusual, though Cora did so more often than most of the mers. No one but her brother said anything about her frequent visits to Barnacle Bay. She wouldn't care if they did. Who were they to complain? None of the mermaids offered her the same sort of friendship Beth did. Possibly because Cora didn't enjoy the same things the mermaids enjoyed. Cora liked to fish and clam with her brother and Kaile more than she enjoyed listening to chitchat while making baskets. Peara hadn't been talking to her much lately but Cora was pretty sure she knew why. Peara snuggled up next to Ko in a crevice near the water.

Cora stepped into the deep pool they called the Cradle and splashed magic water on her legs. Scales appeared and her tail fin took form. Her body relaxed as she became a mermaid again. She dove into the sea and swam for a while, ending her plunge by settling on a cluster of cool boulders formed along the cave wall.

She awoke to the moon shining its beam directly into her eyes. The sense of someone near alerted her.

"Cora?"

At first she thought it was Ko, but when she looked around she saw Tas treading the rising surf near her. Though partly shadowed by the night, the moon exposed his frown.

"Tas?"

"The tide is coming in. Aren't you worried?"

"No Tas, you forget. Pouraka gives us the ability to breathe underwater while we sleep."

He dove quietly and surfaced again nearer to her. "Where did you go today?"

She blinked and sat up. Was she dreaming? "I went on land. To Barnacle Bay."

"You went on land? Where men dwell? How can that be?"

"Our pools are magic. We can change form and walk like humans."

The gentle splash of surf against the sand broke the silence as Tas floated with the rise and fall of the soothing breakers. "Why would you do that? You're not afraid of humans?"

"I have no reason to be."

Tas let himself wash ashore and slid next to her. He searched her eyes with a grave concern in his.

"Why are you looking at me like that?"

"I'm troubled."

"About what?"

"Your safety."

His words were both disturbing and comforting. Cora resented criticism for visiting her friends, yet the fact that Tas cared enough about her to be worried for her safety pleased her in an unfamiliar way.

"Thank you for your concern, Tas. I appreciate you looking out for me. But I'll be fine. I've been visiting my human friends for over a year and they've never posed a threat."

He opened his mouth to speak, but took a breath instead. Inching back into the water he muttered, "I'm sorry. I didn't mean to wake you." He turned to swim away but she stopped him.

"Tas, wait. Don't go! Please. Aren't you sleepy?" she asked.

"I nap during the day so I can keep guard at night."

"That's not necessary. You don't need to keep guard in Pouraka. We're safe here." Cora replied.

"No mer is safe anywhere, Cora. But I'll do my best to make sure you are. I'll watch out for you as you sleep."

"No! You don't have to do that. Get your rest. There's no danger here. Look." She nodded at the sleeping mers scattered throughout the cavern. "Who else is worried?"

Tas followed her eyes for only a moment and then looked at her so intently that his penetrating stare made her shift uncomfortably. "I don't think you or your people know what dangers lie in wait, nor what men are capable of doing."

"No?" Cora hated arguing with Tas, but with a statement like that, a dispute was inevitable. "Terrible things have happened to mers, and I'm sorry for what has happened to your clan, but not all men are the same. I know that for a fact."

"What do you know about men?"

"Come sit by me and I'll tell you." What an opportunity! This was a perfect time to have a conversation with Tas about her friends in Barnacle Bay. He let the gentle waves bring him onshore again and with a sweep of his tail fin he curled next to her. He had a strong presence, a pleasing ocean scent and gentleness in his eyes.

Cora told Tas about Beth and Leni and the wonderful town that protected Pouraka's secret.

6. The Good People

Tas listened to every word she said, though it was difficult to keep from being distracted by her beauty. Her black hair shone like obsidian in the moonlight. Her skin was silk; her scales glimmered like jewels in a pirate's treasure chest. Thick black lashes framed her hazel eyes, and a dimple creased her cheek when she smiled.

Her voice rang like music in his ears, but what she said brought discord. She was in more danger than she realized. He worried for her safety. "Let me see if I understand you correctly. You can change into a human?"

Cora nodded excitedly. "Yes. With Pouraka's magic waters. All you need to do is visualize your body becoming human."

"And then you go on land and talk to people?"

"My friends, yes."

"Why would you do that?"

"Well, for one, Beth is teaching me things that I never knew before. She works at a place called a university where they study everything in the world. And also, all the people of Barnacle Bay love us. They really do. And there's Leni, Beth's father. You would appreciate Leni. Leni takes fishermen out on his boat and brings back deep sea fish like tuna and halibut. When he has extra he trades with Kaile for ocean gems, coral or sea shells. Kaile brings fish home for us."

"Kaile goes on land too?"

"Yes, of course. Lots of us go there. Ko has too. Not very often, but he's been there. Leni's an asset to the mers of Pouraka. He protects our waters."

"How?"

"He keeps the big fishing boats away. We've never had the same kind of trouble that your people have with harpoons. And ever since merfolk came to Barnacle Bay, Leni has posted 'no diving' signs on the beaches. The people of Barnacle Bay are our friends, Tas."

"I find what you're telling me difficult to believe." He shook his head in bewilderment. How could men know about merpeople and call them friends? More, how could mers befriend a man?

"Just as there are different kinds of merpeople, there are different kinds of men," Cora insisted.

She lay in the sand and gazed at the light that shone from the mouth of the cave. Her innocence reminded him of days long gone. How tranquil life had been when his mother was alive and his family lived in their own magical cavern. The moonlight, the summer tide as it crept along the shore, and the sweet sound of family sleeping. Was it even possible to live in peace again? As nostalgic as this evening was, the drumming of war beat within his heart. He feared for Cora, and for her people.

She spoke again before he changed the atmosphere of the evening, before he voiced his fears. "Maybe someday you could come there with me and see for yourself. You can't judge people without knowing them. It's not fair."

Fair? The idea of going ashore and walking among men seemed preposterous, and yet because Cora suggested it, Tas was slow to answer. She sat up.

"Please? I think it would calm your fears and give you a renewed hope. That's what you need, isn't it? Hope?"

He needed something more than what life had dealt him. Perhaps that's why he was here talking to Cora. The attention she gave him soothed the pain in his heart.

She reached out and touched his hand and his whole body trembled. He drew back, but his eyes remained steadfast on hers.

"You've been hurting for a long time." When she tilted her head he saw a teardrop glisten on her cheek. "I'm sorry you've seen so much trouble. But I do believe men and mers can coexist. I believe it with all my heart. Please come with me and meet these people?"

"That's an arduous request, Cora. The sorrow mankind has caused me is insurmountable. I can't forget what they've done."

"I'm not asking you to forget. Only to forgive."

That was enough. She had no idea what she was asking him to forgive, nor how vulnerable it would leave his kin were he to absolve the wrongs mankind had committed against them.

Her naiveté may even destroy Pouraka. He's seen it happen before with his own cavern, Sameri. There was no reason for him to grow legs and walk as a man. Man was his enemy. Tas learned long ago that trust had to be earned.

"You should sleep now, Cora. I'll watch over you and keep you safe." With that he slipped into the water.

7. Division

Kaile kept his thoughts to himself concerning the foreign mers who now lived in Pouraka. He'd heard their stories and though it was obvious the clan had seen hard times, he agreed with Cora. These new citizens of Pouraka should visit Barnacle Bay before they pass a final judgment against the people who lived there. What disturbed Kaile the most was that Ko, whom he had considered his best friend, had already established a relationship with Tama, and Tama was influencing Ko. Ko had never been threatened, so why was Ko speaking against men?

Tama's wound had already healed. The longer the foreign chief stayed in Pouraka, the bolder he became. So bold that Kaile found himself withdrawing from his friend as a result. Tama was outspoken and soon became a competitor to Radcliff. Though there had never been any physical conflict, Kaile often felt the waters tremble when the two were near each other.

Kaile usually woke before the other mers. Morning was his favorite time of day since the early hours were so serene, especially when the tide was low. He had left Pouraka's shelter before sunrise and gone for a swim beyond the tunnel, as he did each morning, enjoying the fresh air and heavy current of the breakers, an invigorating wake up.

However, this morning was different. Not that there was a lot of activity along the coast, or that anything looked unusual. The surf rolled to shore as always. Gulls chased clams as the shellfish tumbled across with the waning waves. But an energy was in the air that alarmed Kaile. The dolphins sensed it too and acted strangely, lingering near Pouraka's tunnel when they should be feeding.

"What's wrong, bud?" Kaile patted the nose of a dolphin before entering the tunnel. "Go eat. Go. Take your pod with you!" Kaile pushed the dolphin away, but he resisted.

The mers would be leaving this morning to replenish Pouraka's food supply. With the addition of the southern clan foraging expeditions had doubled. The rainy season approached. Soon dangerous storms would rumble up the bay and the mers would depend on rations gathered during fair weather.

Kaile dove into the tunnel to wake Ko and get the excursion started. The earlier they left, the more productive they would be.

Instead of coming upon a sleeping cavern, Kaile was surprised when he heard angry voices echoing through the hollow.

"Don't argue with me." It was Radcliff's coarse demand. "I said all of your people are coming with us; Every last one of them. If it weren't for you folk, we'd have enough food to last us months."

"Most of our people are women and children." Kaile recognized Tama's voice and wondered where Ko was. "Whatever rations they would bring back would be minimal, and would not warrant the danger we'd be risking by taking them with us."

"Tama I am sick and tired of hearing you talk about danger. You and your brother have been spreading needless anxiety in Pouraka. My people have changed and not for the better. It's your fault fear is running rampant. I say the only thing we have to fear is you and your ranting! Pouraka didn't have any enemies before your arrival. Now suddenly there's an enemy in every crevice according to you and Tas."

"I'm sorry you don't believe us, but there's more in this world than your tight little cave. There are dangers that you can't even fathom!" Tama bellowed out.

"I'll prove you wrong! This trip will teach you and your people to fear less and assert yourselves more. I certainly hope so. Bring your clan or I'll send the whole lot of you away from here and you can find your own magic waters."

Kaile was stunned. He'd never heard Radcliff speak so callously. He could see them now in the shadows.

"Very well. I will respect your authority only because we're guests. But not for long." Tama dove into the tunnel with a violent splash, leaving Radcliff alone in the cave.

Though this was not the first time an entire clan joined a foraging outing, Radcliff's demands had been ruthless. Weather was changing and unpredictable this time of year. Tama's clan, though much healthier than when they arrived months ago, were still fragile.

Kaile followed Tama into the cavern and stopped when he saw Ko near the Cradle.

"Ko! Did you hear?" Kaile asked, hoping Ko could change Radcliff's mind.

"I heard. They woke the whole of Pouraka with their squabbling. Is there anything I can do to help you, Tama?"

"No. It's settled. I'm gathering our people now." Tama swam throughout the cavern in search of the merpeople that belonged to his tribe. They rose slowly from shelves, crevices and crannies as he shook them awake. The clan consisted of no more than twenty mers, including Tas.

"Come on. We all have to go." Tama nudged at Tas. "Even you. I'm going to need your help with the mermaids and kindermers."

Tama pulled Tas away from the others but Kaile listened in on their conversation.

"As soon as I am able, I will be searching for a better home for us. I'm tired of being treated as a burden, Tas. I'll put up with it today, but I can't handle this guy's arrogance any longer."

Ko swam to Tama, interrupting him before Tas could respond. "There's no need to go to extremes." Ko said. "Let me talk to Radcliff. We can work this out."

"Extremes? You don't think taking the last of our clan out into treacherous waters with no preparation isn't extreme?" He bolted away from the three of them and waved his people on.

Tas joined Kaile and followed the congregation out of the cave. Radcliff waited at the mouth of the tunnel and when the school of mers reached him, he led them on.

8. Collision

As soon as they hit open waters, Kaile knew something was wrong. The sun had risen and with it a wind that stirred the sea violently.

The dolphins were still near when the school of mers trailed out of Pouraka, and they followed the mer clans.

Once far from shore, past the pier and well out of the bay, Kaile fell back to swim with Tas. The mermaids and kindermers strove to keep up; their frail bodies struggled against the churning waters.

"Something's wrong." Kaile whispered to Tas.

"I'll say. I didn't expect to wake up to an exodus. Tell me again why all these kindermers are coming with us?" Tas took the hand of one child who struggled with her basket.

"Radcliff says it's time for them to carry their own weight."

"Seriously? They're lucky if they can swim in this current, much less carry anything."

When another kindermer tumbled past, Tas grabbed him before he was carried away with the current.

"I'm taking them deeper where the water isn't so rough. This is ridiculous. Are you with me, Kaile?"

Kaile had no time to answer. Tas had already dived, beckoning the mermaids and kindermers to follow him. Before they could form a school in deeper waters, Radcliff's voice bellowed from above.

"What are you doing?" He directed his glare at Tas.

"I'm taking the mermaids and kindermers to a depth they can handle."

"You stay with us."

Tas' face reddened and his jaw set. Kaile saw a fight coming if someone didn't intervene. He spoke up. "Come on, Rad! Give them a break. You know that surf is too turbulent for the kindermers."

"If we don't stay together we won't accomplish our mission. This surf is bringing in food from the south and everything we need to gather is close to the surface. Have the mothers hold onto their children and they'll be fine. I can see the kelp from here. Swim up this way, all of you!"

Radcliff's voice held authority, baffling the mermaids. Some of them took their children's' hands and swam toward Radcliff, others lingered behind with Tas, a few hovered in between. As Kaile attempted to sort his own confusion the sea darkened.

"Look out!" someone roared.

Harpoons shot through the water, and before any of them realized what was happening three mers from Tas' clan were hit. Another harpoon spun through the water at Radcliff. Tama intercepted, pushing Radcliff away. The projectile slammed through Tama. The shaft broke and the arrow dangled in the water from its splinter. A stream of blood dyed the sea a brilliant red as Tama struggled for a moment, his face stiffened in agony, and then his body went limp. Lifeless, he hung suspended as Kaile stared in shock.

Chaos exploded! Mermaids and kindermers screamed and rushed to the wounded mermen. Ko cut Tama free from the line on the harpoon.
Regaining his senses, Kaile sliced through the rope attached to the harpoon embedded in another wounded merman. His wife and children followed the bloody stream as the fallen mer sank into the depths. So thick was the red water that Kaile had no idea what was happening below them until he heard another scream.
Sharks charged into the deeper water preventing an escape. The tail fins of four Mako stirred silt, sea and blood into an indistinguishable cloud, enveloping everything that moved. Dolphins soon attacked the sharks but there was so much commotion it left Kaile stunned. All he remembered later was Ko pushing him into a cold current at great speed, and the look on Radcliff's pale face as he trailed in their wake.

9. Impact

Cora watched with a heavy heart as Radcliff and Ko lowered Tas into the Cradle, the two having taken human form for the purpose of lifting him into the pool, and carrying him to the beach. Cora had confidence that the magic would heal his injury, but can the enchantment heal the sorrow when Tas discovers he is the sole survivor of his clan?

Tas' blood spiraled to the surface of the healing pool, and dissipated as his wound closed. He was still unconscious, but at least he was alive and mending.

"If the dolphins hadn't charged at the Mako the moment the shark bit into his chest, Tas would have met the same fate as the rest of his people." Kaile helped Radcliff lift Tas from the pool and carry him to the beach. The mermaids spread Curing Kelp over the sand and there they laid Tas.

When Radcliff and Ko stood to leave, Cora lingered by Tas' side. "I don't know how to help him. He'll be so despondent when he wakes."

Ko knelt next to her and took her hand. "You can't. He'll hurt for a long time, if not for his entire life. Give him as much love and kindness as you can. He's going to feel pretty alienated and very lonely when he wakes."

She stroked Tas' temple with her hand and brushed a granule of sand from his cheek. How much agony was this merman going to go through? "What do I tell him when he asks what happened?"

"Tell him what you know. He fought bravely. Don't let him blame himself. There was nothing he could have possibly done to prevent what had happened."

Cora spent the evening by Tas' side, pulling the seaweed wrap toward the water as the tide receded. The kelp acted as a wick, soaking in enough water to keep him damp so that his scales didn't dry out. As the night cooled and only stars were seen through the mouth of the cavern, Cora lay down and rested her head next to his; pushing his curls off his face.

He opened his eyes. She kissed him on the forehead.

Tas didn't speak, but his eyes grew more probing until Cora put her finger over his lips. "Shh. I know you have questions. We can talk in the morning when you feel better. When you're stronger."

As she massaged his brow he relaxed and took her hand in his. His touch was warm and gentle. Cora snuggled closer to him; his hand covered her cheek and played with her hair until the two fell asleep.

Fog seeped into the cave and filtered the morning light, whispering the coming of a new day. Cora woke to Tas staring at her with a solemn frown.

"They're all gone, aren't they?" he asked.

There was no denying what had happened, and he knew anyway. She nodded.

She'd never seen a merman cry before. Tears flowed out of his eyes like streams pouring from the rainy cliffs on the coast of the northern shore. She took his hand and he clasped onto hers so tightly it hurt. But she bore the pain because she knew his agony was greater. She wanted to tell him that it would be okay, that he had a home in Pouraka. She knew how insignificant those words would be. He wasn't crying for himself. His sorrow was for all the innocent mers that had died, and for the loss of his brother. She let his tears dampen her shoulder, combing his dark silky hair with her fingers.

Finally he pulled away and wiped his cheeks, though tears still gushed. "They didn't stand a chance. It was a slaughter."

"I know. Ko told me."

"I should have died with them."

"No. If you should have died, you would have."

Tas moaned, rolled over and sat up. He threw the kelp off of him. "Forgive me for this display of weakness."

"Tas. It's not weak to love your family and to mourn the dead."

Neither of the two saw Radcliff approach. Cora's cousin swam silently in the gentle breakers that teased the shoreline. Cora looked up.

"I came here to apologize, Tas." When Radcliff spoke, Cora stiffened. Why should Tas ever talk to Radcliff again?

Radcliff shot Cora a worried grimace and continued. "But I don't think there are any words that can relay how sorry I am."

Her cousin emerged from the water and slid onto the beach. "It was my fault your people perished. If I had known what was going to happen, I never would have called your people out. If I had listened to Ko..." His voice trailed. Cora looked away.

"Your brother saved my life, Tas. I am indebted to your people."

There was still no response from Tas.

"I'll understand if you hate me for the rest of your life."

Tas didn't lift his head, nor did he move at all. Cora held her breath and let her gaze remain on the foamy ripples of sea water.

"I'm sorry, Cora."

She looked at Radcliff. His eyes were red and sunken. He must not have slept at all. Still, his torment-induced apology wouldn't bring the kindermers back home or cause the mermaids of the south to sing again. What good was 'sorry'?

Radcliff dove back into the water and swam away.

***

Only time could heal his heartache, but Cora was determined to help. Their lives grew closer as time passed. They swam together, foraged together and as hard as it was to persuade him, Cora finally got Tas to play. Not for long, and not often, but enough that after a month, Tas smiled for the first time.

They'd been playing tag, and Cora teased him, hiding in the seaweed. When she surprised him, he laughed. He pulled her to him and embraced her.

"Let me take you somewhere," she pleaded.

"Where?"

"Just follow me."

Cora led Tas to the magical pool and splashed out of the sea. Lifting herself onto the ledge of the Cradle she slipped into the clear turquoise waters.

Tas hesitated.

"Come join me! Think beach!"

"What?"

"Think about being on the beach out there." She pointed to the mouth of the cavern. "Come and watch the sunset with me."

Tas was unresponsive but still he didn't shy away. With a little more coaxing she might be able to convince him so she asked again. "Please? For me?"

"You know how I feel about that world, Cora. Why do you ask me to go there?"

"Because I trust the people in Barnacle Bay. And I trust that you've an open mind."

"And if I refuse to go with you, then I don't have an open mind?"

"You've been hurt deeply, Tas. I can understand that. But you're hurting yourself even more by letting bitterness keep you away from what is good."

"Good?"

"Yes. Good."

She had touched a tender spot in him and she could see he was fighting through that pain. She read it in his eyes. "Please? Just once?"

"Are you going up there now, even if I don't?"

"Yes."

She held her breath through the silence and exhaled when he finally answered.

"I guess I have no choice, then." He slid into the pool and let Cora sprinkle him with the magic waters. "I'm doing this for you."

"Thank you."

He took her hand. "Because you've done so much for me and have never asked for anything in return. I trust you."

His tail fin divided, his scales floated to the surface filling the pool with glittering color as his body transformed. A look of shock spread across his face. "I can return to being a merman, can't I?"

"Of course you can."

Tas ran his fingers through the sparkling water as the scales returned and adhered to him in the form of clothing. "It feels odd."

"I know. But you'll get used to it."

"No. I won't get used to it. I'll change to human form once. For you. Only once and then I'll return to my natural state. I'm not making any promises that I'll ever do this again."

"That's okay, Tas. You'll see. This will be a good thing for you. There! See? You're a man now. How easy was that?"

She helped him stand, though he tottered as he gained his balance and followed her out of the pool.

"I won't ever ask you to do this again if you don't want to, but I'd like you to meet my friends."

Cora led Tas up the rock stairs out of the cavern into the world of man. She pointed toward the cliff rim that descended to the white shores of the coast. Breakers beat against the sand, the hum of which was carried on the wind.

"Over there is the pier." She pointed to a long wooden wharf that stretched past the foaming surf and branched into a landing stage for Leni's fishing boats. "And down this way is Barnacle Bay." She nodded toward the trail to their left which ended at the highway. Across the street from the trailhead were the gas station, deli and bar. "Those clusters of shops are what Beth calls downtown. There's a boutique, a market and a post office."

"I have no idea what any of those things are," Tas said. Of course he didn't. It was all new to him.

"You'll learn."

"Cora." Tas pulled her back gently. "Listen to me. I don't care to know details about this town. I don't care to learn about what your friends study or where they go when they aren't here. Do you understand? I will meet them today only because you are special to me. Because I love you. That's the only reason I'm here right now."

His declaration of love stunned Cora for a moment. Their eyes locked; his look was intense. She was lost for words but finally breathed, "I love you, too."

The confession seemed awkward, not because she didn't feel a burning desire to be with him for her entire life, but because this wasn't the right time. Tas was experiencing man's world for the first time. Their discussion shouldn't be about love, but rather about mermaids, and men, and friends, and Barnacle Bay and whether they should be standing on the beach with two legs rather than swimming in the ocean with fins.

"And I don't see what the problem is."

"This is man's world, Cora. Our enemy. That's the problem."

"You're wrong. These people are not our enemies. They know us and they protect us. The secret of the mers won't ever be uttered to a stranger here. Beth and her father swore an oath of secrecy the first day they saw the mermaids on the beach. And I believe they will do all within their power to uphold that oath."

The conversation was over. She'd said all she could in defense of her friends. "That is the convenience store." She pointed to the old wooden building across the highway, breathing in the aroma of fried burritos and chicken from the deli. "Smells good!" Cora added with a smile. "Mr. Bradbury gives me samples whenever I go there. But we won't go there today. Come." She was too excited for Tas to meet Leni and worried he'd be opposed to her eating a burrito anyway. She pulled him down the sandy trail.

Once at the bottom of the hill, she broke into a run.

"Cora! I'm not used to these legs, you know." When Tas caught up to her he grabbed her hand.

"Sorry." She'd forgotten how clumsy she was the first time she had walked.

Tas was gentle, his hand warm against her cheek when he took her chin and turned her face to his. His breath smelled sweet, his lips tasted like sea salt when he kissed her. "If I have to be here, at least let me be here with you."

They walked hand in hand after that, trudging through the deep sand that had already absorbed the day's sun. When their legs tired, they strolled to wetter ground where shells, pebbles and sand crabs made long shadows on the beach, grabbing ripples of foam as the shallow surf rolled over them.

"It is beautiful up here." Tas admitted, but he wasn't looking at the sea, or the gulls that floated in circles above, or the hills across the bay. His eyes were on Cora and she could feel them without even looking up.

"How do you know? You aren't even looking."

"I don't have to. The view is beautiful wherever you are." He slowed and lowered his voice. "Cora, I'm a merman. Walking on the beach feels uncomfortable to me. I have no intention of changing my life anytime soon. I'll meet your friends, but I'm not making any promises about coming back here."

"I know."

Cora led him through the sand to the mussel crusted pilings that supported the wharf, and up the stairs where Leni's boat bounced alongside the end of the pier, its orange buoys squeaked in rhythm with the rocking platform as they were pinched against the dock. The smell of steamy wood from the planks filled the air and mingled with the odors of fish. Seagulls swarmed and Leni shooed them away.

"Hey, there! Cora!" He greeted them with a grin.

Leni was a friendly fisherman, short in stature, dark in color with sun-dried skin that wrinkled in a continual smile. He returned Cora's wave and jogged to them, holding a welcoming hand out to Tas.

"You must be Tas. Cora's talked so much about you. It's a pleasure to meet you. A real pleasure!"

Tas fumbled for words and shot Cora an accusing glance. "She told you about me?"

"All good, believe me." Leni lowered his voice and spoke with compassion, taking the merman's hand with both of his, shaking it gently. "She told me about what happened. I'm really sorry. Really sorry. What those harpooners did doesn't say much for the integrity of human beings." Leni ended his handshake with a friendly pat on the shoulder. "If there had been a way to intervene, I would have, I promise you that. I'm sure your people were much farther south than what Benson and I patrol. There hasn't been a harpoon in these waters for years."

Tas merely nodded and put his hands in his pockets once Leni released them.

"I keep an eye on the fishermen who come up this way. We don't ever let harpooners in the Bay. If I had known something like that was going on, I would've chased them down. Cora knows to tell me when there's trouble, not that we've ever had any. Right, Cora?"

Tas looked away. The grief was still too fresh for him to talk about what had happened.

Cora changed the subject. "Leni, why don't you show Tas the Sea Quest and tell him the precautions you take to protect our waters?"

"You up to that, Tas?"

"I suppose that's what I'm here for."

Leni took them aboard. Cora lagged behind hoping that Tas would ask questions, that he and Leni would get to know each other and become friends. Leni showed Tas the captain's cabin, the GPS, depth finder and navigating system, though Tas looked puzzled during the tour.

Leni patted him on the back. "I know you have no way of knowing about these things. I can teach you if you want. Come see our rigs." Back on deck, Leni walked him to the helm. "The Sea Quest is a charter boat. We take our clients out for bottom sturgeon, lingcod and sometimes salmon. There are limits to how many fish we can keep and when wereach our limits we come home. We don't disturb the natural habitat down there. By 'we' I mean both Benson and our commercial charter boats. Granted, there isn't a lot of policing on this island, no coast guard to keep people in line so we're on the honor system. Folks like those who attacked you have no honor."

"So, you don't kill merpeople?"

"Sir," Leni took his hat off and grabbed Tas' arm. "We have a deep reverence for sea mammals and your species is, in our eyes, endangered. None of our boats will harm your dolphins, or any orca that come up this current. Not only that but if we catch anyone pursuing your kind off the coast of Barnacle Bay, I have a loaded rifle I'm not afraid to use."

"A rifle?"

"A firearm. It explodes, shoots bullets, and makes a lot of noise. I'll show it to you if you want? Heck, I'll teach you how to use one."

Tas cracked a smile. Cora breathed a sigh of relief.

"How about it? Want to do some target practice?"

"Not today."

"Okay, not today but sometime soon we'll get together and I'll show you how to use a rifle. Anything you kids need, simply let me know. I'm here to serve."

"Thanks, Leni."

Each year, shrimp drifted near Pouraka, and tradition was that only mermaids foraged for prawn. Tas and Ko waved goodbye to Peara and Cora early one morning during shrimping season and watched as they strapped their baskets to their backs and around their waists.

"You think they'll be safe?" Tas asked Ko as the two mermaids dove into the dark water of the tunnel and swam away.

"They'll be fine. They don't go far nor do they travel deep, and the dolphins are right behind them. Look."

The pod had been in the shadow of the cavern where Tas couldn't see them before now. Once the last of the mermaids dashed through the tunnel, dorsal fins caught the light. A swift rush of moving water told Tas the pod was close behind.

"This relationship you merfolk have with dolphins is unusual."

"Is it? Your clan never communicated with our brothers before?"

"Not that I know of. My father never talked about it if they had. The dolphins were driven away from our shores long ago."

"That's interesting." Ko had been chewing on a sliver of gum kelp and offered a piece to Tas. "Then you don't know about the changing."

"What changing?"

"There's a certain ceremony our people perform once in a great while. A few of our ancestors have gone through it, each for different reasons."

"What sort of ceremony?"

"Given the perfect circumstances, and with approval of the elders, a mer will change into a dolphin."

"How?"

Ko nodded to the glistening waters in the Cradle. "Magic."

Tas had never heard of such a thing. He had observed the close communication Pouraka mers had with the sea mammals, but never once had he guessed that a select few of the dolphins might have been mers at one time.

"Why would one choose to be a dolphin?"

Ko lay on the sand, his tail fin splashed gently in the water. "My great grandfather thought it was a better, more pure way to live. Others feel that by being a dolphin they are empowered to better protect their clan. Others seek to travel. Dolphins can go where mers cannot."

"So you're related to some of these dolphins?"

"Yes. Some of the pod are relatives of ours."

"And they stay here because you're family?"

"Dolphins live close to us for our sakes. If there were no merpeople, the pod would move to deeper, safer waters."

The idea of merfolk having a pod to protect them enchanted Tas. "I wonder if our clan had a pod to protect us at one time?"

"It's possible."

"Where we come from dolphins were slaughtered seasonally. Now they are no more."

"Then you probably had a pod to protect you. Dolphins will make that sacrifice for their clan, if it means keeping them safe."

"But why? Why would they risk extinction for us?"

"Love?"

Tas studied Ko as he tossed pebbles into the surf. "And how could a mer ever return that love?"

"I don't know, Tas. It's a sacrifice on both of their parts. When a mer goes through the ceremony, it isn't like changing into human form where you can come and go as you please. The change into a dolphin is forever."

Tas murmured, hoping his question would be in confidence. "Have you ever considered taking that step?"

"I have. More so since I met your people and heard your stories. I don't trust men, either."

"Not even the men at Barnacle Bay?"

He looked Tas square in the eyes. "I don't go to Barnacle Bay. That's my sister's fetish. I've told her how I feel. She and Kaile are both foolish."

"So, if you chose the life of a dolphin, what would be your reasoning?"

Ko sat up again and leaned toward Tas. "Let me confide in you. I believe you and your people were sent here as a warning. An omen. You've opened my eyes. What happened to your clan can happen to any of us. This danger is like a plague. Someday that disease will hit our coast. There are safer waters for mers somewhere out there. You said your people divided into three groups. Where are the others?"

"They may have perished, as we did."

"Perhaps. Or they may have found another magical pool. Or..." His dark eyes searched Tas' before he spoke. "Or they may have changed."

10. Ko

"Someday we'll gather coral from a shallow reef where we won't have to hide from men." Ko's fins shimmered in the ray of broken light as he plucked twisted white stems of coral from their stony bed.

"What shallow reef, Ko? There aren't any shallow reefs close to Pouraka." Cora found it amusing that he would have such delusions.

"There are other magical coves where merpeople live. I'm sure of it. Safe places. Just think, Cora, shallow reefs that shimmer with colors you've never even seen! The dolphins will find them and I'll be with them when they do."

"You're dreaming."

Ko frowned as he slipped a handful of coral into her basket. "You doubt the pod?"

"I doubt that it's wise for you to join the pod. You'd have to change. That's silly. No one does that anymore. Times have changed."

"Are you trying to discourage me?"

"Yes, I am. Why would you want to be anything other than what you were born to be?" She turned to face him, his green eyes lost in another world.

He tilted his head slightly and touched her cheek, giving her a smile that only a sympathetic brother could. "There's so much you don't understand. I hope your naiveté doesn't bring you ruin, little sis." He tapped her on her nose and she brushed his hand away.

"It won't. I trust humans. It's foolish to believe gossips."

"Gossips?" His smile faded. "Who is a gossip, Cora? Tas?"

She looked away. Tas didn't spread rumors but other mers had and Cora was getting tired of the dissension. What happened to Tas' clan was real and tragic, but the harpooning didn't happen in these waters. The mers were safe in this bay.

"I only want what's best for us," Ko offered.

"And you think I don't? What's best for us isn't you floating around with a dorsal fin. You're a mer so don't do anything foolish."

"Foolish? What is foolish? Doing what's natural?"

"Natural?"

"Yes. Natural. Is the ocean foolish for flooding Pouraka during a storm? No. So too, it's also natural for me to want to find a safe home for our people, and for my sister."

She pushed his hand from her cheek. Where did he get such notions? "I hope you and Tas aren't collaborating on doing something horrendous!" She glared at him. She'd die if Tas changed into a dolphin. "Where is this idea coming from?" she asked.

"Me, Cora. It's coming from me."

11. Pouraka's Magic

The elders called it music, but to Cora the noise rattled her senses. The song bounced off the cavern walls and echoed through every cavity in Pouraka's hollow.

"Stop!" Cora covered her ears though that did little to ease the pain. Her pleas proved a worthless effort in preventing the coming procession.

Six elders appeared in the dark tunnel, swept into the cavern by the coming tide. Their white hair swirled underwater, glowing like moon rays in a starless sky. Strings of seashells adorned their necks and ceremonial belts of rust colored kelp floated around their waists. Clusters of red coral streamed behind them, clattering as they lifted their torsos from the water. They announced Ko's arrival in song. Drifting aside they bowed as Cora's brother passed.

Ko's tail fin swirled in the clear waters as he entered half submerged in the rising waves. His scales were polished to a shine and glittered green. Rainbows from their reflection danced above Cora's head, a strobe of color, hauntingly beautiful.

The entire tribe had come to wish Ko good fortune, something that Cora didn't understand. Friends and family should have prevented this, instead they encouraged him.

"Why don't you stop him?" Already Cora was hoarse from her outbursts, her meager attempts to stop the proceedings. Yet if anyone heard her, they ignored her. "You could have kept this from happening! All of you! Any of you!"

Radcliffe looked up from his position in the parade. She was certain he saw her but his stare was vacant and non-responsive.

She leaned forward nearly falling from the rocky shelf. "Ko!" If only she could reach him she could grab onto him and beg him to stop. Surely he'd have pity on her and change his mind; but the drop was too far, too rocky and the elders had formed a wall below her.

Ko swam from the sea, riding the surf as it rose over the deepest of the magical pools directly below.

The Cradle. The place of Change. Always turquoise and large enough to hold several mers. The magical pools contained healing and transformation in their waters. Tonight they held Ko's destiny.

"Ko, please! Don't do it!"

Tas' strong arms slid around her waist and he pulled her away from the ledge. She struggled against his hold but he only embraced her tighter. Mussels on the rock cut her scales as she fought against him. "Don't let it happen! Tas, please stop him!"

"It's too late." Tas' breath was warm in her ear as he hugged her. "It's for the good. Let your brother live out his dream. Just let him go."

How could she 'just let him go'? The two had been inseparable their entire childhoods. How could Tas even suggest she release him?

Cora hated the magic that changed the merpeople. She'd only seen a transformation once before and even then the incantation hurt her head.

This time was agony. This was her brother. Her heart sank as Ko slid into the Cradle. Waves splashed and a gentle mist of fog seeped in from above as high tide arrived.

Why were friends and family so complacent? They loved Ko for who he is...was. Why don't they stop this insanity?

Kaile could do something! Cora scanned the cave until she saw him cowering on a ledge, curled into a crevice with his hands over his face, his tail fin tucked under him. He'd be no help. She couldn't blame him. She'd be immobilized against the rock as well if it weren't for Tas. Tas wouldn't let her curl. He had asked her to sit next to him while he joined in the chorus.

The booming ballad beckoned the sea which now rose with abnormal speed, climbing past the first rocky ledge and splattering into the three sacred pools. Salty droplets of ocean lavished over Ko.

And then she saw them.

The dark forms of dolphins suspended in the breakers, spiritual cousins entering the cave to celebrate. These beasts of the sea knew the merpeople's incantation all too well. What Cora was losing tonight, the pod would gain.

Cora's affection for the dolphins failed to deter her resentment toward them. It wasn't fair. Ko should be a merman; he was born a merman, not a sea creature. The pod had no right to claim her brother as its own.

As the ancient language heralded magic, the sea grew more and more violent. Rain fell like pellets into the mouth of the cavern and Cora cringed, worried for her friends in the town nearby, hoping they were safe in their cottages far from shore because no man could survive a storm that the sirens summoned.

Ko's black hair swirled in a halo above his head. His shiny green tail fins faded another shade each time the waves surged over him. His green eyes pierced her heart and sent a chill up her spine.

Tas held Cora so close that she could feel the melody resound in his chest. She detested the song that he sang. The warmth of his body would have been comforting, but this wasn't a time for her to feel good. This was about Ko leaving when he shouldn't, and he would never return.

On the ledge next to the Cradle, Peara lamented. The mermaid's voice could be heard above the sound of the tenor's chant. Bent over, tail fin beating furiously against the stones, she sobbed into her hands. Today was the end of Peara's dreams. Never again would she and Ko hold each other in their arms. She would never bear children unless she too underwent the same ceremony. It was unfair for Ko to leave her alone. Peara wasn't ready. Even if the mermaid wanted to Change, the elders wouldn't approve. She was too inexperienced. She'd never explored the sea nor fought a predator, two of the requirements needed to pass the test.

Cora's vision blurred from both the tears that welled in her eyes, and the fog that crept into the cavern through the skylight. The pool became a haze and Ko a black dot submerged under the tide.

A sudden breeze from the violent surf pushed the curtain of mist aside. Ko's once shimmering body was now dark, his arms melted into his torso. Cora buried her head in Tas' chest. He squeezed. His strength assured her they would suffer through this together. She peeked out in time to see a dolphin spin from the pool and dive into the surf with a turbulent splash.

The pod was gone.

The music ceased.

The hammering breakers were now all that encroached upon the cave. Harder and harder the swells beat against the rock, rising, spitting foam over each ledge as it swallowed the pools, filling every tunnel with foamy liquid. The merpeople dove into the wet torrent and swam for safety lest the raging ocean pulverize them against the jagged rocks. Tas pulled Cora up against his body, and pushed off as the water rose over their heads. Dragged and tossed into the white wall of thundering surf, Tas found the current. He held Cora tightly with one arm and swam away from the cavern along the cliffs to a crevice. There he braced himself and protected her from the vehement sea. Cora wrapped her arms around his torso and closed her eyes.

12. The Cradle

Tas had carried Cora and laid her in the early morning sunshine after the waters ebbed. She felt his presence and turned to see steam rising in a misty aura from his body. He lay next to her, propped on one elbow and curling a strand of her ebony hair around his finger.

"Good morning." His breath smelled sweet, like sea grapes.

"Morning." The words barely escaping her lips. Having changed into human form, Tas wore shorts that glistened the same green and blue tint that his scales did when he was a merman. Seashell buttons sealed his pockets. His white shirt that Leni had given him a week ago hung open and framed his suntanned chest. No longer opposed to walking in man's world, Tas had made friends with the fisherman and here was proof that he was willing to visit Barnacle Bay alone.

"You've been on the beach already?"

"You slept in. Look, the whole world is awake without you."

Cora's head still ached from the ceremony's noise and the pain brought visions of her brother, his crooked smile, his smiling eyes, and his raspy voice. She winced. Since when was heartache so physically painful? "I don't want to wake up. The will to live has left me."

"I'm sorry, Cora." Tas sighed and lay down next to her, shifting his weight until he found a comfortable place to relax. "Perhaps you should try to understand the reasons behind his transformation."

"Does it even matter?"

"It should."

"What matters is he's gone."

He touched her cheek with his thumb, his brown eyes full of sympathy. "But Ko isn't gone. He's here as a dolphin. And he hasn't left you alone." He brushed her hair out of her face and set his lips tenderly on her cheek. "Don't torture yourself, Sea Rose. We all suffer loss."

Unable to contain the tingle that spread through her body, Cora took a deep breath as tears finally trickled down her cheeks. Tas pressed his lips against hers. She pulled back. This wasn't about loving Tas, this was about her brother. "Tell me you'll never, ever do to me what Ko did to Peara. Promise me!"

Tas moved away without answering. His nudge was abrupt when he sat up and nodded toward the rocky beach. "Don't be so dismal. Look at those two!"

Cora sat upright and nestled next to Tas as he wrapped an arm around her. His body had been warmed by the sun while he was on the beach that morning and now that same heat soaked into her.

Smooth boulders shone wet from the storm waters that rained into the cavern the night before, and remnants of kelp and broken shells dotted the stony ledges that the tide abandoned in its surge.

Below, Peara swam in the shallow waters near a pod of dolphins. Cora smiled at their playfulness, but sobered when she saw Ko nudge Peara's hand. The mermaid caressed his head.

The affection between the two turned Cora's stomach. "Why did he change, Tas? Look at him now? They'll never be a family. Why did Ko leave Peara?"

"It's not only Peara that Ko cares about. He cares about all of us. His purpose for leaving was greater than his own life, or Peara's. The two will never have children and that's for the better. Living as merpeople has become difficult."

"What are you saying, Tas? That Ko had good reason to turn into a dolphin?" A wave of worry flooded her heart.

"I can't forget what happened."

"Are you saying you believe that this is the answer?"

"We might be successful exploring the deep, finding a home where men don't go. Members of my clan may still alive."

Cora's heart was heavy. His words scared her. "So we wait for Ko to find us a new home?"

"Yes. For now."

"You're justifying his actions, then?"

That same faraway look Ko had given her the day before the ceremony was in Tas' eyes.

"Don't tell me you have the same thoughts. I won't accept it. I don't want to leave Pouraka. Besides, there's as much danger in the deep ocean as there is on land. Sharks and sting rays and other predators threaten mers. What about the abyss? What about the monsters that loom in the darkest depths?"

Tas rolled his eyes and sighed.

"We're more fortunate than any living creature in the world to live here. Of course they're risks, and tragedies. But look at the rewards. We have the sea to swim in, the land to walk on, and Pouraka that makes the magic happen. Why would you want to give all of this up?"

"You forget what happened."

"No, I haven't forgotten. I know that if you change form, my whole future changes."

"Don't worry. If I decide to change, I'll let you know ahead of time. Then you can make plans to either come with me, or not. It will be your choice. No one will force you one way or the other."

"Oh?" Cora's mouth dropped. "I can't believe that's the sum total of our relationship. Here's your choice Cora! Come with me or not!"

"Stop it Cora! Why do you question my love for you? Do I question yours?"

His eyes were too intense to hold onto. She looked away.

"I would expect you'd come with me." he added, shattering her world. "I wouldn't make the same decision Ko did unless it was essential to our existence. I wouldn't change into a dolphin because I don't love you, but because I do."

Cora swallowed her tears, her words came out broken and in a whisper. "I love you, too, but it's not my desire to be bound to the sea and the sea only."

He took her chin in his hands and turned her face gently, exploring her eyes with his as he spoke. "Men are a threat to everything we are or ever hope to be. Can't you understand that? They don't care about us." Before she could respond, he kissed her. It was a cure-all kiss meant to ease any strife between them.

It didn't work.

Cora loved Tas and everything about him. She understood his feelings toward humans. But that bitterness came from tragedy. Cora had friends in Barnacle Bay. They were good to her and Beth was teaching her things she never would have known. Tas was wrong, just wrong.

"C'mon, Sea Rose." He forced a smile and slid into the Cradle, splashing the turquoise water on his legs. His shorts dissolved as scales appeared sparkling in the sun making his tail fin whole again. "We shouldn't be arguing. Ko's made a decision and it's final. There's nothing anyone can do to bring him back. We both need to respect your brother, not hurt his feelings." Tas took Cora's hand. "We've work to do. We told Leni we'd trade and the coral is still on the reef. Are your spirits strong enough to dive with me?"

Cora peered out from behind her hair, a grin slowly rounded her cheeks and she wiped a tear away. It would be foolish to stay angry at Tas, or refuse his invitation. "I think a swim to the reef would be refreshing!"

"Then let's go!"

Tas dove from the pool into the sea, his broad strokes and thrusts with his caudal fin sent him springing ahead of Cora. Still his iridescence glistened brightly in the dark channel. Once outside of the tunnel where the sun beams danced in the water, he waited. His smile sparkled as brightly as his scales, his hair floated in circles over his head and his shoulders glided gracefully as he lowered himself deeper. When Cora caught up to him, he led her to the coral reefs.

Tas spoke merlanguage, sending voice vibrations through the water. "I know an untouched drop-off further up-current from here that I think you'll enjoy. The scenery on the way is enchanting."

"I'm up for an adventure!"

Cora coasted alongside Tas. Adapting to the deeper water took more effort for Cora's body than it did for Tas', an already seasoned swimmer (seems like all mers would be seasoned swimmers). As they descended the water darkened. Lone gray pillars of rock poked above the sandy bottom, harboring anemones and sea worms that swayed with the current. The scattered pillars became more frequent until a tunnel formed where no light beams reached and the temperature cooled. Tas rolled over and swam on his back, pushing with his tail. He wore a grin of contentment, but Cora shivered until her body adjusted to the chill and she became one with the temperature of the water.

"What are you smiling about?" she asked, suspended above him.

"merely the feeling of being free, that's all. The ocean is magnificent, abounding with treasure."

She couldn't argue. She hadn't really explored as much as Tas, nor had she found anything she would consider treasure.

Spots of light danced on the parapets above them before the pillars ended, indicating an open sea ahead.

"I've never been this way before."

"You've kept yourself pretty sheltered, it's true. You should explore the ocean as much as you do land."

"Why? I find exploring land less dangerous, though both are equally intriguing. That's where we differ, Tas. You've came from waters far from here in search of a home. Of course you've seen more." She skimmed the bottom of the sea and inspected the dunes scattered with Conch shells, Knobby whelks, and a field of red flat-grass kelp which swayed gracefully in the current, tickling her arm as she brushed by.

"And while I discovered as much as I could about our home, you walked among men learning their way of counting the seasons." Tas coiled in and out of a bed of stony formations and waited for Cora to catch up.

"True. I've been learning how to recognize summer and winter and I've also learned some marine biology! I bet I could pass the same tests that Beth takes at the university."

"Seriously? You have to study about the sea in a university? Why can't you learn marine biology here by coexisting with nature?"

"I do. But there's more to learn about marine life than simply living around plants and animals. Beth's been very generous with what she knows. She's studying about diseases and working at the lab now too, you know, earning money and everything. Someday I may help her and make money too!" Cora pinched a leaf of Sweet Kelp from a swaying branch and broke it in half, offering a bite to Tas.

"Money? Why would you need money?" He opened his mouth and let her pop the tasty leaf on his tongue.

"Money would buy those burritos at the deli."

"Why would you need burritos? All the food you need is right here." He sped away into denser waters.

"Burritos taste good." Tas was too fast for her so she didn't even try to match his speed. Distracted by a sparkling white shape in the sand, Cora spun her tail fin under her to stop and reached for the thin translucent shell. So smooth to the touch and a perfect shape for a bead, she toyed with it, admiring its beauty and then noticed the ocean bottom was covered with others exactly like it. "Tas, look at these! Has Kaile been here? He would go crazy over these things."

"I'm not sure if Kaile has. He's like you. He spends more time combing the beach for shells than he does the sea. It's a shame too. He'd find more jewels here than on land."

Cora curled next to a rocky incline to rest and gather a handful of gems to take back to Kaile. "I think he's working on a necklace to give to Beth. I think those two are sweet on each other."

Tas swam into the open. "That's not right."

"Why isn't it right?"

"How can Kaile be sweet on a human?"

Cora shrugged, contemplating on the idea. "It just happens I guess."

"Cora, don't you understand? How can the two pursue a relationship? Can Beth grow fins? Would Kaile leave his kin to live among humans? Don't you see what's happening to us? We're compromising our existence by mingling with men."

"I guess they aren't thinking too far in the future."

"Indeed! I'm guilty as well. I'll be making my visits to Barnacle Bay less frequent, and I'll have a talk with Kaile."

"Don't, Tas. Stay out of it. Let Kaile be who he is. Who are you to interfere?"

Tas curled next to Cora and took her hand. His voice lowered. "I shouldn't have ever dipped into the magic waters. I can't tell Kaile what to do. I can't even tell you what to do. But I'm concerned about what I see happening to you."

"What's happening to me?"

"When your scales turn to clothes, your face lights up like a kindermer finding a pearl. Sparkly things lure you and it troubles me. You're like the dragonfish prey as they chase the predators' glow, unaware of the danger. You are very much like my mother."

She glared at him and then plucked a leaf of seaweed from its branch. "This kelp would make good basket material."

"You're ignoring me."

"Only on purpose. You're being mean to me."

He moved nearer to her. "I loved my mother, Cora. Her death crushed me. I love you. I want to protect you, not hurt you."

Cora tore another length of seaweed off the leaf and turned to see his expression. Tas only met her glance and swam on. She dropped the kelp and followed Tas into the deep unknown water.

"We've been arguing too much today, Cora. Let's stop. I've brought you here to show you something."

Cora dove after Tas to another drop-off where they touched bottom, stirring up silt and sand. Tas circled behind Cora and grabbed her waist. He pushed off with his fin, propelling her forward. She laughed. The speed that he carried her was faster than she'd ever gone before. Soon the turquoise channel they had taken was lost in the haze of underwater, and a mystery of blue lay before them.

"I love to hear you laugh." He nibbled her ear and she squirmed in his arms.

"Stop."

"Why?" He kissed her neck.

"Because you're too irresistible and we're on a mission."

"Oh, so now you're with me."

"I've always been with you. And look where you've taken me. I've never been this far from home."

"I didn't think you had."

They charted the gradual descent of the ocean floor. Quiet and mysterious, the disturbance of current and climate never reached this part of the world, though sunlight still rippled on the surface as dots of light and guided their way along the dappled bottom. Tas slowed as they neared the rock cliffs of an atoll.

"Is that another island?"

"A small one, yes."

"How much farther are we going? I thought we were going to a coral reef."

"Don't worry. We're almost there."

Out of the mud a towering unnatural shape protruded in front of her. Larger than Tas, and thickly coated with mussels and sea worms, the tip of the statue curved in a half circle and its armature leaned into the current. Cora swam around it, ducking under its arch. Solid and cold to the touch, she followed its form, to the chain that fastened it to the ocean floor. Curious, she asked, "What is it?"

"Something made by man. There's more. Follow me." Tas ran his hand along a muddy railing and plucked a mussel from the pole, tossing it at Cora. She caught it and followed him around the ruin. The structure had once been a ship, similar to the one that Leni piloted, only larger and older. Broken in two, and resting on its side, the vessel melted into its grave. Seaweed clung to the rails and streams of kelp floated in thick masses harboring a school of blue cod. Cora could see a dark hollow with a door that hung open, swinging freely with the current.

Tas slithered inside. Schools of fish rushed from the safety of the cabin. Cora stayed. The merman peered out of the opening. "What are you waiting for? Come see how your human friends used to live!"

The passage was narrow and covered with silt; the water was cold and smelling of decay. The ship had lost its form, morphing into a mass of sea stars and barnacles that clung to the vessel's surface and hugged the deep as though it had become the ocean bottom. Tas continued farther in, but Cora lingered behind.

"Tas!" she said.

He answered with a turn of his head.

"I think we should go. I don't like the feel of this place."

He didn't argue, yet Tas took his time getting back to her. "There's more to look at in the other half."

"You've been here before?"

"Your brother and I came here once. There's really nothing to be afraid of in this old ship. I think an octopus lives in the captain's cabin, but he's pretty harmless."

They floated up and out of the hatchway, and followed along the starboard side of the craft. Sunlight danced overhead, flickering off and on as the current moved.

Tas stopped short before he reached the stern, nodding at a shadow that crept steadily along the wreckage. "Stop!"

Cora gasped and her heart stopped. The shadow slithered along until it was directly overhead and sealed out the rays of light. Without moving as much as a finger, she looked upward. A shark circled above them. She held her breath and stayed as still as she knew how. Tas froze a few feet away, yet his eyes darted about in search of an escape route. He spoke quietly in the water language.

"There's a porthole a little way up ahead. It's closer than the hatchway we left a moment ago. When I say swim, follow me as fast as you can and don't look back. Don't!" he reiterated. "Look back!"

If they remained in the open, the shark would attack. If Cora or Tas moved, the shark would attack. Common knowledge had been passed through their culture that a mer could outswim a shark. She had heard stories of narrow escapes before. Agility gave the merpeople an edge, but it wasn't a race Cora coveted.

The Mako stopped circling; surely it sensed their presence. If it would only change direction for an instant they could flee!

Cora's eyes met Tas'. She was certain the shark heard her heart race. He was an ugly creature. His mouth hung open and rows of pointed teeth glistened. Black eyes surveyed his surroundings as his pointed nose swayed back and forth. He turned his back to them with a jerk.

"Now!" Tas said and with a thrust of his caudal fin he jolted ahead, Cora on his wake.

They hadn't fooled the predator. The Mako dove directly at them. Tas grabbed Cora and bolted over the shark's head, escaping from its jaws a second before they were sucked into its mouth. Clumsier than the graceful merpeople, the unsuccessful shark retreated, preparing another attack. Tas sped toward the portal of the ship, but he had miscalculated. There was no hole that led inside the shipwreck. Cora fought the urge to look back though she didn't need to. Tas had seen the Mako coming at them again. The merman's eyes flew open wide, his face paled. He grabbed her again, but Cora pushed him away.

"I can keep up. Let me swim!"

Tas sped away. Cora swam by his side and mimicked his turns, zigzagging so quickly the shark snapped and missed several times. Tas and Cora dove into a crevice between the hull of the wreckage and the sea floor. There they waited in the shadows as the shark hovered near.

Cora's heart beat frantically. She pressed against her confines, and dug with her tail fin into the sandy bottom. Tas watched the predator with anxious eyes, positioning his body in front of Cora. After what seemed like forever, the shark swam away. Still they waited.

"I think that one has eaten mermaid before," Cora finally sent her feeble words to Tas through ripples in the waves. "Or he wouldn't have been so intent on catching us." When she saw that Tas had relaxed, she asked. "Do you think he'll find us again?"

"If we can make it back to the reef we'll be safe. There are plenty of hiding places for us there. We can gather enough coral for Leni and then go home. But we'll have to be quick once we move past this wreck and on to the island. It's a long swim. Are you up to it?"

"I am."

"Then let's go while that Mako is out of sight."

The moment the two emerged from under the ship, the Mako reappeared. Though its distance was greater than before, his speed overpowered them. Within seconds both Cora and Tas would have been dinner, were it not for a barrage of objects thrust on them all.

A sudden pain on her shoulder and a scrape across her face sent Cora spinning downward, her vision fading in and out. For a moment she saw the open mouth of the shark close in over her head and smelled its insides, but it failed to clench its jaws on her. A cord around his nose yanked him away seconds before she became his lunch.

The Mako screamed and twisted violently, whipping its body in vicious circles, slapping Cora upward. She fell across his back and slid toward his tail. Again the Mako spun. Nylon cord tightened around his nose as the shark battled for freedom.

If Cora didn't get away soon she would be caught in the same net. She grabbed onto his tail fin. With the shark's next convulsion, she let go, flying away from danger.

The shark was too tangled to follow. Bruised and exhausted, Cora swam away from the net to the nearest stand of seaweed and watched; the shark was now immobilized in a muddled mass of cord and kelp. A low rumble shook the waters as the mesh rotated upward, trapping bluefish and bass by their gills.

Their cries were drowned by the hum of the pulleys. First relieved, and then awed, Cora's mouth hung open. This wasn't Leni's boat. Leni didn't fish so deep and indiscriminately. Cora stilled her racing heart and watched the catch be hauled to the surface. Then she remembered Tas. Was he in that tangled mess? "Tas!" Cora called, sending panic laden sound waves through the water. "Tas!"

The rumble of the pulley stopped. The nets floated well above her head, the shark limp. Cora glided across the ocean floor in search of Tas yet keeping watch above in hopes the nets wouldn't be lowered again until after she found him

"Tas, where are you?" she called.

A splash drew her attention. Bubbles broke the surface above as a stream of red spiraled through the water. The fishermen had killed the shark and thrown it overboard. Cora panicked. Other Mako would smell the blood and be here soon.

"Tas, Tas we need to go. Where are you? Answer me!"

Cora swam in circles. She had to leave to save herself, but she couldn't leave Tas. It would be sure death for him. Her eyes welled with tears. If she gave up looking for him, the sharks would find him. If she stayed they would find her. "Tas!"

The body of the Mako slowly drifted to the ocean bottom leaving a thick red trail. Overwhelmed with fear Cora scanned the ocean floor one last time. Had she not seen a flicker of green sparkle and movement under the sand, she would have given up. Once the glistening color of scales caught her eye, she raced to the wounded merman and turned him over. His head fell back across her lap, revealing a bleeding wound. Cora maneuvered herself under his body, balancing Tas on her back. With strong, forceful strokes, she swam toward the cliff.

She hadn't cleared as much distance as she wanted by the time the sharks came. When she looked over her shoulder she saw twelve of them devouring the dead Mako's flesh. She also noticed a stream of Tas' blood suspended in the water, leaving a trail the sharks could easily follow once their Mako feast was over. Cora swam harder, relieved when the dark form of rock appeared. e wouldn't make it home carrying Tas on her back. She could not outswim a school of Mako with such a burden. Already spent from her own injuries, she slid into the first crevice she found, slithered out from under Tas and with her hands under his arms, pulled him deeper into the underwater cave. With her palm pressed against the bruise on his temple, she stopped the bleeding.

Back and forth the sharks swam outside the narrow inlet as Cora held the unconscious Tas in her arms. She shuddered. The trauma of all that had happened was taking a toll on her. She would need to breathe soon, and still she was far from Pouraka with a school of Makos patrolling her passage home.

13. Merchants

Time passed. A mermaid's breath could last for days under less stressful conditions. But when traumatized, retention of air diminished. There were ways to conserve. Cora practiced the survival exercise she had been taught as a child by calming her thoughts. She leaned back against the barnacle-laden rocks, and closed her eyes as she consciously absorbed the oxygen in her body. Tas would be fine. He rested unconscious, stress free, his head on her lap. From her perch she could see the narrow slit that opened out into the sea, and the dark figures of the Mako sharks that passed by. Hopefully they would abandon their chase before she or Tas ran completely out of air.

Next to her lay a harmless spotted leopard shark, suspended over a tiny ledge. Oblivious to any danger, the fish hovered motionless. Sea stars clung to the rock above it, and several anemones swayed gracefully with the movement of the sea. Cora could lay quietly too, but she lacked the same peace as her companions. Fatigue and despondency sickened her.

Never had she been in such a dangerous predicament. Never had she had such worries as now. She glanced at Tas, his eyelids sealed closed, unconscious. He looked so serene, like the leopard shark, without a care in the world. She visualized Pouraka and the warm sunbeams shining on her.

If only she were back home sunning on the rocks, or making baskets with Peara. Perhaps that's where Tas was in his dreams. She closed her eyes wishing she were in her human form walking on the beach, breathing the salty spray from the breakers, watching the golden sunset ripple across the wet horizon. Cora fell asleep.

A loud cry sent waves through the crevice, and the sound of an undersea battle woke her. Forgetting where she was, Cora lunged forward and Tas rolled off her lap.

"Cora?"

She spun around. The merman lay helplessly on the ground, blinking his eyes. Thrilled that Tas was awake, yet drawn to the commotion outside the cave Cora turned toward the opening in time to witness a pod of dolphins attacking the Makos. Two of the sharks sped away with dolphins pursuing them. The other shark was pinned to the rocks, a dolphin's nose driven through its gills. The victim squirmed and cried in pain. The dolphin rammed it again, blood tinting the water in spurts. When the dolphin backed away, the shark rolled over, lifeless.

"It's Ko, Cora!" Tas slipped by her, inspecting the dead shark for only a moment. Ko nudged Tas and then Cora.

"Ko saved us!" Cora hugged the dolphin's head.

Tas pushed his hair away from his face and looked at her, his eyes glazed over. "What happened?"

"You were unconscious, Tas. Let's go home. I'll tell you when we get there."

Ko nudged her.

"I think he wants to escort us back to Pouraka. Let's go before the Mako return."

"Mako?"

Pouraka had never appeared more beautiful than when they returned home that afternoon. The light that beamed from above made the whole cavern sparkle with life. The rocks glistened, the reflections of water danced on the walls, the mosses and ferns hanging from above glittered a brilliant green. Even the grass that hung over the edge of the cavern mouth gleamed with color.

Cora gasped for breath as they floated in the shallows, thankful to be alive. She surfaced, wiping her face with her hands. Tas sprawled half on the beach and half in the water next to her and stared at the skylight, blinking drops of sea from his lashes.

The cavern was empty but for one person, Kaile, who sat alone near the rock steps that led to the upper world. He made no indication he saw them slide into the cave, keeping his head bowed, his hands folded on his lap.

"It must be midday." Tas shielded his eyes from the sun.

"I'm surprised it isn't later than that. We were held up in that crevice all morning."

"We were? I can't remember a thing that happened," he finally admitted.

Cora wondered if she looked as exhausted as he did. She pushed her wet hair over her shoulder. "I'm not surprised. You were unconscious."

"I was? From what?"

"The nets that were dropped had heavy weights on them. One hit me and I think one must have knocked you out."

"Weights?"

"They were powerful, like rocks falling from a volcano. Look, one made a gash on my shoulder."

"Come here." Tas sat up as Cora scooted closer. He inspected the wound and even though he was gentle, she cringed when he touched her. "That needs tending! Come near the pool."

They floated on the next wave and when it crested they grabbed onto the rock shelf surrounding the pool, lifting themselves to the Cradle's ledge.

"If that weight had hit you on the head, neither one of us would have made it home. Let me soak that." Tas' strong arms lifted Cora into the pool. She hadn't realized how weak the adventure had made her until she felt his arms supporting her. His hold was warm. Reassuring. He slowly lowered her into the pool. "So tell me about those weights. How were they attached to the nets? Did you see them?"

With cupped hands he scooped up the magical waters and let the cool droplets stream between his fingers onto her shoulder. Instantly the pain lessened. He repeated the process slowly and gently. With each application the swelling eased and the flesh healed.

"Yes, I saw them. They were large and heavy and slammed to the bottom of the sea. The nets were equally bulky and threatening and stretched until I could no longer see their ends. How far, I couldn't tell you. Once the weights hit bottom, the nets started moving, ensnaring everything inside. I was cut off from the shark because of the nets, but what the nets did was horrible! The Mako panicked and thrashed about wildly. Black cord wrapped around dozens of schools of fish. The poor things fought and cried, caught in between the gaps by their gills, helplessly struggling to get free and all the while being pulled to the surface."

"Gill nets. Didn't Leni say he would protect us? What happened? Where was Leni? These waters are too rich with delicate creatures to be dredged so indiscriminately." Tas said.

"I don't know where Leni was."

Tas rubbed her shoulder and then kissed where the injury had been. "There. All better!"

Cora smiled and stroked his face. "Thank you. I was so worried that I had lost you."

"Tell me more."

"You'd been knocked out by the weights, I guess, and you were rolling in the sand when I found you. Completely out of it, I might add." Cora dripped the magical water on his temple. Instantly the bruised flesh lightened in color.

"So that's what this knot is?"

"You were bleeding, leaving a savory trail for those sharks."

"How did we escape?"

"I swam you to safety on my back."

"With sharks chasing you?"

She nodded.

"I'm indebted to you for your heroism."

"What was I going to do? Leave you? You are the world to me, Tas. I feel as though we are one."

Tas kissed her neck. "We are. Forever."

A slight cough took them by surprise.

"Excuse me." Kaile stood over them, a sheepish grin on his face, and his hands in the pockets of his shorts. He forced another cough. "Sorry, I didn't mean to interrupt, but the sun is high and if we don't leave soon we might miss Leni. He was expecting us this morning. Trade? Remember?"

"I remember, Kaile. But things didn't go the way we expected. We have nothing to trade. We ... we were detained." Tas squinted up at Kaile.

The sun was bright behind the young, lanky merman's back. His sandy hair hung over his face and he shook it away. "I have extra. I went diving this morning after you left. I thought you'd be down at the reef too, but I didn't see you, so I harvested some of the coral and came back. I guess I took more than I should have. You're welcome to half of it."

"Thank you, Kaile." Tas peeked at Cora.

"See!" She nudged him. "You like going to Barnacle Bay."

"I like seeing Leni. He's a wise man. Without Leni we'd never know what kind of vile things men are doing down south. I wish he could patrol beyond the bay."

Cora wished that as well, though she didn't add to Tas' doubt. "He does his best."

"Let's go. Leni always has a bite or two of some tasty fish that we merpeople are too slow to catch." Kaile said.

Cora was the first to slide into the magic pool. Scales swirled with the stir of the water, floating briefly like gems freed from their bezels, and then clamping as magnets to her skin, wrapping around her newly formed shape as pants and a tank top. Tas dove and quickly changed into human form, grabbing his shirt from the rock shelf as they exited the cave.

The three climbed up the rocky cavern and out the skylight mouth of the cave. Kaile, usually quiet, his woven seaweed pack swung over his back, talked the entire hike.

"I'm sorry about avoiding everyone yesterday during the ceremony. I was pretty upset last night. I mean it really hurt me what Ko did. I'd been angry with him since the first day he made his decision and we didn't get along well after that. Still, I don't think the finality of his change really hit home until I saw him swimming in the water last night. It's a lot to handle."

"You don't need to explain." Tas patted him on the back.

Cora followed Tas and Kaile from the cavern into the world of man and the bright light of a midday sun. The narrow mouth of Pouraka opened to a rocky ledge that stood high above the sea. It had become Cora's favorite place to view the ocean. Here she could pretend she owned the world.

Cora took a deep breath of salty air as it blew against her face. Always so refreshing! Her eyes took in the turquoise sea, the puffy white clouds and fog rolling in the distance. To the west the purple mountains formed the bay that quieted their stretch of the island. And when she turned south, green hills trundled gently off into the horizon. Nearer to them nestled the quiet little town of Barnacle Bay. Some of the houses were painted with blues and yellows, some with red trim, but most were gray seasoned wood laced with vines and baskets and colorful wheels that spun in the wind. The road wound through the town like a ribbon of seaweed swirling in the tide, and a few cars bounced sunlight off their windshields. This was life! With the ownership of both the land and the sea, what other creature on earth was so fortunate and so rich?

Cora listened to Kaile's ramblings and wished he'd stop talking about her brother, especially in front of Tas. Neither of them had suffered like Tas had. Kaile's chatter rang intrusive. She peered at Tas who was exceptionally patient and nodded occasionally.

"He was my mentor, you know? I mean, everything I learned about life I learned from Ko, both on land and in the sea. I don't know how to take it." He brushed his sandy hair out of his face and sheepishly nodded at Cora. His blue eyes glistened behind his blond lashes. "You know what I mean. He was your brother."

"Yeah." Cora mumbled. "He's still my brother. Look Kaile, if it's any consolation, Ko saved our lives this morning. So I guess that's reason enough to forgive him. And if I can forgive him, than you should too." She smiled at Kaile, though it wasn't easy. "I'm good with it."

"No lie? He actually saved your lives? That's what was going on while I was gathering coral? Where were you? What happened?"

Cora and Tas took turns telling the tale as they walked down the grassy footpath. Kaile listened intently, absorbing every word that painted his friend as a hero.

"That's Ko, all right. He's always there when you need him the most. He's still one of us!" Kaile concluded.

"You could put it that way, yes." Though it sounded awkward, Cora agreed.

Tas led Cora and Kaile away from the road and down a set of stairs onto the sand. The dip onto the beach blocked the view of town.

"The road is quicker," Cora argued.

"I don't want to take the road." Tas took her hand. "The more we are seen in town the more questions people will ask. Eventually they'll ask to see Pouraka."

"They don't know about Pouraka."

"They know we live somewhere."

"I agree with Cora, Tas." Kaile stopped and grabbed a handful of sand at his feet, letting the granules trickle through his fingers until a cluster of bleached seashells were all that remained in his palm. He quickly slipped them into his pocket and jogged to catch up. "I spend lots of time with these people and I don't think their curiosity goes beyond being friends. I like them, too. I'd like to spend more time here. I've been seriously thinking about asking Leni if I can be on his crew. More than that I'd really like to go on Benson's fishing tours."

"You aren't serious!" Tas' voice was sharp as he dug his feet into the sand and turned to confront Kaile.

An argument was not what they needed, not now. Cora took Tas' hand. "Tas! Don't be mad at Kaile. Let's keep our voices down or they'll hear us on the wharf. Do you really want an audience? Come on." Cora didn't wait for an answer but ran ahead to the stairwell and jogged up the old steps, bleached and worn from the wind. There she waited and watched Leni's crew prepare the vessels for the day's voyage, hoping Tas and Kaile would forget their squabble and follow. When the two mermen joined her she skipped to Leni's boat.

"Leni!"

Leni waved to her and pulled his cap tighter onto his head. "Well look who's come to wish us luck!"

"We have some wares for you."

"Come aboard!" He waved the three on deck and met them by the helm. "We'll be taking off in about an hour but I have time to negotiate with three of my favorite young people." He smiled at Cora. "Let's see what you brought."

The merpeople followed Leni into the cabin where Leni's daughter Beth stood by the hatchway and greeted Cora with a hug. "So good to see you! I wish I weren't on my way to the city. I'd stay and talk."

"I'll come visit you next week, Beth. That's all right, isn't it?"

"Of course, Cora I'll be looking forward to it. We can make tacos." Beth nodded a greeting to Tas.

When Kaile stepped into the cabin Cora heard Beth whisper. "Hi Kaile."

"Hi," he returned. "How's the prettiest girl in Barnacle Bay doing?"

Tas turned sharply but Cora gave a tug on his hand and scowled at him. It was none of his business how Kaile and Beth felt about each other.

"Sit down." Leni motioned to the table, unaware of the drama taking place.

Quarters were tight but comfortable in the cabin. With room for only a sink and a table with a bench that curved around it,

Cora scooted across the cushions and Tas followed her. Leni sat at the other end and Kaile set his seaweed pack on the table in front of them. He pulled out two bundles of cloth, pushing one toward Tas.

Before he sat down, Kaile unwrapped his bundle. Several delicate coral branches glistened with color and he set them carefully on the table. He looked up with a grin spreading across his face. The old fisherman released a low whistle.

"There aren't many of these. Funny you can't find them anywhere else but this special reef where..."

Cora's eyes sprung wide. He dared not tell Leni their secret. Rainbow coral only grew near a magic spring and as far as anyone knew, Pouraka bore the only magic pools that existed anymore. "I was careful not to thin them too fine." He looked up at Leni. "We haven't brought you anything this precious in a long time, Leni. I was hoping I could work out a trade with you."

Leni nodded as he touched the coral with his fingertips. Without saying anything he stood and shut the hatch, sealing out any eavesdroppers and then returned to the table. "I know you kids don't have any idea what this sort of thing is worth to us." His tone roused a fear in Cora. "Don't go showing this coral to anyone else, you hear?"

Kaile laughed nervously. "Why not?"

"Well, because folks will be all over you wanting to know where it came from. There are stories about this stuff. Legends. Tales that link rainbow coral to pirates, sunken ships and ..." Leni studied each of them, catching their eyes with his. "And mermaids."

Tas sat back with his arms crossed as he studied Kaile's reaction.

"If you cherish that sea bottom of yours, and I know you do, you don't want that kind of invasion, let me tell you. The folks here at Barnacle Bay respect you and have sworn to protect you and your culture. You know that. But we can't keep big industry out if they think you have a commodity as precious as a rare coral. And if that commodity has a legend about merpeople behind it, well, then you're asking for real trouble."

Kaile sat down, his shoulders sank and a pout stiffened his face. "Then you don't want to trade?"

"I didn't say that." Leni fingered one of the pieces again. "What do you want for only one piece? Fish? I can get you plenty of fish."

"I want to go out fishing with you. Actually I want to go out fishing on Benson's tour boat, the one he takes to South Point. I want to be part of the crew on the big boat!"

"Kaile!" Tas' mouth flew open. "You can't do that!"

"Why not? Why can't I do that? I have every right to learn a trade. I've been thinking really hard ever since Ko..."

"Stop it!" Cora shouted. How dare Kaile reveal a sacred ceremony to a human? Even though she liked people, she knew that was wrong. "Stop thinking of yourself, Kaile. We need the fish. We'll trade for fish."

Kaile's face reddened. "You have your own bundle that I gave you."

"Settle down, kids!" Leni raised his hand, his eyes wide. "No need to get upset. I never pry into your business. That's why I'll tell you right now, Kaile, as much as we like you, there's no going with Benson. It isn't going to happen." He shot Tas a knowing look, and then his voice softened as he talked to the sandy haired merman. "Not because we don't think you can do the job. You're a good hand and we could use you. If you want to go with me, I'm taking a couple of fellas out sturgeon fishing tonight and you're welcome to come along. We'll probably need help reeling in the big ones. But you can't go with Benson. I'm not sending you south. Now as for fish, we have some for you to take back. Barracuda this week. We had a good catch this morning. That works, eh Tas?"

Tas nodded, still observing Kaile's reactions.

The fisherman took one piece of coral, pushing the rest of the bundle back to Kaile. "Hang on to that. Maybe something else will come up. You never know."

Kaile glared at Tas as he took both of the bundles from the table. Leni rose. "I don't mean to get you kids riled against each other."

"It's okay, Leni. It's not your fault. We had a hard night last night." Cora gave both of the mermen a scowl. "We lost something really special to us."

Leni nodded. He could never guess what she was talking about, but his grimace showed his concern. "I heard the sirens singing in the storm. I worry about you kids on nights like that."

"Thanks, Leni." Tas nodded, his frown grave. Kaile left the cabin and stomped up the stairs, but Cora stopped long enough to see the fisherman grab Tas' arm.

"That boy can't go on the fishing tours with Benson. The south end is growing faster than coconuts fall in a hurricane and Ocean Bend is selling out to the oil riggers. Strangers from the mainland have settled in. They're even building a new marina. It won't be long before the commercial guys start coming up this way. Already I've seen a suspicious fishing boat past the bay. You folks need to stay low key and as far away from the south point as possible."

"Really? Fishermen?"

Leni nodded with a scowl.

"They wouldn't happen to have a gill net would they?" Tas asked.

Leni stared at him with his mouth open. "They better not! If I see them again, I'll motor out that way and check on it."

14. Tas

Moonlight shone through the skylight, creating a haunting blue glow in the cavern. Cora was fast asleep but Tas lay staring at the stars. The tide was out and he could hear the sound of the surf in the distance outside the cave. Other merpeople slept on the rocks, the sandy inlet, in crevices and adjacent caves. Kaile sat at the stairs looking out at the moon.

It was time to talk. Tas slid carefully over the damp rocks and scooted next to Kaile. The young man brushed his hair behind his ears and gave Tas a quick glance, though it was clear he didn't want to share his thoughts.

"You're still in human form."

Kaile folded his legs under him. "I'm never going to do what Ko did. Never."

"That's not a requirement for being a merman." Tas assured him.

"I don't see why I can't stay this way. I don't need to swim. I don't need to live underwater."

Kaile's pain was so evident, Tas chose to listen to him rather than argue. He made himself comfortable against the rocks and gazed at the same moon that held Kaile's attention.

"I could be a fisherman. No one would ever know I was born a merman. I don't ever have to change back to a half fish. You know?" His blue eyes met Tas' though it was doubtful he was seeking an answer. "You didn't have to tell Leni I shouldn't go with Benson. You could have stayed out of it."

"Going to Ocean Bend is not a good idea."

"Why? What do you think will happen?"

Tas shrugged. "That place is dangerous."

Kaile spat on the ground, his violent reaction surprised Tas. "I saw what happened the day your people died. But you can't judge all humans by one event. That was a fluke. And your clan didn't all die by man's hands if you remember. There are other predators out there."

"I remember." Tas pulled away from Kaile's piercing stare. His voice softened. "But I've seen more than that 'fluke'." The word hurt. Kaile's anger hurt. "I'm not trying to spread terror. I'm trying to caution you."

Kaile didn't argue but his sigh was abrasive.

"Cora tells me you and Beth are developing an interest in each other."

"Leave Beth out of this."

Kaile's retort was so hostile that Tas held his tongue.

"What? You're afraid of a merman and a girl falling in love?"

"It would cause complications."

"Like what?"

"Think about it Kaile." Though he was certain Kaile would not dwell on any negative repercussions that might occur from having a relationship with a human, Tas let the matter rest. Cora had warned him not to interfere. Tas let another silent moment pass before he continued. "Why would you want to spend so much time with men?"

"They're intelligent. They do things we can't do. They invent things and make things we don't have a clue how to make. Ships!" He scooted up against the rocks, his arms folded across his chest. "They make ships."

"We don't need ships."

"Depth finders."

Tas peered at him. "Surely you jest."

"Airplanes. Trucks."

Tas sighed. "We don't need mechanical things for our way of life. We're sea creatures, Kaile. Merpeople. And the dolphins..."

"Don't tell me about dolphins." Kaile's retort was quick and piercing, his lips bent in a sneer.

Tas took a deep breath. "Okay. I understand what Ko did is too fresh in your heart. Don't stay bitter over his changing, okay?"

"I'm not." Kaile's eyes narrowed. "You aren't part of our clan, Tas. You and your family came here from the south and ever since then you've had a big influence on Pouraka and on our traditions."

"You think I had an influence on Ko's transformation?"

"Yeah, I do. Before your people came, no one in our clan ever transformed because they wanted to. Ask Cora."

"I know that."

"Do you? You talked to Ko about changing, didn't you?"

"We had a conversation. But it was Ko explaining the ceremony to me. I'd never heard of it before."

"Likely."

"I don't lie, Kaile."

"In any case, your fear mongering has not done anything for Pouraka's safety. And as far as I can see your tactics are off. If you trusted men more, they'd be more likely to be kind to you."

"You think that? You should know what happened to my mother. Maybe it will give you some insight as to how much you can trust a human."

Kaile didn't answer; he only stared at the moon again. Tas took his silence as an invitation to continue. "This isn't a pleasant story, but if I can save you from the evil of men, the pain is worth it."

"I don't need any stories."

"No. You need the truth." Tas took a deep breath before he began. "My mother was a beautiful mermaid. As pretty as any you've ever seen. As pretty as Cora. As pretty as Beth."

Kaile glimpsed at him but remained silent.

"My mother loved to visit the atoll and had a special fondness for the shallows. She never sensed any danger swimming in the same waters as men did. She was fast and easily hid in the reef if she needed to. That was after we had to leave our cavern because men had invaded it with their tour guides and cameras. We lived along an underwater island off the southern coast, on the far side of what is now the shipping lane. Our cavern was quiet before humans came with their ships and road runners."

"Cars, you mean?"

"Yes, cars. Divers came to the atoll, a few at first. We saw them and they saw us and they seemed friendly. No one ever considered them a danger. In fact, there were days when mother would come home with stories about how near she had been to the divers. I think she would have loved to swim with them if she could."

"Don't tell me anymore." Kaile shifted uneasily. "I know where you're going with this. I've heard rumors."

Tas shook his head, tears forming in his eyes. "Let me tell you the whole story Kaile. You need to hear it." Kaile gave Tas a cold look before he leaned against the rocks and closed his eyes.

"More and more divers arrived. They started to bring hunting gear, lances and harpoons. One day my mother didn't come home when we expected her. Dad searched both night and day, but by that time we knew something was terribly wrong." Tas took a deep breath. "He finally found her. It appeared the men had chased her into a cave. She was so fast and smart they were unable to capture her. But I guess they were intent on bringing her back dead if not alive, so they used a harpoon. Mom swam as far back into the rocks as she could so they'd never be able to get at her. There she died. How long she suffered, I don't know."

Tas watched the remnants of waves ripple in, and listened to the constant hum of the sea outside the cavern.

Kaile spoke softly. "It's over, Tas. You've seen death and now Pouraka is your refuge. None of us regret that your clan came here. But you didn't have to drill fear into our hearts."

"Kaile, fear is the only thing that protects us. We can't fight men. We're powerless against their machines."

Kaile's sigh echoed the whisper of the breakers as the pulse of the sea clutched and released the sands below. "I'm sorry about your mother, Tas. Things like that shouldn't happen. And I'm not angry at you. Hurt. Ko was my friend, that's all."

"And humans are not our friends."

Kaile shifted again, tucking his legs further under him and brushing his shorts. How the story of his mother affected Kaile, Tas couldn't say. Maybe it would make him think, maybe not. "Your friend is still alive and free."

They listened to the surf for a long while. Tas thought about his mother. Perhaps Kaile was thinking about Ko.

After a long quiet moment, Kaile changed the subject. "There was a ship last night that came to the docks when I was working with Leni."

"A ship? What kind of ship?"

"Another fishing boat, but not like Leni's. They wanted to dock but Leni wouldn't let them. The stranger got kind of irate. Said they'd be around for the weekend. Claimed that Leni didn't own the waters here."

"Did they say who they were?"

"No, but Benson said later the guy's dad is a boss on one of the oil rigs."

The oil rigs! Tas had heard Leni and Benson talk about the oil rigs. Tas had never seen one. His clan had migrated north shortly before the rigs were built.

"I'm curious, Kaile. If those men are the gill-netters that Cora and I came across, they killed a shark for no reason. They lack respect for life and most likely are the same sort of men that killed my mother. They would probably kill any one of us given the opportunity."

Kaile shuddered; his wide eyes followed Tas. "So you think the gill netters were on that boat right there at Leni's dock?"

"It's quite possible but I don't know. If they were, and they're moving up the coast, Pouraka's in danger. Everyone here is in danger." Tas considered the cavern and the mers sleeping soundly on the rocks, the moonlight shining on their silky skin and glistening scales. His eyes rested on Cora and his heart jumped. She was as vulnerable as his mother had been. "We'd have a chance to keep our people safe if we found out exactly what they're doing."

"That's always been Leni's job. He's always kept strangers out of these waters, but I don't think he wants to get in a fight. Those men were pretty hostile."

"Leni's not a fighter even if he does have a rifle. He's a fisherman."

"What do we do then?"

Tas looked at the moon, and then again at the cavern and the merpeople that slumbered peacefully in its light. They were his kin now. Having seen his own people slaughtered, he couldn't let Pouraka perish. Dawn would be upon them soon. What dangers daylight would bring Tas didn't know. "If we found out more about those men, who they are and why are they here... Are the men that you saw threatening Leni the only ones? Or are there more? If we knew those things, we'd be able to guard what is sacred to us."

"How?"

Tas shrugged as he thought. "I don't know. Destroy their nets?"

"So how do we find out their numbers? What do we do?"

"We find them and follow them. You wouldn't feel like going for a swim this morning, would you?"

"What? Where?"

"South. To the oil rigs."

"South? There are sharks in those waters."

Tas laughed. "Sharks? They are the least of our worries." He patted Kaile on the shoulder. "We have dolphins!"

Kaile broke a smile.

15 Riggers

When they reached the open sea, Tas whistled. Though he'd never called them before, he was thrilled when Ko's silky body spun out of the water and fell against the swells with a splash. Soon the entire pod danced in and out of the water, spinning and rolling toward them with Ko in the lead. Tas raised his hands and the pod frolicked around the two mermen.

"I think they're ready to go!" Tas laughed as he grabbed Ko's dorsal fin. "We're headed to Ocean Bend, Ko. Would you like to take us there?"

Tas swung himself onto Ko's back and wrapped his arms around the dolphin. Ko whirled high above the surface, flipped and plummeted back into the sea, stirring whitecaps and splattering Kaile with a wall of saltwater. Ko plunged deep, never slowing, and then the dolphin surfaced again. Tas clung to the dolphin through the surf. The sun warmed his back while the sea breeze cooled his face. He peeled his wet hair from his eyes and grinned at Kaile.

"Pretty cool, eh?"

Kaile rode another dolphin and the rest of the pod skated through the surf alongside them, stretching their glossy bodies southward, putting a great distance between them and Pouraka in a short amount of time. Though storm clouds darkened the sky behind, the day ahead was bright with flickers of sunlight bouncing off the surface.

Tas had not been to the southern tip of Talbatha Isle in a very long time, and even then swimming in these waters warranted caution. "Slow down, Ko! There could be danger ahead and I'm as concerned for you as I am for the merpeople." The dolphin obeyed, signaling the command to the pod with a flap of his tailfin. Many of the dolphins dove deep at that point, but Tas, Kaile and their mounts glided along the surface.

No longer did they see Blue Mountains and the serene waters of the wild country that crowned Barnacle Bay. These were rugged waters with ships of all shapes and sizes dotting a path as far as the horizon and beyond. Sailboats and cargo ships, seaplanes and yachts. The bluffs on the coast of the island were laced with houses, buildings and fences. Piers stretched beyond the beaches, harboring an assortment of vessels and masts that poked at the sky. The fresh salty air had a heavy smell and a bitter taste that coated Tas' tongue.

Tas slid off of Ko's back and nodded for Kaile to do the same. Though they were still far from the busy scene, Tas was not a stranger to spyglasses and binoculars, having seen such tools in the hands of the tourists that had overrun Sameri. It would be a fateful occurrence for the mermen to be spotted in this part of the world through the eye of a lens.

New to the vista was a man-made island resting awkwardly on stilts. The tall metal structure cut a strange profile into the hazy sky. Coming from the platform was a monotonous hum that vibrated through the water. A disturbing sound, it made the ocean tremble and Ko's body shake nervously. Tas patted him gently. "It's okay, Ko. We won't stay long."

"That's an oil rig, you think?"
"Must be."
"What does it do?"
Tas couldn't think of any real purpose for the man-made island other than marring the seascape and making a hideous noise. "It's a mystery to me. Men are a strange lot."

Over the hum of the rig came the noisy rev of a motorboat and the voices of men shouting and laughing as the vehicle sped toward them. Tas directed Ko underwater and Kaile followed, joining the other dolphins deep below the surface.

"Did we see enough to come to any conclusions?" Kaile's mervoice vibrated through the current and Tas sensed his nervousness.

"Only enough to whet my curiosity."

"You mean you want to go further in?"

"Not necessarily. Ko is upset by the sounds, and it seems you are as well."

"I can think of a lot safer places to be than riding a dolphin under a harpoon boat. Another reason I wouldn't mind keeping my legs."

"That's your solution? Become like them?"

"Do we have to discuss this now?"

This was neither the time nor the place to enter a debate with Kaile. Tas patted Ko's quivering body; the vibrations of the oil rig had a significant effect on the dolphin who seemed confused and nervous. The pod they had traveled with was gone. "No. We should go back. This isn't good for Ko. Did you notice there's another piling being built farther south?"

"No. But I did see the gill netter moored near the oil rig."

"I saw that too. I wonder if it's safe to assume there's only one." Tas said.

"What do we do now?"

The water above them churned as the motorboat sped over their heads. "They're headed north. Let's follow and see what they're up to."

Tas moved silently and slowly north following the pull of the rising tide. Cloudy waters and rising temperatures alluded to a coming storm. Tas fought the temptation to surface and check the weather; instead he kept a keen eye on the wake of the motor boat.

"The weather's getting rough out there." The water tasted sweet, feeding his suspicions. Rain pounded against the sea. He could see the pod of dolphins in the water far below them, sinking slowly toward the ocean shelf. Tas would have to let Ko go if the storm were to escalate. "Let's swim home, and let these guys retreat."

Tas dismounted and pushed Ko's head around toward the other dolphins but the cetacean didn't budge. "Go with them."

Kaile's dolphin left without being coaxed, joining the others of his kind, sinking deeper into the murky blue.

"Go!" Tas pushed Ko again, but the dolphin nudged back with his nose, and patted Tas' shoulder with his fin.

"He's not acting right." Kaile grimaced.

"Didn't he assume the instincts of a dolphin when he changed?" If a storm was forming the pressure would harm Ko, and the saline imbalance would make him sick. He needed to go with the pod, but the dolphin refused. "Let's swim on. Perhaps he'll stop following us."

Though they swam quickly, the plan wasn't working. Ko swam alongside the two mermen.

"Is he trying to tell you something?" Kaile asked.

"You mean besides the fact that he's as stubborn as he always was?"

"He's not stupid, Tas. Let's go home and see what happens. We shouldn't be out in these waters either. The current is already trying my strength. Wasn't there a group of merpeople killed during a storm some time ago?"

"From the eastern waters, yes. But they were farther out at sea and rumor has it they encountered a cyclone. Nevertheless, I'm for being safe at home." Tas ducked his chin to his chest and with a sweep of his tail fin caught the current north. The sea churned so violently that though they swam well below the surface, swells opened up above them exposing the mermen to rain and hail. The wind whistled so loudly it nearly deafened Tas while salty spray slapped his face and blinded him.

When the wind eased he opened his eyes in time to see the speedboat they had been following fly overhead and crash into the crest of a swell. With a loud crack the hull splintered. Men screamed, their voices lost in the whistle of the wind. Another swell sent the bow nose-diving into the waves tossing the men in the air, only to collide with the sea again.

"They're going to die if we don't do something." Tas spoke in merlanguage that rumbled with the sounds of the storm.

Without any further discussion he seized the underside of the bow and pushed it upward, keeping it afloat on the swell of the next wave. Kaile rushed to his aid and together they struggled to hold the vessel above water. Tas felt the footsteps of the men moving in the boat above his head, and heard them calling to one another as they bailed water over the stern.

"There's a fish under us!" one of the men yelled.

"Well we're lucky for that if it's keeping us afloat," another answered.

Tas released his hold with one hand and with a scowl, pointed at Kaile's tail fin flapping next to the hull. Kaile pulled his fin under him and kept it tucked.

The task of preventing the rig from capsizing or splitting in half became more difficult as the storm strengthened. If only Tas could surface long enough to see where they were in relation to the coast, perhaps they could maneuver the men to shore. But that was risky. When Tas had spent his strength and was about to call off the rescue, Ko appeared. The dolphin pushed his back into Tas, Kaile and the hull, using all of his strength to propel the vessel sideways pointing it into the swells. Once stabilized, Ko dove under, circled and came back again leaning his weight into the mermen, moving the boat forward until they eased it into protected waters.

"We're going to make it!" a man yelled from above. "There's the beach!"

Tas and Kaile dove away, Tas being careful to keep his tail submerged, but Kaile was clumsy and flipped away from the vessel, breaking surface.

"What was that fish that saved us? Look, there it goes!"

"That was no fish, Oscar! That was a mermaid. I swear to Neptune!"

After those words were spoken, even Ko had difficulty catching up to the mermen.

16. What's this about Mermaids?

Kaile walked the beach early the next day. So many shiny surprises lay hidden in the sand, and he had a keen eye for spotting them. He tossed his most recent find, a piece of clear blue stone, into the air and caught it. Another gem to string around his neck. Or he could use it in the necklace he was making for Beth.

Kaile's pockets already bulged with shells and colorful pebbles. The sandy beach, still damp and cold under his feet, spread out before him shaded only by the wharf. Littered with logs and kelp and unfortunate jellyfish which had floated to shore and been left to dry under the sun, the shoreline hinted at unfound treasure. Crabs scurried away from his toes as he walked under the pier.

The wharf was quiet, reeking of creosote and decaying kelp. Leni's boat wasn't there. He must have gone fishing at sunrise.

Kaile's shoulders drooped as he eyed the empty berth. He'd give anything to be a steady employee of Leni's. He yearned for the life of a fisherman, waking early in the morning and drinking a hot cup of cocoa with the guys, weighing anchor and then working hard all day under the sun.

Adventures on a boat far outweighed swimming with sleek gray beasts that can't talk. Ko had been a hero last night when he helped maneuver that motorboat to shore.

Still there was something repulsive about his friend having changed into a beast. He considered his own transformation into a human and back to a merman again as vile. People ought not to switch around like that, Kaile thought. An individual should be one form or the other. They should make a choice. Every day Kaile wished he could choose to be a man. Forever! He wouldn't have any other choices to make if he could be a human.

Kaile wandered past the wharf toward his favorite resting spot, a quiet cove filled with tide pools and shaded sands. There he would be alone to meditate over what had happened in Pouraka these last few days. He looked ahead, down the coast at the rocky cliffs where the waters were protected by a jetty. Beyond the jetty was moored a fishing vessel he assumed was Leni's, though at this distance he couldn't tell for sure.

When Kaile neared the cove his smile faded for he could see that his favorite hideaway was occupied. Though he had no way of recognizing the intruders in the brilliance of the morning sun, still their silhouettes struck a chord of familiarity. The tallest of the three bore the stature of the fisherman who had encroached on Leni's dock the day prior before.

If Kaile's eyes did not deceive him, the agitator was the same man Benson had identified as the oil rigger's son. What was this person doing on the shores of Barnacle Bay, and in Kaile's favorite cove no less? Kaile planted his feet in the warm sand, his hands in his pockets, and watched.

A dark haired man knelt on the ground, his brightly colored shirt hung loose as he leaned over an object. The other two were bare-chested, muscular and tanned. They seemed to be instructing the man kneeling.

At first Kaile thought they were hovering over a sea otter so Kaile moved closer. If these rogues were hurting an animal he would have to meddle. They weren't. The center of their attention was nothing more than a deflated rubber raft. The kneeling man's face shone bright red as he huffed air into the collapsed vessel, his efforts meeting with little success.

"Hurry up!" The oil rigger's son said. "We don't have all day! We're missing the best fishing."

"Hang on, Tom," the man responded.

Kaile squinted again at the sparkling white fishing boat he had mistaken for Leni's. This was probably the gill netter that had caused so much trouble. Were these the men who killed the shark? Striking up a conversation might give him some answers why they were so far north when the oil rigs were on the southern tip of the island. If so, he could take the information back to Tas.

"That yours?" Kaile nodded toward the moored boat.

The men turned sharply, surprise on their faces. The rigger's son, the one called Tom, straightened his back and looked Kaile up and down with a smirk.

"It's my dad's. One of many." He paused; his piercing blue eyes sent a chill down Kaile's spine. "Didn't I see you last night on the pier? You were with that cranky old wharf hog who wouldn't let us dock."

"I thought I recognized you." Kaile took offense at the insult, but held his temper.

"So what's with the old man that he can't be friendly to his new neighbors?"

Kaile shrugged. He couldn't speak for Leni, nor did he want to make excuses for his friend. The reference to Tom being a new neighbor was disconcerting though.

"Well you can tell the old man we're here to go fishing whether he likes it or not!"

Kaile raised a brow, but maintained his composure. "I don't see him regularly. I only work for him sometimes."

"Hey, Tom, I'm getting nowhere with this. We should go into town and see if that gas station has an air pump." Tom's friend stood and brushed the sand off of his shorts; squinting at Kaile briefly, he asked Tom, "Who's this?"

"Some local that works with the old coot who chased us off the dock yesterday."

"The name's Kaile." Kaile held out his hand in friendship. There was a moment of hesitation before Tom accepted Kaile's handshake.

"All right. I'll shake your hand since you say you only work for the guy. Not your fault. Although you might want to think about the kind of the people you hang with. Chasing off strangers is not always wise. Especially folks that own as much of this island as my dad does. My name's Tom."

Kaile choose not to respond to Tom's curt comments. No one needs enemies, but this guy's boasting was a bit much. "What happened to your raft?"

"It appears we ran this dingy over a sharp rock when we beached this morning. It's out of air, obviously. We patched the hole but I guess we'll have to drag it up to that gas station to put air in it. Looks like a long hike in some pretty hot sand." The dark haired man stood, still staring at the raft.

"This isn't a real good place to beach something inflatable. Too many shells and sharp rocks."

"We see that. Well, if you'll excuse us." Tom snickered and nudged his friend. "Let's get moving then."

"You're all barefoot and the sand's hot. It's a long walk to town across the beach." Kaile nodded toward Barnacle Bay barely visible beyond the shimmering heat waves that dazzled the shoreline.

"No shit." Tom spat in the tide pool at his feet.

Kaile chose to ignore his vulgarity. "Why don't you let me help you?"

"Nah, it's not your problem. We're okay." The third man picked up one end of the dinghy and lifted it onto his shoulder.

"It wouldn't be a problem if all you need is air. I'd be glad to help."

Tom held out his hand for his friend to stop wrestling with the raft and studied Kaile for a moment, a leery glint in his eyes. "Okay, then. Some fresh breath is what we need, eh Pat? Give the kid a shot."

Pat dropped his bundle back on the rocks and stepped away. Kaile knelt next to it. He'd never seen a raft deflated. "Where do I blow? Right here?"

"What are you, stupid? Yeah, that's the place."

Once again, Kaile ignored the man's insult and held the tube to his mouth. He slowly eased his mer-air into the vessel. The rubber squeaked and hissed until it popped up, fully inflated, all within seconds. Tom and his friends stared wide-eyed.

"Whoa, that's enough, stop before it bursts! Wow, man."

A grin spread across Kaile's face as the men took the raft from him and replaced the seal.

"Where are you from, fella?" Rick asked.

Kaile flinched and eyed the beach the way he had come. "Barnacle Bay."

"You have quite the set of lungs!" Tom said and slapped him on his shoulder. "Once Dad starts building the east oil rig he'll be needing a diver to set the lines. You dive? With lungs like that I bet you do!"

Kaile felt his face flush. He nodded. "Yeah, yeah I dive sometimes."

"Come apply with us up if you're needing a job. Especially if you've got a license for Saturation Diving."

"I'll do that." Kaile had no idea what Saturation Diving meant and his face must have shown it.

"You know, deep diving. You have to prep for it."

Kaile beamed with a sense of satisfaction as the men lifted the raft off the rocks and set it in the water. "Are you fishing today?"

"Sure are. Why don't you come along? We've been meaning to meet the locals on this side of the island. The friendly ones, that is. You can clue us as to where the best fishing spots are. Come on!"

Kaile thought for a moment. Fishing with Tom and his friends would unveil the men's fishing methods and answer the questions they've been asking. "Really? Well, yeah, I'll come." Kaile helped Tom push the rubber dinghy away from the rocks into the gently rolling surf. When there was enough water to keep them afloat he jumped into the raft with the others. They paddled to the sparkling white fishing boat, tied the dingy to cleats at its stern, and climbed up the ladder.

Nearly twice as large as Leni's boat, Tom's trawler was polished and new, with huge pulleys both port and starboard and a mound of nets resting on the deck. Eyeing the pile of cord in front of him, Kaile wondered if these were the same nets that had almost killed Tas and Cora.

"Welcome to the Beeracuda! You drink?" Rick handed him a can, cold to the touch. "Go ahead and relax. We have to secure the dinghy and then we'll fire up the engines."

Tom flipped open a lounge chair for Kaile and sat across from him, popping open his beer. "We're new to these waters, so why don't you be the navigator?"

"Me?" Kaile sneered at the unusual request. "What are you fishing for?"

Tom shrugged. "Pan size perch, snapper. Something for dinner, mostly. Dad won't let us sell fish yet. Something about a license."

"I can show you where to find some rock bass if you like." Kaile pointed to the jetty. If he kept these guys away from Barnacle Bay and Pouraka, he'd be doing the merpeople a service. And he wasn't lying. Rock perch were everywhere especially around the jetty.

"That sounds like a plan! Rick, weigh anchor!" Tom stood and called to his friend at the helm as he peered through a pair of binoculars.

As the engines fired, the noise drowned any further conversation. Rick turned the ship about and headed south away from the cove. Once they came to the far side of the jetty that outlined the bay, Kaile held his hand up for Rick to stop. Out here wouldn't interfere with merlife or Leni's fishing territory either.

"You could cast your nets down current, away from the rocks." Kaile suggested.

Tom laughed as he handed Rick the binoculars and nodded south. "That's not quite how it works. We don't cast our nets. We lower them. Pat!" Tom signaled to the third man, who stood and released a latch on the pulley, dropping a massive pile of net into the water. Rick took the helm, steering the slow moving boat in a large circle southward.

"There aren't that many fish out here." Kaile looked nervously at the net wall being made in the water. "I thought you simply wanted dinner."

The grin on Tom's face sent a shudder down Kaile's spine. "We have a big family to feed."

Kaile wasn't sure how to ease out of the situation without stirring up trouble. But as he watched the nets lower into the turquoise water, another sight disturbed him. Dolphins frolicking in the distance were heading toward them.

"Well, would you look at that?" Tom laughed and shot Kaile another wicked smile. "A whole pod! How many would you say, Rick?"

Rick answered with a smirk.

"Please!" Kaile swallowed before he spoke, taking a moment to catch his breath and control his voice. "Please pull in your nets while the dolphins are near? Please."

"Sure, boy, anything you say. We owe you for inflating our raft, after all." Tom chuckled. The rigger's son gazed into Kaile's eyes longer than was comfortable. "Did you hear that Pat? Pull in the nets."

Already the nets had trapped a few rock bass that wiggled frantically as they were brought aboard. Pat freed them and tossed the fish on the deck. Tom picked one up, showed it to Kaile, and threw it out to sea, toward the dolphins, enticing the cetaceans.

Kaile shot glances between the dolphins and Pat's control on the pulley as the boat drifted further south. Pat took his time retrieving the nets. Too much time in Kaile's opinion. Dorsal fins soon broke the surface near to the boat as Tom continued to toss bait to the dolphins. "Here ya go fellers, come and get it."

Kaile jumped from his chair and raced to the winch. "Let me help."

"Hey, steady there, Kaile. We have it under control." Tom chortled.

"Your control is what's making me nervous. You don't intend to net those dolphins do you?"

"Would I do something like that?" Tom strode over to the pulley and flipped a switch, activating a motor that reeled in the nylon grid. "But now I see your colors. This little town of Barnacle Bay is nothing but a tribe of sea huggers, isn't it? No wonder the fisher dude who owns the dock is so uppity. He's trying to protect his babies."

Kaile straightened and set his jaw. The man faced him, his breath hot on Kaile's face. He smelled foul. "You're the kind of people who put guys like my dad out of business. You care more for the dumb animals than you do your own kind. Well, it isn't going to work on this island. Not anymore. We own the place now."

"Take me back home, please."

"Home? Where's that?"

Did he know? A wave of heat traveled through Kaile's head. How could he know he's a merman? Impossible. "Barnacle Bay."

"Ha!" A spray of spittle flew from Tom's mouth and landed on Kaile's cheek. Drool rolled down the fisherman's chin. "I ought to make you swim back to land with the dolphins!"

That would have been fine for Kaile who fought the urge not to dive into the water. Kaile's stomach was queasy from the smell of Tom's breath. He wiped his cheek.

Pat interrupted them. "Hey Tom, leave him alone. He hasn't done anything."

Tom watched Pat as the man put the last of the fish in a cooler. "I think we should be respectful to the local people. Stop trying to start a war with everyone you meet. Your dad's coming up this way sometime soon and you don't want the locals shooting at him when he gets here. Who knows? This place might have more possibilities than Ocean Bend. From what we've just seen, there's a gold mine up here. You know the price Arnold's relatives pay for aquarium specimens."

Kaile's heart skipped a beat. They do have plans! Pat's words were richer than rainbow coral, and just as terrifying! Kaile had something to take back to Tas, now.

"Okay. You're right. I concede." Tom held his can out and offered another handshake to Kaile. "I'll be friendly to you and to your dorsal finned partners out there too." He laughed at himself. "Sit down. Go ahead. Sit down. Tell me about these friends of yours." Tom jerked his chin toward the ocean that now stirred with the movement of dolphins gathering around the fishing boat.

"What do you want to know?" Kaile's eyes darted between the men.

"People say they talk. You ever hear a dolphin talk?"

Kaile breathed out a laugh.

"Have you?"

"No. No I haven't heard a dolphin talk."

"That's what I thought. People say all sorts of things." He took another slug of beer, his Adam's apple bouncing as he held his head back and drained the can. Kaile's eyes were glued to the man. "Hey Rick, toss me a beer."

Rick brought another chair, unfolded it next to Tom and sat down, handing him a can, which Tom immediately popped open. "Some guys just last night said they saw mermaids in that storm." He shot out a laugh, spewing spit and beer all over himself. "Imagine that! Ever see a mermaid, Kaile?"

Kaile stared at him. He'd never told a lie, not in all his life. It wasn't something that merpeople did. They were too pure, too cleansed by the turquoise waters and magic of Pouraka to lie. So Kaile stared at Tom waiting for the oil rigger's son to change the subject.

"Two fishermen, friends of my dad's got trapped in a storm and bit the bullet. They came back pale as ghosts. Darn fools said mermaids brought their boat to safety. Right here on these beaches."

"Dolphins, Tom. They said they saw dolphins push them ashore." Rick corrected.

"Dolphins and mermaids." Tom raised his voice. "I heard them say mermaids."

"Is that why you're here?" Kaile asked, cautious that his voice didn't reveal anything.

Tom laughed again. This time he had swallowed his beer first and wiped his mouth with his arm.

"I told you why we're here. We're fishing. Once Dad gets the rigs built, he's setting me up a business. I'm already making connections with some distributors. I admit I have some things to learn, like what kind of fish swim around here. We've got the best, most efficient nets in the industry right here on the Beeracuda!" He lifted a buoy from the pile.

"Well, those nets can be dangerous for some of the habitat." Kaile spoke softly and cast a glance at Pat. The man sided with him once before, perhaps he would understand.

Pat nodded. "You don't have anything to worry about. I doubt Tom will even be on any of our expeditions. He's merely financing them."

"Hogwash! I plan on being the helmsman."

Pat winked at Kaile, but the nicety was not convincing.

"Okay. So let's make a deal. You tell me where the dolphins live. That way I can avoid them. If I avoid the creatures, they won't be a nuisance. These rigs aren't cheap and something as big and clumsy as a dolphin will get tangled up and tear the nets. That will cost me money. So, where do they live?"

"What do you mean, where do they live? They live all over these waters."

"Come on, man you know what I mean. Where do they hang out when they aren't prancing around like this? How do we avoid them?"

Kaile watched the pod that had moved a distance from the boat, jumping and splashing in the sea. Some of the dolphins started to spin. They were a beautiful sight with the sun shimmering on their backs. Kaile recognized Ko among them, one of the fastest swimmers. "They have feeding hours when they're most active. Don't fish during those hours."

Tom chortled and took another drink. "Okay, so don't fish at dinner time? Where are they the rest of the day? I wouldn't want to accidentally bump into their home, if they have one. Where do they live?"

Kaile leaned back in his chair, shifting his weight uncomfortably. The three men's eyes were fixed on him prodding him for an answer. Tom, red faced and drunk sat smugly across from Kaile. Rick's blue eyes pierced his with inquisition, and Pat, now at the helm scrutinized all three of them quietly. "They live near Barnacle Bay. Leni's protective of them. That's why he was angry with you. If you leave the dolphins alone, Leni will be your friend. I promise. He's a good person to have on your side."

Tom nodded. "Fair enough." He spat across the deck. "Yes sir! Fair enough indeed! Still want to go home?"

"Yes, please."

17. Confrontation

Last night's storm had washed tidewater into Pouraka, and though the cavern wasn't flooded, still the moisture cooled the air. Tas had asked Cora to sit with him in the sun on the hillside. Exhausted from his adventure the night before, he napped in the sun while she picked flowers, made little stone houses with pebbles, and sat absorbing the serenity of the vista, marveling at the beauty of the glimmering sea. When late afternoon sparkles tickled the waters with color, Cora spied Leni's boat heading for home. She smiled at the sleeping merman, and kissed him on the cheek.

Tas opened one eye. His black hair was tied back with kelp lace, but a curl dangled over his forehead. Cora flicked the ringlet away from his lashes and laughed quietly.

"What are you staring at?"

"You're just so handsome."

His face flushed and he pulled the curl behind his ear, closing his eyes again.

"Wake up. They're coming home." She shook him gently.

"Who's coming home?" Tas mumbled and brushed her hands away from his shoulder.

"Leni."

With a low groan, Tas sat up and wiped his face. "How long did I sleep?"

"Almost all day. Are you awake enough to meet with him?"

He gave her a nod and stood, offering her a hand. She gathered the baskets that she had woven earlier that week from strips of kelp and strapped them over her shoulder.

"I like that sand dollar in your braid."

Cora flinched when he touched the shell near her ear, not expecting the attention. Tas had been understandably grumpy lately. For him to notice and mention something about her appearance surprised her, but also made the sun shine a little warmer.

"And I like the way that curl hangs down over your forehead." She laughed when his face turned red. He pushed the curl behind his ear again.

They walked along the grassy trail that led to the beach. She slipped her fingers in between his with a renewed appreciation for him. She had almost lost him twice in the past two days, but Providence had spared his life and hers, too. For that she was thankful. She couldn't imagine what life would be like without Tas.

Neither of them had seen the boat approach the pier. Their eyes had been fixed on each other so they didn't notice that the vessel wasn't Leni's, not until they walked up the steps to the wharf and Tas pulled Cora back. "Wait!"

She gasped. The fishing boat was twice as large as the Sea Quest, with huge pulleys on either side and nets piled high on the deck. A stranger jumped onto the dock, another tossed a can into the water and waved directions at the helmsman as he tied the lines.

"What's Kaile doing with them?" Tas asked.

Cora hadn't recognized Kaile until Tas mentioned his name. But there he was, leaping from the deck of this stranger's watercraft.

"So we'll see you again, buddy?" Tom called to Kaile from on board. "Come see me about that diving job too, okay?"

"Just remember my request, that's all I ask." Kaile's gesture was more of an appeal for their departure rather than a friendly goodbye. The sound of another engine drowned any more conversation. Trouble came by way of Leni's boat as it approached the end of the pier from the north.

"Get off my dock!" Leni bellowed. "Bandits. Get out of here!"

"Get lost at sea, old man! You don't own the world! You don't even own this island." Tom shouted back as he tossed his line into the boat, hopped aboard and steered the Beeracuda toward the sea. "I'm returning one of your deckhands back to you. You ought to thank me for that. I had half a mind to make him swim!"

Sparks were flying so rampantly Cora wasn't sure whether to run to Kaile, to Leni, or back down the stairs. Tas' hand slipped into hers and he pulled her back to the stairs. Leni revved his engine and a cloud of black smoke streamed into the air. The Sea Quest backed up and rolled over its wake. Leni's hands flew over the helm as he turned the boat about and drove it to the other side of the dock. Cora coughed from the fumes of diesel that now blackened the end of the wharf. The sound of motors drowned out angry voices.

"Get your dolphin-killing gill netter off of my property or I'll call the cops right now." Leni jumped from his boat onto the pier, a rifle in his hand, leaving his crew to secure the Sea Quest.

Tas tugged at Cora's arm. "Let's get out of here. Let Leni take care of this."

"He might need our help!"

"Cora!" His strong arms swung her around. His dark eyes demanded her attention. "Get off the dock!"

Anger burned inside of her, but when Leni's gun went off, she jumped at the sound. Tas pulled her down the first two steps. Kaile stood between them and Leni.

"Kaile!" Tas called

Kaile turned and when he recognized them he raced toward them.

"Go ahead and run, you wimp!" Tom threw a can at Kaile, hitting him in the arm. The contents exploded across the wooden planks.

Leni fired his rifle into the air again. "Dial 911," he ordered his crew.

"You'll pay for this, you worm!" Tom waved his fist at Leni and jumped aboard his boat as his gill netter drifted away from the pier. "I won't forget! And keep your nitwit deckhands to yourself. He's useless anyway."

Kaile followed Tas and Cora down the stairs. It wasn't until they were clear of the pier and halfway to Pouraka that anyone spoke.

"What in Neptune's name were you doing on that gillnetter?" Tas blurted the interrogation that Cora had been rehearsing in her mind.

"It's a long story, but the short of it is I was investigating the practices of these visitors from the south, like you suggested."

"What practices? Their beer drinking habits? You think I couldn't have found that out myself? It shouldn't be too difficult to see they drink beer and kill our habitat without going onboard their ships and partying with them."

"I wasn't partying with them, Tas. I wanted to find out what else they're up to. I mean, besides the obvious."

"Well, now you know. And now you've got Leni all riled up and he's probably as angry at you as he is at that crew."

"Why? Because I was on their boat?"

"Well, yeah, Kaile!" Cora chimed. "That says a lot, you know."

"What? What does it say?" Kaile bent over and seized a piece of driftwood on the beach, slinging it out into the breakers. "I tried to make peace with them; got them to consent to leave the pod alone when they come up here to fish."

Tas stopped short in the sand and froze. His stare stunned Kaile into silence.

Cora slowed.

"You made a deal with them?" Tas' voice was no more than a whisper, his eyes burned fire.

"Not a deal. I just asked them not to disturb the dolphins during feeding time."

"What else did you tell him?"

Cora stopped on the beach and regarded Tom's rig which had halted a good distance from the pier, his engines quiet.

"That's odd. Why would he kill the engines there? You'd think he'd want to get away what with Leni chasing him."

"Is Leni chasing him?" Tas asked, shielding his eyes from the blaring sun.

"No. Leni's still at the dock."

"Tom's engines are still going. I hear a hum." Kaile stepped into the water to get a better view.

"That's not his engines." Tas noted.

"No. It's not." Cora recognized that deathly noise too. "It's that same sound we heard when that Mako was captured."

They stood on the beach trying to decipher what Tom was doing, but the boat was so far in the distance all they could see were dots for men, although Cora was certain she saw one of them waving their arms.

"Nets." Kaile muttered, still staring. "They have a pulley that lowers their nets. They did it when I was with them. And then they baited the pod. They pulled the nets in before they took me to shore. Now they've motored right back to where we saw the pod. Look!" Kaile pointed.

More disturbing than Leni firing his rifle into the air, or angry words exchanged on the dock, a roll of water swelled toward the boat. Dorsal fins. The dolphins were spinning toward the Beeracuda.

A black plume of smoke spiraled by the pier as Leni's engine started. The Sea Quest sped toward Tom's gill netter. Kaile lunged into the water and Cora followed, wading into the surf to get an unobstructed view of what was happening.

Above the sound of Leni's boat, Cora heard shouts and laughter.

"Come and get it, old man!" Tom mocked. "You want this one? How do you want it? Sunnyside up?"

"They have a dolphin!" Kaile was waist deep in the water when he turned to shore, his face pale and his voice cracked.

Several figures on the boat held the large struggling shape out of the water. More laughter, a sudden splash, and then the roar of an engine followed by rolling wakes as the gill netter sped away, the Sea Quest fast behind.

When Cora spun to face Tas, he was already halfway to Pouraka.

18. Mourning

Though it was a long, steep climb to the entrance, Tas didn't stop for breath once, nor did he look back to see if Cora or Kaile were behind him. He dashed up the rocky cliff, slid down the damp staircase and slipped into the Cradle. His heart was beating so hard the act of splashing water on his mer body was like a dream, though the cold water of the pool shocked him back to reality. Pouraka was empty save for several kindermers playing in the water, splashing their tales at one another and giggling.

"Where is everyone?"

"Someone sounded the conch. We were told to stay here." The oldest of the children answered and then pointed south.

"The conch?" Tas was not familiar with the northern merpeoples' tradition.

"The horn of death. It's blown only when the blood of a merdolphin is spilled. The sound sends a tremor more rattling than the mermen's siren. Everyone can hear the conch no matter how far away. You should go, too. All the adults have gone."

Tas dove into the channel just as Cora stepped into Pouraka.

"Tas!" she called, but Tas ignored her.

The waters were exceptionally blue. Light flickered and danced below him as the sun rippled on the surface above.

Tas swam hard and fast. When he reached the pilings of Leni's wharf he halted and listened, wondering where everyone had gone yet worried his innermost instincts might be right. A sound played in the movement of the current, a low and mournful hum.

    Mermusic was reserved for ceremonies only, and this song was a lament. Tas followed the quivering, passing several mermaids. They sang with their heads bowed as they gathered bundles of kelp from the ocean floor, another indication that something was dreadfully wrong. Slung over their shoulders were strips of Taruweed, flat kelp used only for burials. Tas watched the gatherers for a dreadful moment.

    He passed other merpeople as he traveled through deeper, darker waters. The song grew increasingly louder as he swam to a group of mermaids and mermen clustered around a body. Peara was with them, crying feverishly in the arms of her sisters. Tas' heart broke.

    "No!" He choked on his words and hurried to her, touching Peara's shoulder gently. Her eyes confirmed what he feared most. The dolphin slaughtered had been Ko.

    Already mermen had wrapped Ko in kelp, working quickly so that sharks and predators would not sense a death and tear into his body. The ritual was ancient. The dolphin would be bound and then buried under the sandy ocean floor.

Tas joined the mermen, lifting and turning Cora's brother into a cocoon. They brushed away the sand with their tailfins, moving in rhythm to the music, digging a grave in the ocean floor. Once Ko was lowered into it, the mermaids swept the sand over the mummy, tossing shells and sand dollars on the mound.

Tas, immersed in the ceremony, saw Cora take the sand dollar from her braid. She kissed it gently and set it next to the other shells. When she turned to him he hadn't the heart to meet her eyes. Anger boiled within. He would be of little comfort to her. With a powerful thrust of his fin, he left the scene. Cora followed.

He did not return to Pouraka. The wrath that churned his blood kept him away. His home was too precious, his hate too strong. Swimming along the cliffs of the island, he passed the coral reefs, through schools of fish and above a lone octopus that hovered in the ebon shadows. Tas turned into a narrow channel, through a tunnel and into a dark cavity, a hole under the sea where he could be alone and grieve. There was so much to sort out. So many deaths.

Still Cora followed him.

She moved silently into the crevice, settled herself on a ledge next to him, bowed her head and covered her eyes. His desire to be alone was overcome by her need. He could never send her away. Life was too short. They stayed there together in silence for what seemed like eternity and until the music could no longer be heard.

Finally he spoke. "This isn't the end." The vibrations of his voice broke the stillness of the water. "They will kill more of us. They are the same kind of people that killed my mother."

Cora said nothing.

"Ko didn't deserve to die like that."

Cora wiped her nose, and then her eyes. She buried her head in her hands and curled up close to the wall, camouflaged by the dark, surrounded by anemones that clung to the rocks.

"Cora?"

She shook her head and curled tighter.

"Cora, come here." He spoke softly, floated to the ledge where she sat and wrapped his arms around her. "Come on, Sea Rose. I know you're hurting."

She placed her head against his chest. Her dark locks swirled around his fingers, soft and flowing. She shivered as she wept and clung to him. Her scales glistened silver blue and green.

"He was my brother, my flesh and blood. I never wanted him to be anything but Ko."

Tas searched for words, but there were none that would be of comfort. He stroked her hair and kissed her head.

"We were like twins growing up. Everything we did, we did together. When we were little we'd play hide and seek in the atoll. I could always find him because he sparkled so." She wiped her eyes with her hands. "When it was his turn to hide, he never buried himself in the sand like I did. I think he did that on purpose just so I'd find him. Playing tag was his favorite part of the game."

Her head fell back on Tas and her tears warmed his chest as he stroked her cheek. "I could never ever catch him he was such a strong swimmer. So strong."

"I couldn't keep up with him either," Tas whispered.

"You couldn't?"

"No."

"He always made time to be with me, always. That's why I couldn't understand why he would want to go off and be something other than who he was. I just wanted him to be Ko. That's all. Why did he have to change? Why did he have to go where I couldn't go?" Tears welled in her eyes again.

"He wasn't rejecting you, Sea Rose. Don't think of it like that."

"He was my only family."

That wasn't quite true. Ko was her brother, but not her only family, not as far as Tas was concerned, but now was not the time to argue.

He kissed her hair. "Someday you won't see it that way," he said, not sure if Cora could even hear. It didn't matter. She needed to grieve. Nothing would bring Cora's brother back. Ko's changing to a dolphin had been hard on her, and now this. Unjustly slaughtered, Ko was forever gone. Merman or dolphin, he was now buried at the bottom of the sea. Tas would bring justice, but not yet. He squeezed her tighter. He'd stay by her side as long as she needed him, his own wrath would have to wait.

19. Moonlight

Kaile didn't follow Cora into the water. When he heard the children tell Tas about the conch, there was no mistaking who had died. What other dolphin had been so newly changed that he was considered a merdolphin? The merpeople would offer a lament and a ceremony but Kaile refused to go. He'd had enough ceremony. He climbed back into man's world and waited for the stars.

The moon was comforting, and would hide his tears and listen to his musings. No one else would.

Kaile was alone on the beach when Beth sat down beside him. She didn't say anything, she just sat there. She had no way of knowing what was on his mind, what had happened under water, or why he was even on the beach alone. She didn't ask.

Why he felt he had to speak, Kaile wasn't sure. Possibly to acknowledge her presence or to tell her more. He certainly didn't know how.

"He was daring and brave." Kaile tossed a stone at the waves as they rolled in, though it didn't hit the water but only splattered onto the wet foamy sand. "He always stood out from the others."

Kaile could feel her eyes on him, but he didn't look at her. If he had he'd probably break into pieces like the empty shells that had been scrubbed into fragments by the weight of the sea.

"Funny how one person can mean so much to you and when they're gone you feel so empty," he said, more to himself than her.

"It's not funny," she whispered. "Not at all." Her eyes were set on the moon too, and in a way it made him feel better, like he wasn't alone. "I don't know what happened, but I can tell you I felt the same way when my mom died. She meant the world to me. Not just to me but to Dad and Sasha too. She's what kept our lives in order. Always there to wipe a nose or tie a shoelace, or give a comforting word when we were down. She slipped away so suddenly. I don't think anything in the whole world will ever replace her."

Did Beth understand?

"I don't know who you lost, Kaile. It's not my place to ask."

Kaile wouldn't have answered anyway. Beth knew who Ko the merman was, but she didn't know who Ko the dolphin was and that secret still belonged to Pouraka.

"I just want you to know that you aren't alone in your pain." Beth zipped her sweatshirt up, flipped her hood over her hair and tied the lace under her chin. With a quick smile she stood and caught his glance before she turned away. Even in the moonlight her eyes were radiant. If his throat hadn't been so dry he would have thanked her, but the words wouldn't come.

"If you ever just want to talk, or if you want to visit, you're welcome to come to the house and have some cocoa. Though I agree that the beach is a serene and comforting place to be when we're down."

Kaile nodded and watched her walk away.

20. Distress Call

"Tas!" A merman's voice thundered through the water.

Cora opened her eyes. She must have fallen asleep in Tas' arms, but for how long, she didn't know. Determining the hour of the day was impossible in the deep waters where they had hidden. Daylight beams could not reach inside the narrow fissure.

"Tas!" The vibrations echoed again. It was a merman's voice. She wasn't sure who called, but when she felt another tremor she knew more than one person was searching for him.

Tas was not waking up. Black lashes sealed his eyes, and his smooth skin revealed none of the grief he suffered the night before. She hated to disturb him, but the call rang urgent.

"Tas? Tas?" she said softly and touched his cheek. "Tas, someone's calling."

He smiled, squeezed her tighter, and his lips touched her hair. "Shh. Sleep, Sea Rose."

"Tas, wake up. Some mermen are out there calling for you."

With a blink the contented smile washed from his face. "Who?"

She pushed herself away from his hold. "I don't know but their voices are frantic."

The call sounded again. Alarmed, Cora led Tas through the cleft and into the open. Figures emerged from the turquoise depths. Tail fins glimmered irregularly as a group of mermen swam toward them.

"Tas, we need your help." Radcliff spotted them first. "Nets have been lowered in Phantom Bay and an entire pod is in danger. The boat has been chasing the pod all morning. The dolphins are exhausted and helpless."

"Our pod?"

"Not ours. A southern pod. We heard the cries all the way from the atoll. There's blood in the water. Already some of our people and our dolphins have gone to see if they can rescue the pod."

"Did you gather the spearheads from Pouraka? The weapons?"

"We did." When Radcliff handed Tas a kelp sheath and a knife carved from whalebone he ran his hand over the smooth white handle and looked at Cora with an expression she had never seen before. It wasn't fear, but there was resolve in his eyes and it frightened her.

"What?" she asked.

"Go back to Pouraka and wait for me." He pulled the sheath strap over his shoulder and swam away.

"You're not leaving me, Tas." She trailed behind him. "I can help."

Tas stopped abruptly and turned to her. He took her by her shoulders and swam her away from the others. "Go to Pouraka and wait for me."

"No!"

"Cora, just do as I say. Please!"

"You're not leaving me behind to wonder where you are and if you're alive."

"And I'm not leading you into harm's way."

"No, Tas."

"If you see any mermen at Pouraka, have them join us if they can. But you!" Tas squeezed her shoulders. "I want you safe."

His lips met hers in a warm and passionate kiss, nearly pushing her over backwards. Cora melted in his arms though the fervor ended more quickly than it began. "I can't lose you. Go to Pouraka. Please!"

Tas left Cora both stunned from the fire of his kiss, and angry from the rejection. "I can fight, Tas! You're forgetting I saved your life."

If he had heard her, he ignored her. The merman soon vanished with the others leaving Cora burning inside.

Following him now would be foolish. No mermaid swam into the deep currents alone. There were too many dangers and the memory of that shark attack was still too vivid in her mind. As much as it humbled her, she headed for Pouraka burdened with an uneasy feeling.

Though no mermen were present, the great sea cave was bustling with activity. Today was basket making day but the calamities of recent events distracted the mermaids from their chores. Many of them huddled in the shadows, whispering. Others stayed near their children, hovering over the young ones as if to ward off some unknown danger. Piles of seaweed had been strewn on the rocks, still only a few mermaids wove the fibers together. Peara was perched on a narrow cliff above the magic tide pool, flattening strands of kelp. "Come sit by me, Cora." She offered a hand to Cora and pulled her onto the ledge.

Cora watched the young mermaid weave the shiny green lengths, tugging the folds tight against one another. Peara's fingers moved quickly, confidently. Cora was not certain what to say to her best friend. They hadn't spoken since the day after Ko's transformation. Peara kept her head bowed, her thick auburn hair concealed her sorrow, yet every once in a while she'd lift her wrist to wipe her cheeks.

Cora gathered kelp from the pile between them and began peeling the strands apart, handing them to Peara. Her friend peered sheepishly from behind her hair, and smiled.

"I'm sorry for your loss." Cora spoke softly.

"And I yours."

Indeed, they shared the same pain.

After a long sigh, Peara brushed her hair aside and patted Cora's hand. "You know, we've got to find the good in this. Ko wouldn't have it any other way. He risked his life for us, and lost it. He knew more than we wanted to admit. And he was right. Men are our enemies. That's why he changed."

"I don't know what you mean."

Peara lowered her weaving; her eyes were red from tears, her expression grave. "You should. Most of what Ko believed are ideas he gleaned from Tas."

"Are you blaming Tas for Ko's death?"

"Blame? There's no condemnation for what Ko did. If anything he's proven Tas right. I only wish I had realized it sooner, otherwise I'd be with Ko right now."

"What? Dead?"

Peara went back to her weaving.

"Changing isn't going to save us. Dolphins are at risk just like we are."

"Dolphins can ward off sharks and swim to greater depths than we can. If it weren't for mermaids, the dolphins would be far from shore. We're bound to the coast, Cora." Her voice was sharp, her brow furrowed. "It's only a matter of time before the men from the south discover Pouraka and its magic. Once they do, they will strip us of everything, even our lives."

"I think you're wrong." Cora handed her another strand of seaweed. "I don't think men are our enemies. Maybe some are, but not all of them." Cora ripped another length of kelp in two. "We can live peacefully alongside men and still be mermaids. We just have to be careful who sees us."

"That's just it. We have to hide all the time. We're in perpetual danger, Cora. Everyone, even the children. Why do you think Tas and his clan migrated here? The only reason we stay in Pouraka is for the magic ponds. If we were dolphins we wouldn't be anywhere near shore."

"And then there would be no mermaids." Cora argued.

"Does the world really need mermaids?"

Cora gawked in disbelief. "Are you serious?"

"I am. I see no functional purpose for us being tortured into seclusion when we could be free."

"We can live side by side with men. Barnacle Bay is proof. We're safe here." Cora assured her. "I know we are. My friends would never hurt us. Beth! Jamie! And the fishermen have sworn to protect us. You should have seen Leni scare those gill netters away."

Peara smirked. "Leni's violence is what killed Ko."

Cora slammed the kelp on the rock, heat rose to her temples. "Leni didn't kill Ko."

"No. But firing that gun prodded those men to do what they did."

"Who told you about the gun?"

"Kaile told me everything."

"Kaile has a big mouth!"

"Kaile is honest."

First Peara denied her heritage and now she blamed Leni for Ko's death. "This is hard to take."

"It is, isn't it?"

Cora pulled apart two short strands of kelp and set them down. "How many other mermaids want to transform?"

Peara scanned the cavern, resting her eyes on the mermaids that worked quietly. "More than you think," she mouthed.

Cora dropped the kelp and brushed her hands. She'd go nuts continuing this conversation especially while worrying about Tas. "I'm going to go talk to Leni right now."

"That's not a good idea."

"Why?"

"What can Leni do that he hasn't already done?"

"You're crazy to blame Ko's death on Leni. Leni loves us and he loves the dolphins."

Cora glared at her with narrow eyes but Peara only shrugged. "I'm devastated over Ko's death. But I would never blame Leni. If anything, Leni was trying to chase the riggers out of the bay. If anything, Leni was defending the dolphins. Someday I hope I can convince you that the people of Barnacle Bay are our allies!"

Words weren't flowing the way Cora wanted them to. Her friendship with Peara was too important to say what she really wanted to say. She'd be misunderstood.

Cora slid into the tide pool, submerging her body into the magical waters until she took on human form. Her scales hung off her shoulders as a shimmering tank top and clung to her legs as pants.

"What are you doing?" Peara asked.

"I'm going into town to tell my friends what's been happening." She gathered her seaweed pack and with one last glance at Peara, began climbing out of Pouraka. The other mermaids in the cavern stared at her.

"Don't!" Peara called, putting her unfinished basket down.

"You can't stop me. I'm so tired of everyone telling me not to do things."

"Tas is going to be mad."

Cora turned sharply and looked Peara square in the eyes. "It's not my duty to control Tas' temper. He'll have to get a handle on it himself. I have just as much right to help our people as he does."

She stormed toward the skylight without turning back.

21. The Fisherman's Daughter

When Cora stepped from the shelter of Pouraka gusts of hot air blew bits of sand into her face. She squinted, blinded by the sudden sunlight and pivoted around to view the coast. Whitecaps danced on the ocean surface beyond the wharf and breakers pounded on the beach below, their music competed with the whistle of the wind. The scent of the sea gave her a sense of home. Still, somewhere out in that blue water Tas was fighting for the life of a pod of dolphins.

"I hope you're successful!" Cora shook away visions of sharks and nets with the toss of her hair.

Cora took a deep breath and set her mind and feet toward Barnacle Bay. A lazy afternoon in the township, no one stirred from their homes, nor were there any cars moving through the streets. She took the less used eastern trail that led directly to the paved highway. Stones and goat heads pricked at her heels sending spasms of pain up her legs. Once at the road she brushed the stickers from in-between her toes, turned her back to the breeze, and crossed into the neighborhood where houses blocked the brunt of the weather.

Beth's yellow and red trimmed home nestled on a corner lot just before the alley. Large purple flowers peeked out from behind trailing vines covering the awning that shielded the windows from the heat of the day. She skipped up the stairs, her feet soothed by the silky warm planks under her soles.

Cora breathed in the fresh perfume of flowers and dampened soil so different than the odors of Pouraka with its kelp and musty salt fragrance. Beth's porch smelled sweet.

The verandah had a display of fascinating objects arranged among the flower pots, driftwood hangings, and antique wrought iron chairs. Next to the door stood a large aquarium, an abode for three baby sea stars, a variety of sand snails, and a hermit crab. The creatures hid among rocks and pools of water in a miniature cove Beth had made for them. One of the sea stars was missing a leg due to a disease. Beth was researching the malady at the university.

Before Cora knocked on the door, she put her nose to the miniature rose in the window box. Of all the flowers she had seen in Barnacle Bay, the rose was her favorite. When she told Tas about the sweet smelling pink and violet petals he responded with, "You are more beautiful than any bush on a human being's porch. You are my Sea Rose." He's used that term of endearment for her ever since. Her smile faded as she sniffed the flower.

Red geraniums adorned the cobalt planters by the door and today the wind chimes sang sweeter than a merman at a wedding. A pang of remorse tingled in her bones as she thought of Tas, and then of her brother. She swallowed the tears forming in her throat, lowered the basket off her back and took out a shell necklace wrapped in sea lettuce, a present she had made her friend.

Merpeople often gave gifts when they were sad. The act of giving eased whatever emotional pain they were experiencing. Cora clutched the parcel tight in her fist and tapped on the door, taking a step back when she heard footsteps and female voices inside.

Good! Beth was home!

The door creaked open and Beth's little sister Sasha peeked out. "Oh! It's Cora! It's the mermaid! You came at just the right time!"

The girl immediately pulled Cora inside. "I missed you! I have something to show you."

"I missed you too." Cora smiled at the child and forgot her troubles the moment the girl's soft white hands slipped into hers. "What do you have to show me?"

"My favorite book of all books. It belonged to my grandma. We found it in mama's trunk last week. You're going to love it!"

Sasha dragged Cora into a cozy but cluttered room lined with bookshelves, aquariums and an overstuffed couch. Thrown over the seat was a red and black afghan and so many pillows Cora had to move them aside to sit. Sasha bounced on the couch next to her holding an old gray book with a torn spine and worn pages falling loose.

"Look!" Sasha pushed the book in Cora's lap.
"It's lovely."
"You think? I don't. The cover is kind of boring and it's falling apart. But read what it's about!"
Cora thumbed through the pages looking for pictures that might give her a hint as to what the story said.
"Here. I'll show you." Sasha took the book from her and flipped it open to a black and white drawing of a mermaid sitting on a rock. In the distance was a shoreline and pyramid-waves that curled at the tips. Beyond that, against the puffy clouds, stood a castle.
"It's about us?" Cora asked. "I thought people didn't know about us."
"It's a fairy tale. It's a story about a mermaid who wants to be a person because she falls in love with a handsome prince. But she can't be with him because well, because she can't."
Cora stared at the image and immediately thought of Peara and Ko. "Why can't she be with him? Because he's different?"
"Yep."
"So what does she do about it?" Was she thinking about Peara and Ko? Or was she really thinking about her and Tas should Tas decide to change? Cora shuddered.
"She goes to the wicked witch that lives in the sea."
"Oh!"
Sasha thumbed through the book and found another illustration. This one showed a young mermaid in a dark cave talking to an odd and ugly beast.

"A wicked witch lives in the sea? Is that her?"

"You didn't know?"

Cora had never heard this story before. She'd heard tales of dark and dangerous things living in the deepest parts of the ocean, the parts where merpeople are forbidden to go. But she never heard of a witch.

"What happens?"

"All sorts of bad things. The little mermaid gives up everything she has for her prince, even her tongue." Sasha stuck out her tongue and made an unpleasant noise. "But the prince marries someone else instead so the mermaid dies and goes to heaven."

"I see." Cora closed the book. "That's a sad story. Why did you want me to see it?"

"Because you're a mermaid. And I just wanted to warn you not to fall in love with someone you can't be with. Or don't go talk to a witch, either!"

The admonition left Cora stunned. "Okay."

"But while you're here, I wanted to ask if you can take me with you next time you go swimming? I've been practicing my dog paddle. I can dive off the diving board now, too." Sasha jumped up from the couch, her sandy curls bouncing on her shoulders as she put her hands on her hips. "I'm ready for you."

"I don't know, Sasha. Perhaps someday."

Sasha pouted. "It's sad to know a mermaid and never see her shimmer under water." Sasha fell back on the couch, pouted and fingered Cora's shiny tank top, the scales glistening with blues and blacks and purples. "I love them. They shine so pretty and I want to see them on you like they're supposed to be."

"Sasha, I can't promise you when, but someday you and I can go to the beach and I'll let you see me as a mermaid. Maybe. But not now. I have something important to tell your sister."

"Sasha, are you bugging Cora again!" Beth peeked out from behind a bedroom door.

"Not bugging!" Sasha insisted. When she saw her sister's grimace she backed away. "Sorry."

"Come on in, Cora." Beth ushered Cora into the bedroom and Sasha trailed close behind.

"Go color or something, Sasha. We're having a big girl conversation now. Go on!"

Sasha stopped in the doorway and waved at Cora. "Remember!"

Cora smiled.

"Remember what?" Beth asked as she shut the door.

"Oh Sasha was telling me a story."

"The Little Mermaid I bet? She's obsessed with that story now. She's been wanting to show you that book for over a week. She's afraid that something bad is going to happen to you. She keeps waking up at night and having bad dreams."

"Oh, I'm sorry, Beth. What are her dreams about?"

"Mom, mostly. I think the storms really scare her. The one the other night was horrid. Sasha said she heard voices singing but I told her it was just the wind or the wind chimes on the porch." They stared at each other for a moment.

Beth's best friend Jamie sat on the bed, a makeup case by her side. Dark curly hair, and big brown eyes, Jamie reminded Cora of an angelfish, perfect and graceful. She'd been applying lipstick and looked up when Cora walked in.

"I knew you'd come today! I just knew it!" Jamie slipped the cover onto the tube of her lipstick. She tossed it in the case, patting the bed next to her as a gesture for Cora to sit.

"You did? How did you know?" Sasha's mermaid story didn't make Cora feel any better and now with Beth mentioning her mom, how could she tell her two friends the sad news about Ko?

"I'm really glad you're here, Cora. How have things been going with you?" Beth bounced onto the bed next to Cora.

Cora didn't answer, she only shrugged. Where could she begin?

"How's Kaile?" Beth's face flushed when she asked.

"He's fine. The same as always I guess. Why do you ask about Kaile?"

Beth shrugged. "I saw him last night. He seemed, I don't know. Sad. He didn't come into town with you?"

"No."

"Is everything all right with you folks?"

Cora shrugged and twisted the wrapping on the gift she had brought.

"There's something Jamie and I wanted to talk to you about. Look!" Beth pulled a newspaper from the chair by her bed and opened it. "Read this!"

Cora gazed at the paper.

"Okay. I'll read it to you. But brace yourself. It isn't good news. Think of this article as a warning. You merpeople have got to be more careful! This newspaper comes all the way from the big city of Ocean Bend and it says this..." Beth cleared her throat and held the newspaper at eye level in front of her.

"The headline says, 'Is Barnacle Bay Hiding a Secret?'" Beth gave Cora a blue-eyed scowl, and then continued; all the while Cora's heart began to race.

"Nestled safely along the coast, the barely noticeable habitat would be missed by a weary passerby unless the gauge on their gas tank read near empty, or their stomachs hungered for a hot oyster sandwich from the local deli. Barnacle Bay fishermen keep the town alive, but barely. Still, with marine traffic increasing, the township is gaining more attention. Why? Well, some boaters from Ocean Bend claim sightings of unusual sea life. And some of them are insisting the glittering tail fins are those of mermaids."

Beth slammed the paper on her lap. "Cora, are you folks getting careless about where you swim?"

Cora's mouth dropped. Stunned, her gaze jumped from Beth to Jamie and back again. "Our people are careful."

"Do you know what this means, Cora?" Jamie took her hand.

Cora shook her head.

"This paper is the Ocean Bend Chronicles. The big city! Everyone in the big city is reading this story and now they're going to think mermaids live up here."

Cora's cheeks were suddenly warm as her friends stared at her. "I ... I didn't do anything!"

"No one is blaming you. But how many merpeople are there, Cora? We only know a few, you and Kaile, and Tas. We never met Ko and Peara but we know about them. Are there more?"

There were hundreds more, but not all merpeople believed in communicating with humans and it would be criminal for Cora to expose them. She stared back, speechless.

"People from Ocean Bend are going to be coming up this way now, you know that don't you? Tourists, boaters, trespassers!"

Cora bit her lip; tears welled in her eyes. She focused on her hands that now pulled and twisted at the gift she had brought. She smoothed out the wrapping and offered the present to her friend. "I made this for you." She hadn't the courage to look Beth in the eye anymore. She stood. "I should go now."

"No, Cora, don't leave. We didn't mean to make you feel bad. We wanted to warn you. You're right. These sightings were probably not your fault. But still it isn't good news for any of you."

"I'll let them know." How she yearned to tell Beth and Jamie what had happened, but it didn't seem relevant any more.

"Wait!" Beth jumped up from the bed, taking Cora's arm. "We didn't mean any harm. Honest!"

Cora wiped her eyes and peeked at Jamie who smiled sympathetically.

"You had something to tell us. What was it?" Beth brushed Cora's hair over her shoulders and combed it gently with her fingers. "What?"

Words were not coming.

"Cora? What's wrong?"

She couldn't hold the tears back no matter how hard she bit her lip or blinked her eyes. Beth wrapped her arm around Cora's shoulders and urged her to sit on the bed again. "Honey, tell us what's wrong?"

"It's Ko. He's dead."

A hush swept through the room.

"How?" Beth handed Cora a tissue.

"Nets, fishermen, they killed him." The story came out in broken sentences and gushes of emotion. Jamie pulled tissues out of the box while Beth held Cora's shoulders.

"Did the fishermen see Ko before they killed him? They saw a merman?"

Cora shook her head and blew her nose. It would be wrong to tell them he was a dolphin when he died, they didn't need to know. They'd ask too many questions which would lead to spilling out the truth about Pouraka. When she had relayed the entire event, Cora took a deep breath. "Do you remember that day you and your friends stumbled onto our secret?"

"You mean last summer, when we saw you in the cove, sun bathing as merpeople early in the morning?" Beth shared a smile with Jamie. "I could never forget how beautiful a sight that was, how you all glowed, with your scales shimmering in the sun. We've come to love every one of you. I'm so sorry for Ko's death. If I could do something..."

"No. You can't. There's nothing anyone can do to bring him back. But..." Cora's eyes met Beth's. "I want you to know that no matter what happens, I'm not ashamed that you know who and what I am. We're friends."

"Of course, Cora. Everyone loves you."

"No! I mean you and me. No matter what happens with anyone else, you and I are friends. You too, Jamie."

Jamie nodded and then frowned. "What's going to happen?"

"I don't know. But..." How could Cora tell them that the mermen were getting nervous? That Tas mistrusted all humans, men, women and children? That Peara blamed Ko's death on Leni? That if things continued as they were, Barnacle Bay would never see any of them again? "I don't know," Cora said.

"Well no matter what, we'll keep your secret. I promise." Beth squeezed her hand.

22. Knots

Tas heard the commotion before he saw what was happening. He swam faster toward the hollow hum of man's machine, the whistling screech of dolphins, and the slap of their flukes. The water thickened with mud and silt, stirred up by the rotating nets.

Through the haze Tas discerned two captive dolphins amongst a school of cod struggling on the inside of a net. Pushing against the knotted prison with fins rubbed raw and noses bleeding, they cried in agony. His heart feared for them, and that fear turned to anger. First Ko's death, and now this. When will these people stop this brutal attack on sea life?

The harder the poor creatures fought, the tighter the ropes entangled them. Tas charged at the net with his whalebone, and sawed at the threads in a desperate attempt to free the terrified creatures. He clung to the ropes with one arm as the net whirled him around.

Kaile and the other mermen each attacked a different part of the net, freeing fish small enough to wriggle through the loosened macramé. Yet the snarled mass of line could not be compromised enough to release the dolphins or the tuna. The main rope was coarse and strong and held a great resistance to whalebone. Bodies of captive fish slammed into Tas. Each collision knocked the blade out of its groove and Tas had to start his cut over again while the net dragged him and its contents across the ocean floor.

Above him the dark underside of the boat blocked the sunlight. Higher and higher the net rose, and tighter it pulled together. Fish wrestled against each other in an effort to escape, their gills snagged, their mouths opened and thrust against the bindings by the weight of the dolphins.

"Tas! Help! I'm caught!"

Tas stopped his cutting and leaned away from the net enough to see the extent of Kaile's ensnarement. The merman's fin was entangled in the net and pinched against several large tilefish. Though Kaile pulled and pushed to free himself the tilefish only leaned against him tighter.

Tas stopped sawing and swam to Kaile. He pulled on the net in an attempt to make enough room for Kaile to slide away but Kaile couldn't move. Tas sawed the rope of the fiber wall frantically and was able to loosen several knots.

"I'm going to die." Kaile's breathing was labored more from terror than exertion.

"Don't panic. I'll get you out of this."

The color from Kaile's face drained as the net moved steadily higher. "I didn't want to die in the sea, Tas. I swear I didn't want this."

"No one wants to die, Kaile." Tas worked harder. His hands were numb but saving Kaile was more important than the dolphins now. It was only a matter of minutes before the ball of net and its catch would break surface. "Don't panic. I'll get you loose." Tas assured him.

Daylight glinted above them and the water warmed. "Duck, Kaile, don't let them see you!"

Kaile crouched as Tas snatched the netting again, adrenaline empowered him this time. The threads finally broke loose and ripped in his hands. Kaile slid free and dove. Tas turned to follow, but when one of the captive dolphins shoved his nose into the hole Tas had made, he turned to free it certain that with another sweep of the blade, the dolphin could be saved. When Tas enlarged the hole enough for the dolphin to push past him the net sprung upward. Tas lost his balance and fell in among the tonnage of sea creatures. Water gushed over him as the net was pulled out of the water. Stunned and blinded from the sunlight that shone in his eyes, Tas swung with the captive sea beasts high above the sea.

Not until he heard men shouting underneath him did he gain a sense of what had happened.

"Look at that! Look what we caught! Holy Persephone!"

Tas scanned the many hands waving and pointing at him. He rammed against the lines that held him above the boat. If he could break past the net he could dive and swim away. He had lost the whalebone, though, and his strength was spent.

Men on deck huddled around the pulley, lowering the net as fish dropped onto the boat. One of the dolphins spun overboard, but the men didn't seem to mind. Tas was their prize. Once within their reach, men's rough and greedy hands grasped his tail and tried to yank him through the mesh.

"Stop! No, let him go!"

Kaile called from the water. Several of the crew leaned over the railing starboard and jeered but Kaile didn't seem to understand that his life was also in danger.

"Kaile go!" Tas shouted above the noise of the pulleys and the shouting of the men.

"Please? He's done you no harm. Let him go."

"Look, another one! Get some line, make a lasso. The harpoons!" The sailors scrambled, tossing line and a life raft into the water. One man whirled a rope and slung it at Kaile.

"Go, Kaile!" Tas shouted again as he landed atop a mound of fish on the deck. He made eye contact with Kaile for a split second. "Go!" Tas ordered with the last of his strength, relieved when Kaile disappeared under the water. Tas dropped against the wet wood floor, helpless and muddled with hundreds of dying fish.

Spent and dizzy from exhaustion and pain, the world darkened as he fought to keep his eyes open. Men surrounded him, swiping fish off of his body, poking him, gawking, talking into cell phones and taking pictures. Finally Tas lost consciousness.

23. Pouraka Compromised

    Cora had originally planned to walk to the wharf and tell Leni about Ko's death, and to see if he could help the dolphins that were in trouble. But after talking to Beth she was so discouraged that all she wanted to do was go home. Nothing made any sense. Who were the careless mers that had been seen and what kind of danger did it put the rest of the clan in? She should return to Pouraka, warn everyone, and forget her plans to go to the pier. She would tell Leni everything when she felt better. Tas could walk with her to the wharf in the morning and help her explain.
    Cora hiked up the grassy hill, the crest of which concealed the cavern entrance. The salty wind gave her goose bumps and with the chill, a sick feeling came over her. What if Tas was right? What if the merpeople should flee to the deepest parts of the ocean? They would never be able to dive that deep and that far away in merform. They'd have to change.
    Cora loved the beach, the reef, and the magic pools. She didn't love the dark depths of the ocean, its mystery or its danger. She was terrified of the abyss and all that might lie below the green water. And what if there was a witch like in Sasha's story?

"I would never make baskets and jewelry, or feel the ground under my feet. I'd never roam the beaches picking up seashells, or visit with my friends." She gazed out over the ocean again. "I'd have to say goodbye to Beth and Jamie forever. But the worse thing is..." She wiped a tear. "I would never be in Tas' arms again because he wouldn't have any arms." She shuddered. There was only one way to convince Tas not to lead her people to change and that was to convince him men and mers could coexist.

Unfortunately, with Ko's death, the odds of proving that any humans could be trusted were against her.

Before Cora reached the narrow opening of Pouraka, she turned to Barnacle Bay, the beach, the wharf, and the highway. The sun was low in the sky, making all the colors of the earth glow golden. A car sped toward the town on the lonely shoreline highway, its radio blaring. Envy crept through her as she watched the red vehicle speed down the road. Those people were having so much fun. Beth would get her license soon and had promised to take Cora for a ride in her dad's truck. Cora had been anticipating that day.

As the vehicle neared the bend where she stood, it slowed and the headlights flashed. A girl leaned out the window, her hair flew in the wind and Cora heard the other passengers laugh. They pointed up the hill at Cora. Cora thought they were waving so she waved back, though she didn't know who they were. The horn honked. Cora took a step backwards not certain what to make of the sound. The windows closed and the car sped away.

"Cora!"

Cora jumped, startled as Kaile appeared from out of Pouraka and onto the hillside.

"Cora! I have to tell you something."

She spun around with wide eyes. Kaile panted as he approached, his hair was wet, his face pale. He'd been scraped on the cheek and he had bruises on his hands.

"Kaile, what happened?"

"Tas was captured."

"What?"

"There's a search party going out right now to try and save him. I would have gone with them, but I had to find you."

"What do you mean captured?"

"The fishermen. It was a gill net. Possibly the same people that caught that shark but I don't know. Look." He pointed toward the southern waters. On the horizon a tiny dot of a ship danced on the sea. "They have Tas."

"Oh no." Though Cora wanted to hear the story, her heart raced so fast she held Kaile's arm to keep from fainting. She took several deep breaths. "You didn't help him?"

"There was nothing I could do, Cora. He was in the net and hoisted into the air, hanging above the boat before I knew. He told me to go. We've got to tell Leni. I thought we'd go tell Leni and ask for his help even if the boat is that far south. I thought if we talked to Leni he'd take us out there. I don't see how the mers can rescue him without his help." Kaile wiped the blood that still oozed from his cheek. His hands shook.

"And what would Leni do?"

"Leni could ask that they give Tas back."

Cora shook her head. Truly Kaile was as naïve as they come. "Kaile, if they pulled him out of the water and didn't put him back in, why do you think they would release him to Leni?"

Kaile shrugged.

"Where were you when Tas was caught?"

"In the water. I had been tangled in the net and Tas freed me. He reached in to free one of the dolphins and that's when the net pulled him and a lot of other fish out of the water and into their boat."

"And you were far away by then?"

"No." Kaile blushed. "No, I watched."

"With your head above the surface?"

The veins in Kaile's temple pulsated, his blue eyes paled.

"They saw you, didn't they?"

"I pleaded with them to let him go but they started throwing things at me. Tas told me to leave."

"Great. So if they see you on Leni's boat they'll know that Leni knows about us. They know your face and they know you're a merman. Were these people the same men who dropped you off at the dock that day Leni fired the gun? The day Ko was killed?"

"Tom and his friends? No. I don't think so. It might have been the same boat though, I don't know."

At that moment a horn sounded again as the red car approached from the other direction. Cora clutched Kaile's arm, dragged him to the mouth of the cavern. They dodged into Pouraka and rushed down the damp rocky ledges. Several of the mermaids still lingered but most of the basketry had been put away, the new woven vessels shelved to dry. Already the cavern was cool in the evening shadows.

"Who was that?" Kaile asked between breaths.

"I don't know but they drove by just before you came. They waved at me like they knew me but I'm pretty sure I've never seen them before. At least I've never seen that car before."

They stopped talking when they heard voices. Cora surveyed the other merpeople in the pools. Alerted, the mermaids dove quietly into the water, with several children who splashed in after them, and swam away. If the humans were coming into Pouraka, it would be too late for her and Kaile to take on mermaid form. The voices were too near. Cora took Kaile's hand and pulled him into an adjoining cave before four people leaned over the edge above the stairway. They were young adults, two men and two women, not much older than Tas.

"Wow, look at this place. Do you think that girl came down here?"

"Spooky."

"Let's go in. I bet she's one of those mermaids."

"You're crazy Jake, you don't really believe that hype? I'm sure the newspapers were scamming people to sell oysters at that convenience store. You know marketing these days!" They laughed.

"I'm going down there," one of the men said.
Kaile inched further into the shadows.

"Wait, Jesse. You might be sorry you did."

"Why's that?"

"Caves like this can fill up with water when the tide comes in."

"Chicken. You climb out before the tide comes in. It's just a friggin' cave. Allison, you in?"

"Lead the way, oh great leader."

Cora hugged the wall of the crevice they were hiding in, but there was no guessing how curious these people would be. She held her breath, listening, exchanging fearful glances with Kaile.

"Look at this!" Allison's voice echoed clear. She sauntered ahead of Jesse, and when she found several of the mermaid's baskets she picked one up. The other two humans lingered behind on the steps.

"This is cool! Karen, come check this out! Whoever lives down here makes these things." While fingering the basket Allison jumped back, dropping the hamper to the ground. "Ew! Slimy."

"It's made up of seaweed, of course it's slimy."

As Cora peeked around the corner the man named Jesse approached the Cradle.

"Those pools are so clear! I wonder if they're hot springs." The stranger stepped up to the ledge of the center pool and leaned over.

"No, dummy, hot springs aren't clear like that." Allison kneeled near the ledge.

Cora panicked. They mustn't touch the sacred waters. She took Kaile's arm and pulled him to her.

Kaile pulled away.

"Kiss me," she said, her voice well above a whisper.

"What?"

Cora pulled him to her, took his head in her hands and planted her lips against his, inching him toward the light, keeping an eye fixed on the strangers. Kaile was hesitant to touch her at first, but then he sighed and squeezed her tighter, his lips pressed harder against hers. She closed her eyes and felt his heartbeat, his chest pulsating against hers.

Karen tapped Allison on the shoulder and pointed at Cora and Kaile. Jesse cleared his throat. "I think we found our mermaid."

"Oh! A love cave," Allison said and took Jesse's arm. "Let's go and leave them alone. It's kind of creepy in here anyway and it's getting dark." She called out to Cora and Kaile. "Sorry!"

Not until the foursome stumbled up the rocky ledged steps and disappeared into daylight did Cora release Kaile. She waited until she no longer heard their footsteps before she sighed.

Kaile smiled and licked his lips. "Wow! Okay. That was good, Cora. I didn't realize there was anything between us."

"Don't be ridiculous." Cora slapped his arm. "That was show."

"Was it?"

"It got them out of here. That's all it was meant to do. Although, the damage has been done I'm afraid. Pouraka was compromised. I have a feeling things are going to get worse. We have to rescue Tas and we need to do it now."

"We do. And we need to hurry. I'm afraid for him."

She searched Kaile's eyes. They could do what Kaile suggested and run to Leni, have him run down the boat that Tas was on, but then what? Would Leni start shooting like he did before?

"What?" Kaile pressed. "Why are you looking at me like that?"

"Because we can't do that."

"Do what?"

"We can't just race off and get Leni and have him start shooting. What if they do something to hurt Tas?"

"Cora, they could have already."

"Don't think like that. We can't think like that, Kaile."

He nodded, his eyes glued to hers. "I'm trying hard not to. But what do we do?"

She stepped away from him and paced toward the Cradle. The turquoise water sparkled as it caught the last of the day's sunrays from outside. The answer had to be in the magic of that pool.

She picked up the basket that the stranger had dropped and rolled her hand over the hollow, fingering the strap so delicately made. Carefully dipping the woven vessel into the Cradle, she filled it with water and strapped it over her shoulders, sealed the lid and stood erect. "Stay here. Or swim away. But don't follow me, Kaile. They know you but they don't know me."

She didn't wait for his reaction. Cora climbed out of Pouraka, stepped into the light and walked toward the wharf.

24. Disappointment

Cora had never walked on the beach at night by herself before. Though not normally timid, tonight she trembled. The breakers pounded unusually hard, unless she was hearing her own heartbeat resounding like drums against the sand. Tas was gone. Where he was, she didn't know but men had taken him away. What would they do to him?

Newspapers had spread rumors about mermaids living in Barnacle Bay, and strangers had invaded the sacred cavern. This was not a good day. Anxiety knotted her gut. She tried to control her imagination but it did no good.

Cora shifted the weight on her back; the only comfort of the night was that she carried the magic waters. Her plan was vague and she had no idea if she'd find Tas, where she'd find him, or if she'd even find him alive.

She didn't walk on the street but rather on the grassy bank above the beach. The lights of the village were ominous, not friendly as they had been the many nights she and Tas walked home together under the stars. She cringed at the first sight of headlights on the road, and jumped off the ledge onto the sand, ducking for fear of being seen. With all this quivering fear, Cora was not herself. She hated being afraid. She hated being vulnerable.

Barnacle Bay could not be seen from the low shoreline nor could the people in the town or on the road see her. The luminous white of the waves breaking on the moonlit shore offered more security than man's electricity. In the distance the dark silhouette of the pier beckoned her and she squinted to see if Leni's boat was docked. It was. A dim lantern moved on the wharf indicating Leni was awake and moving about. She broke into a run staying out of reach of the shallow breakers. The wet sand cooled her feet and allowed her to move swiftly. She held the basket steady on her back, and controlled her breathing so she'd still have some strength left by the time she reached the wharf. The night air cooled her head and by some strange miracle she reached the pier quicker than she believed possible.

Once on the wooden planks, she eyed Leni stepping into the Sea Quest's cabin and raced to catch him before he went home.

"Leni!" She sighed when the hatch opened. He had his pack and had locked his door behind him.

"Good heavens, girl, what are you doing here at this hour? Are you alone? It's not safe for a young lady to be walking around by herself at night. You should know that."

"Leni something terrible has happened and we need your help. I wouldn't have bothered you, but I don't know who else to turn to." Cora paused to catch her breath.

"Settle down there little miss. Settle down. I've got a moment to talk. Sit down." He nodded toward the deck but Cora refused the offer.

"I can't sit down. Not now."

Leni waited a moment as his inquiring eyes studied her "Okay, then what can I do for you?"

"Tas has been captured."

The fisherman's eyes widened, the whites of them reflected the moonlight. "Captured? By whom? Where?"

"I don't know those answers. The southern pod got tangled in nets so the mermen went to rescue them. I'm not sure how it happened, but Kaile saw everything. Tas was caught and they have him on their boat, and I don't know what they're going to do to him. Please help, Leni! Please help me get Tas back."

Leni studied the horizon at the dark and foreboding sea.

"Please don't go with your guns or anything. They might get scared or angry and hurt Tas like they did. . ." She stopped herself before she said 'Ko', ". . .the dolphin. But please help me save Tas!"

Leni brushed his hair back with his hands and focus on the ocean again. Cora followed his eye. Stars cast dancing beams that rippled in the dark. Tiny lights flickered in the distance and the lights of a boat on the horizon spread a beam of color on the quiet waters. Leni rubbed his chin awhile. "I take it he's in merman form?"

The look on Leni's face when she nodded, and the way he shook his head made Cora's stomach churn. "You have to help us, Leni. There's no one else."

"Cora." Leni bowed his head. Cora waited for him to think, to come up with a plan but all he did was shake his head over and over again.

"Leni!" she pleaded.

"I'm not sure what all I can do. If they caught themselves a merman, they aren't going to give him up just because an old fisherman asks them to. If it's that oil rigger's son, he'll laugh and who knows what he'd do to Tas. They don't have any respect for me you know. They don't have much respect for life at all."

"What are you saying?" She couldn't believe his response. Leni had always been so understanding, so available when the merpeople needed him. "Are you saying you won't do anything?"

"I'm saying I can't just race out there and ask them to release Tas. If he's held captive, he's going to be under tight security. Heck, he might not even be on that boat. He might be halfway to Ocean Bend by now."

"Leni!"

"Cora, this is bigger than you can imagine. Men have been trying to catch merfolk for thousands of years! They'll take him to the nearest lab or university and do tests on him. The newspapers will be all over it. The government might even claim him." He shook his head again and met Cora's eyes. A sympathetic pout turned down the corners of his lips. "I'm afraid Tas' fate is out of our hands, Cora. You'd better warn your friends because those people will be coming back for more. Believe me."

"You're not going to do anything? You're not going to try and free him?"

Leni threw his hands out in helplessness. "What can I do? If I try to run that boat down, even if I pull out my guns and start shooting, they're going to laugh at me. They'll know we're hiding something. Scientists, government officials, they'll all be up here harassing folks at Barnacle Bay asking questions. I've got family, Cora. I've got two daughters who need me. I can't have those people knocking on our doors searching for mermaids."

"You swore to protect our secret!"

"And that we did. This wasn't our mistake."

If she weren't so angry she'd burst into tears. Never once did she think Leni would withdraw from helping her and especially when Tas' life was at stake. "You can't let them take him, Leni. I don't care if they know we're mers. I don't care what they think, save Tas! Please!"

Leni didn't respond. She felt his eyes on her as she sobbed and wiped her nose, paced the deck of the Sea Quest and twisted her hair, but he didn't move. His expression was grave and she knew he was feeling remorse, but feelings wouldn't bring back the one she loved. Even her own hysterics wouldn't bring him back. She wiped her eyes again and nodded. "Okay. So you aren't going to help. I can understand and it's okay because it's not your problem. I thought you cared."

"I care, Cora."

"I thought you cared about us."

He took her arm. "I care about you. I care about my family and I care about Barnacle Bay. I wish I could help you, but Tas being captured by a big fishing rig out of Ocean Bend is more than I can deal with alone. If I can think of a way to get him back I will. But right now I'm clueless."

"Well then I'll deal with it. Alone!"

Leni released her arm and spoke in a soft and gentle voice. "Go home, Cora. Tell your people to stay far away from boats. Tell them to hide. I don't know what kind of places you folks have underwater, or if you even have a home. I do know there are caves and things you can hide in. That's what I would do if I were you. Tas is a strong man merman. He's pretty smart too. If it's meant to be, he'll escape. You take care of yourself, and Kaile and your other friends. It'd break my heart to see any more of you rounded up."

He might have meant to be fatherly but Cora was repulsed. She adjusted the pack on her back, wiped her eyes one last time and stepped off the boat onto the dock.

"Go home, Cora."

Cora walked to the end of the wharf, but instead of going down the flight of stairs toward Pouraka, she took the steps that led in the opposite direction, south, toward Ocean Bend.

"Cora, don't be going that way!"

Without another thought she let the night breeze kidnap his warning and blow it far from her. No she will not give up her pursuit. The coast stretched far into the dark, away from the highway toward towering cliffs and rocky coves. The breakers hummed a traveling song and her feet kept beat.

25. Distant shores

Tas woke to the sound of squeaking rubber under his back. The moon greeted him with a catty smile, haunting and vengeful. His first instinct was to jump and swim, but a pain bolted through his arms. He was bound tight, his hands tied. He struggled against the ropes, cringing from the sensation. His tough merman skin that was usually satiny and moist was now cracked. Blisters from dehydration formed on his lips. His stomach tightened. His throat swelled.

"There, there, fella!" A man leaned over Tas. "No need to get upset. We'll find you a home soon." The stranger shook his head as he inspected Tas, running his calloused fingers over Tas' dehydrated fins. "I swear I have never seen the likes of you before. The size of those scales alone!"

"Who are you?"

The man laughed. "Who am I? It's you who should be telling me who or what you are?"

Tas grimaced.

"The name is Arnold. And it surprises me that you can talk. They said you were half fish but fish don't talk."

Tas said nothing. The lack of water drained his energy. He rested his head on the floor of the raft again and closed his eyes.

"I bet you're wondering what you're doing on this raft in the middle of the night."

Tas could only breathe an answer, as his mouth was too parched to speak. "I'm dying."

Arnold didn't seem to hear. Instead he rambled on. "Then I'll let you in on a little secret. You and I are going to Ocean Bend."

Tas peered at Arnold through half opened eyes.

The moonlight cast a pale aura over the man's balding head. Unshaven whiskers dotted his portly cheeks and his nose was scaly from sunburn. A satisfied smile stretched across Arnold's pudgy face.

He sat in the center of the dinghy and rowed with both oars, his body rocking slowly and he chuckled as he pulled and swayed. "Why in a rubber raft, you ask? Well once Tom motored to the fishing rig and saw you, he didn't want to split the profits with the rest of his dad's crew, that's why. He figured he's on to something here. Tom took me aside and said to get you to a holding tank and call my cousin pronto. The sooner we ship you to the mainland, the sooner we'll be rich."

Arnold didn't wait for a response from Tas. If he had paid attention to the merman he might have seen how shallow Tas' breathing was, or how chapped his lips.

"Tom's a smart one though. He figured if there was a man mermaid, there'd be one of those pretty female ones nearby. You know, the ones you see in story books? Seen any of those?"

He gave Tas a crooked smile. "I bet you have! So Tom's staying on board his dad's boat to do some fishing. Can't blame him, really. For whatever price he gets for one mermaid, you know it will double for two. Not to mention any little ones born in captivity." His grin took an evil slant. "You just might be the start of a legacy there fella. Another wonder of the world! Not only entertainment, but science too."

Tas mustered his strength and with great effort rolled up onto his elbow to study the water and get his bearings. The gill netter had drifted farther north, very near the mouth of the bay. Arnold navigated the raft in the opposite direction, south, riding the current along the shore.

"How many of those do you have?" Tas' words were scratchy and hurt his throat as they came out.

"What? Fishing boats? Heck, Tom's old man bought a fleet of them but the Beeracuda is Tom's favorite. That one there, the one that pulled you up, that's the Ransom. Pretty boat but expensive to run. Hence the dinghy. Couldn't get the outboard to kick over so I said what the heck, give me an oar. We've a little bit of a row to Ocean Bend, but it will be worth it." He laughed again. "My cousin will be mighty proud. He owns an aquarium. A big one. He'll go berserk when he sees you! What do you bet he gives you one of the big special tanks? He keeps the orcas in there now. Does your kind get along with orcas?"

Tas glared at the man. If he could channel the anger that raged inside of him, he'd burn the ropes he was tied with, dislodge this demon into the water, drag him to the bottom of the ocean and hold him there.

Arnold chuckled to himself as he rowed. "Guess we'll find out. You know, there's been some wild tales about mermaids, and all this time I thought they were kid stories. Never have I seen the likes before!"

"I'm not a mermaid!"

"What do you call yourself then? Merman?"

"Yes."

Tas tried to move his tail fin but he was bound so tight it had gone numb. Dehydration was setting in. If he didn't get in the water soon, his body would shrivel.

"Cousin Matt comes to Ocean Bend for sea mammals every six months or so, dolphins, orcas. Replenishes his stock now and then. You know, short life span in the tanks. He's not due for a month but if I call and tell him I have a mermaid, excuse me...merman, you can bet he'll drop what he's doing. You, dear fellow will take the cake. This is priceless. Folks from all over the world will come to see you." He squinted at Tas with a crooked smile. "You might have to live in a fish bowl for the rest of your life but that's no sweat off my back. Times are tough on all of us."

Tas stared at the man. How could anyone's thoughts be so wicked?

Arnold leaned forward and squinted at Tas. "Feel like answering some questions?"

"Like what?"

"How many more mermaids are out there?"

Tas lay back down. He would sooner stick his hand in a shark's mouth than tell the secrets of Pouraka to this joker!

"Tom's taking his motorboat out to find that friend of yours in the morning. They're hoping he'll lead them to the females."

Tas wrestled against the rope again, but it was useless.

"What? Does that get your goat? Don't like anyone messing with your lady friends? Don't worry. Matt will probably throw you all in the same tank. He's kinder than I am. I'd give you each your own window to stare out at the public. Solitude would keep you fat and happy. But Matt, he considers the social aspect. Thinks mammals live longer when they're allowed the social fineries. He'll try and find your natural mate. Don't worry; you'll both be well fed. He'll probably teach you some tricks, like jumping through hoops and such!" Arnold laughed. "Yep, Matt has class."

Tas closed his eyes wishing he could close his ears and block out the sound of Arnold's voice. When the man's breath became heavy, Tas peered through one eye. Sweat beaded on Arnold's brow, and his motions were labored. "Seems to be getting harder to move this thing."

"Tide's coming in." Tas watched Arnold, though his stomach churned from his appearance and his ruthless ways. Perhaps this fool would wear himself out.

"Yeah, so it is."

"You should row toward shore."

Arnold steadied his gaze on Tas. the corners of his lips bent in a pout. "Why? You fixing to mug me or something?"

"Mug you? With my hands tied behind my back?"

Arnold scowled at him. "I'm not letting you get away. I need the money, and you glitter gold."

"I won't be glittering if I die."

"Pfft, die! I'm not going to kill you."

"Fair enough. Not purposely. But what you don't know will. Did you notice how dry my scales and my skin are? It's called dehydration and if I dehydrate it will take a long time to replenish the water in my body. I could die before you reach the harbor."

Arnold leaned forward again, released one of the oars and touched Tas' arm. Tas flinched. Without having changed to human form Tas' chance for survival out of water diminished by the minute.

"What's happening to you? You got lungs. You shouldn't die out of water. They say mermaids can live on land."

Tas shook his head and wet his lips with his tongue but the gesture only intensified the pain. The sense of touch was becoming more and more unbearable.

"Well I don't want to bring a dead merman to Matt."

"Lower me into the water." Tas was not accustomed to pleading for anything but tonight he was at this man's mercy. Perhaps Arnold had a soft side.

Arnold sat up straight. "Can't."

Tas' head fell back on the deck. He'd prepare for a slow and painful death. He'd never make it to Ocean Bend in this raft. Not with the current against them, and the physical nature of his oarsman.

Arnold relented and reached over the side to splash sea water into the dinghy. The sudden sting of salt on his cracked scales caused Tas to cry out. No! "Stop!"

"I thought you needed to be wet."

"Not like that." It was difficult to swallow, much less speak, but Tas fought the pain and raised himself on his elbow again. "There's too much salt on the surface of the sea. I need to dive into cool water."

"I can't have you dive."

Tas' eyes locked onto his. "You would have me die then?"

The man faltered for an answer. It was obvious he struggled with his conscience. "Not like that. I don't want you to die."

"Well I'm going to. I won't make it to Ocean Bend like this. I promise you that."

"I don't know what to do."

"There's a cove not far from here; row to shore and let me soak in the tide pools until morning."

"You'll escape."

"How? I'm tied. We've a long row to Ocean Bend and you aren't making much distance with the tide pushing against you." Tas lay down again. "This raft will be invisible in that shipping lane at night. You risk being run over. Ever see a living creature chewed up by a propeller? I have."

There was silence but for the sound of the oar fighting the sea and the rolling of the ocean splashing back at them.

"Go to the cove where you can rest and I can regain my strength. You can bring me into the city in the daylight." When Arnold only shifted uncomfortably Tas added, "Otherwise you'll have nothing to bring your cousin but a pile of bones and a handful of scales."

"I'm not so sure I want you to gain your strength."

Tas sighed, Arnold relented.

"But I don't want you dead, that's for sure." He stopped rowing and shifted in his seat, dipping one oar in the sea until the boat came about. Once the stern faced shore, Arnold rowed with both oars until the surf snatched the raft.

"Toss me overboard here, where it's deep."

Arnold hesitated before he tightened the line around Tas' fin, wiped his hands on his shirt and pulled Tas to an upright position.

He didn't untie the merman's hands. He lifted Tas onto the side of the raft with a grunt; the effort was strenuous for the man.

"Let me roll over the edge. It'll be easier."

"No monkey business!"

"I only want to get wet, sir. It's a thing with us merpeople."

Arnold moved to the other side of the seat to balance the tilt of the dinghy. With the extra room, Tas was able to rotate his body to the edge.

The wet rubber burned his chest as he slid out of the raft into the water, and the rope tied around his fin jerked him backward before he could hit the ocean floor. Arnold eventually cut him enough slack that Tas drifted downward, away from the agitated surf. Though he rocked back and forth with the swells, the cool water soothed his skin and began to soften his scales again.

26. Rainbow Coral

Kaile stood alone in the cavern watching the entryway expecting Cora to return. She didn't. Why didn't he follow her? Because she told him to stay? Tas would never let her wander alone on the beach at night. Shouldn't he watch out for her since Tas wasn't here to keep her safe?

"Fool!" Kaile kicked at the mussels on the rock, stubbing his toe. "What if something happens to her? It'll be my fault!"

Kaile made sure his whalebone knife was secure in the pocket of his shorts, and felt for the rainbow coral still in its pouch. He meant to give the coral to Beth as a gift but he hadn't seen her since that night on the beach after Ko died.

Kaile climbed out of the empty cavern and took one long look into its hollow. Gray in the moonlight, the breakers beat on the sand below crawling steadily toward the pools. The tide was coming in. How far Cora planned to walk, Kaile wasn't sure but the coves along the southern beaches would be dangerous for even a mermaid, more so for a mermaid without the use of her fins.

A sultry breeze hit his face. For a brief moment a radio sounded. Porch lights still lit the fronts of houses; an occasional car would pull out from a driveway. The deli was closed but the bar next to it was open, its neon signs flashed red and blue against the night.

Kaile hoped he'd be able to see movement on the beach, but aside from the steady pound of waves, not even a gull disturbed the sands.

Perhaps Cora was already with Leni. If she were, Kaile might be able to catch up to her. With Leni's help, the two of them could dissuade her from any foolish notion she might have about rescuing Tas alone. She should trust the mermen search party, or procure Leni's assistance.

Regardless of what she should do, Cora was too upset to think straight. He sensed an urgency as the lonely night sent a haunting chill through his bones. Kaile ran down the hill and along the beach.

Deep grainy sand resisted his rush. He kept an eye on the dock hoping to see Leni's lantern, disappointed that he didn't. Still the Sea Quest was tied to the pier, rocking with the incoming tide. As he neared, other movement drew his attention. A motorboat bobbed in the surf on the far side of the wharf next to the Sea Quest. At first Kaile thought it was Leni and Cora taking the dinghy out to find Tas. Excited that there might still be time to catch up with them, Kaile broke into a run but stopped short under the pilings. It wasn't Leni and Cora in the craft but rather two men with a third that climbed from the pier, a short hose in his hand.

"Hey!" Kaile's voice carried over the sound of the outboard. The three turned in surprise.

"Well look who we have here, Rick!" He spoke softly as he tossed the hose into the boat, jumped in and maneuvered the vessel to the beach. Kaile recognized him when his face caught the moonlight. Tom, the Dolphin Killer and his sidekick, Rick. Once ashore the men dragged the boat onto the sand and approached Kaile.

"Does Leni know you're on his boat?" Kaile asked.

"Leni doesn't need to know. He'll find out soon enough." Tom walked steadily toward him, his two friends a step behind. Tom had the smell of gasoline on him. The men's intimidating advance prompted Kaile to step back.

"Leni!" The call was sudden and loud. Leni needed to know about the intrusion, but Kaile was interrupted with a fist in his face. Blood burst from his mouth and out of his nose. He toppled backward into the sand. Rick grappled him by his shirt and wrestled him upright to face the man that hit him. Tom was twice as large as Kaile and all muscle.

"Tell me, kid, where are they?" Tom stuck his face up against Kaile's face; his breath was as foul as his sneer.

"What? Who?" Kaile held his hand over his bleeding nose while the men dragged him out from under the wharf into the moonlight.

Rick laughed when he reached in Kaile's pocket and pulled out the whalebone knife. "Check this out! Seems our friend, here is an artisan." He tossed the blade to Tom.

"Well I'll be a spearheaded mongrel! Whalebone with a driftwood hilt. Kind of aquatic, wouldn't you say?"

"You think this one's a merman?"

Kaile winced when Rick jerked his arms behind his back.

"Fess up… Kaile? That's your name, if I remember right. You're that porpoise hugging kid that blew up our raft, aren't you? The boy with the hot air. So tell us. Are you a merman?"

"He doesn't have any fins, Tom."

Kaile peered into the shadows to see if the third man was Pat but only saw a cigarette butt as it fell to the ground.

"No. Not now. But I'll bet he knows someone who does."

Kaile clenched his jaw when Tom grabbed his chin and lifted his face. The fire in the man's eyes burned for information that Kaile would never convey.

"Where are they? Where are the mermaids?"

"I don't know what you're talking about."

His lie met with another blow to the jaw, this one blinding him for a second. He would have fallen, but the men held him up. Tom punched him in the stomach and Kaile doubled over, the pain unbearable.

"I suspected you might be one, too. All I need is some kind of sign. What else is in his pockets, boys?"

Kaile fell in the sand when they released him.

His head throbbed. Blood and sand trickled from his mouth. He could barely breathe. He was so faint, he didn't protest when the men frisked him, nor did he try to stop them when they pulled the small bundle wrapped in cloth from one of his pockets.

It didn't matter what they took, Kaile wanted to be left alone in his pain. His vision blurred until he saw them as nothing more than blots of dark.

"Well I'll be! The mermaid's bounty. Don't tell me you don't know who I'm talking about!"

An eruption of sand flew into Kaile's face and the sole of someone's shoe met his cheekbone. Before he passed out Kaile heard laughing. And then they were gone.

27. Beth

Kaile woke to a cool cloth pressed against his head and the sun backlighting Beth's golden hair. Leni stood next to her. They both stared intently at him.

"Hang in there kid, the medics will be here soon. When'd this happen?"

Kaile blinked. "When did what happen?"

"Pops, I think he's got a concussion."

"What's a concussion?" Kaile touched her hand as she held the compress.

"Whoever did this to you dumped sand down my engine. I'd like to know who it was, Kaile. They did a felony's worth of damage."

Kaile tried to think. His mind was blank. "I don't know what happened. I'm not sure where I am."

"Dad and Benson found you under the pier this morning and brought you up here on the dock to get you out of the water before the tide rose any higher. Then he sent me a text." Beth's voice soothed the uneasy feeling he had in his gut. "Try to remember what happened last night. How did you get like this?"

"I don't know." He closed his eyes for a moment. Shutting out the light brought the figures back, the scoffing. He remembered. Kaile opened his eyes again and sighed when he saw Beth more clearly. "I set off from Pouraka to find Cora and then some guys jumped me."

"Who jumped you? And where did you come from?"

He stared at her as he recalled the mandate to never mention the cavern's name to a human being.

"From Pouraka!" Kaile stammered, uncertain of the damage he was doing.

"Where is Pouraka?"

"I ... I don't know. Somewhere. Nowhere."

Leni knelt down next to him and interrupted his ramblings. "Your friend Cora took off down the beach last night with nothing but a basket on her back. She said she was searching for Tas. I tried to stop her. Figured she'd be back home by now. Guess not."

Leni stood and paced, searching the roadway that ended at the pier, then the sea, and back to the road again. "She could have swam home, I think. Where are they?"

"Who, pops?"

"The medics. The boy needs stitches if nothing else. And I need to talk to the cops."

Kaile rolled over and pushed himself up on one elbow. Too fast, his head spun. He fell back down. "Oh man."

"You should stay down."

"No. Let me up. I'll be all right. I'd like to leave before the medics get here."

"Why?" Leni came back to his side and knelt down next to him again. "They're coming to see you!"

"Kaile, why? You need to take care of these wounds. You might need X-Rays."

"X-Rays? Do they sting?" Kaile's eye widened and he breathed a half laugh. "Why would anyone use rays for medicine? Most rays are poisonous."

"Silly, not that kind of ray. Photos. Of your insides."

"You're joking, right? That doesn't make sense. You take images on the outside, like with your cell phone. Or when the tide pools are still and you can see your reflection."

The twinkle in her eye made him laugh.

"You're teasing me aren't you?" he asked. "How can a doctor do that to my insides?"

"He has his ways."

"Well, wouldn't he find out I'm a merman? So, what then?"

Beth turned to her father. "What do you think?"

"His cut's bleeding. It needs stitches. What if he's got some internal damage?"

Kaile fought the dizziness and sat upright. He held his head for a moment, dabbing at the swelling around his eye. "Let me go back to Pouraka. I'll dive into the pool and everything will be fine."

He pulled his hand away from his bruise and caught their stares. Something's wrong. He did it again. First he told them about Pouraka and now he mentioned the magic pools. As he brushed his hair away from his face and felt blood still oozing from his forehead, remorse set in. He betrayed the magic cavern. "Just let me go home."

Sirens blared as vehicles with flashing lights pulled up to the end of the pier.

"Stay here, both of you." Leni ran to the end of the dock.

"Those thugs messed you up bad." Beth gave him a sympathetic pout as she brushed his hair away from his wound and held the compress against his forehead again. "That cut doesn't want to stop bleeding. Why would someone want to hurt you like this?"

"I think I was in the wrong place at the wrong time. If they were messing with your dad's boat they had to knock me out so I couldn't remember who they were."

"Can you?"

Kaile shook his head. There was no visual other than shapeless figures in the dark that he could recall, nothing that would help Leni, nothing to tell the police.

He leaned over and whispered to Beth. "Let me jump off the dock and go home." Kaile tried to rise, but stumbled before he could stand and then the men in uniform, their boots clapping on the wooden dock, came running. Questions flew at him. Questions he couldn't answer, or didn't want to.

"What your name?"

"Kaile"

"Where do you live?" Kaile's eyes widened. She rattled her address to him and told the officer that Kaile was her brother.

Leni vouched for him. "Yeah, that's my kid." And then he changed the subject, taking the policeman to his boat to show him the damage. Two of the medics came to him, took his pulse and checked his heartbeat.

"His vitals are fine. We can give you a ride in the ambulance if you want to go to the hospital but I don't see any need for the stretcher."

"No, no need for an ambulance. I'll be fine. Beth can take me in." Kaile said.

"I'll follow you in my dad's truck." Beth suggested. "It's just a cut. My father over-reacted."

"Who did this to you, kid?" An officer moved in between Kaile and the medics and stood over him with a notepad.

"I don't know. Not for sure. It was dark." Kaile's head pounded.

"Did you see the people who assaulted you prior to when they hit you?"

Kaile squinted up at the police officer. The sunlight behind him made it difficult to see his face. "I saw some men climbing off the dock into a motorboat and then the next thing I know I was knocked out. That's it." He did remember now. It was Tom and Rick and another person but if he told the officer, the conversation about mermaids might come up. He shut his mouth tight. He'd already told Beth about Pouraka. That was more than enough. He hoped Leni would divert the policemen's attention.

"I found this on my boat." Leni held up an empty beer can. "I'm pretty sure I know who they were."

"Would you want to come down to the station and answer some questions?"

"Sure, let's go." Leni gave Beth a nod toward Kaile. "Let me get the keys to my truck so my daughter and son can get home."

"You sure?" The policeman addressed Beth and she nodded. "He'll be okay. I promise I'll take him to the hospital if he shows signs of a concussion."

Beth helped Kaile to his feet once they were alone. "Do you want to go to that Pouraka place, Kaile? Would it make you feel better?"

Kaile leaned on her as he fought dizziness. In the distance lay the vacant highway, the corner deli and the bar where the bend in the road disappeared to the right, and where the hills to the left stretched out to the sea, their crest a rocky tip. Somewhere among that black shale was an entrance to a secret cavern, his not-so-secret, home. There he would find relief. "I'd like to go there, but..."

"Your secret's safe with me, Kaile. If you want I can run you up the road in Pop's truck and I'll help you get to where you need to go. If it makes you feel better, I promise I won't peek at your Pouraka place. And when you are done you can stay at the house with us, we have a spare bedroom. Either way is fine with me. Is that okay, Pops?"

Leni shrugged. "If that's what he wants to do. That's a brutal cut though. I still think it needs stitches." He stood with his hands on his hips, scowling with concern, yet with a gentle twinkle in his eye. "If I were a merman I wouldn't want x-rays either. What is this Pouraka place? The beach? Never mind, you don't need to tell me. Go on, I'll see you at the house a little later. Call my cell if you notice any changes in him Beth, if he seems dizzy or something. Don't wait."

"I'll be fine, really, Leni."

The healing waters of Pouraka would fix everything. Kaile could get his scales back, go for a swim, be a merman and curl in a cave somewhere and his troubles would go away. Still the attention Beth gave him was unlike any he'd ever had. Her gentle hand was irresistible, her soft and thoughtful touch comforting.

"You want to take me there?" Kaile asked Beth.

"To our house?"

"No, to Pouraka for a little while. We wouldn't have to stay. Just long enough to have some..." Her eyes were so innocent. She had no idea what Pouraka was. "Just long enough to get some water."

"If that's what you want then I'll help you get there."

Kaile wasn't sure what he wanted; he could barely think at all, but there was a gut feeling inside that he needed to go home. He let Beth hold him up as they staggered to Leni's pickup. The old door creaked when she pulled it open and pushed aside papers, a coffee cup and pieces of knotted fishing net. The truck's strange odors, fish, motor oil and metal all mixed together, gave his stomach a queasy feeling.

Leni stood by the window and handed her his keys after Beth slammed the driver's door shut. "Park by the railing near the stairs to the beach."

"I know pops. I wasn't going to go any farther."

Kaile was silent as she drove to the ramp a few minutes away. She turned left into the pullout and the truck jerked and stalled as she released the clutch too quickly. She laughed with a nervous tremor in her voice. "Sorry. I'm not used to driving a clutch."

Kaile smiled. "I thought this was a truck."

"Yes. It is." Beth jumped out and opened his door. "C'mon, Kaile. Take me to your beach."

"It's not simply a beach. Beth, wait, I have something for you." He reached into his pocket for the rainbow coral necklace he'd made for her. It was gone. He'd been robbed.

"What?"

"It's gone."

This was not the time to talk about missing coral even though it angered him to have his handiwork stolen. He would make her another. Kaile took her hand in his and led her to the footpath.

A wind always blew above Pouraka. Even on sunny days the salty spray rose from the ocean on a breeze. Today was no different except that Kaile was more aware of the refreshing smells. Holding hands with Beth gave him unnatural strength and lifted his spirits. When the two reached the crest of the mountain overlooking Barnacle Bay, he felt like a king. When he stopped in front of the narrow opening that led to the merpeople's sacred ground, he turned to Beth. "Someone came here the other day. They weren't supposed to. They didn't know what this place was, and they'll never know. You are the first human to ever experience Pouraka for what it is."

"I'm honored, but are you sure it's okay to take me there?"

"I have no doubts." He led her down the rocky incline. "Careful of your step. It's slippery."

Once inside, Kaile's shoulders dropped. Never had he seen the cavern so abandoned and his heart broke when he realized how much Pouraka had changed in so short a time. "This is our home, Beth. The merpeople live here. Or they did."

Beth stepped respectfully into the cavern, her eyes wide and mouth agape. "It's a beautiful home."

"It's magical."

"I should say so! But the merpeople are gone, aren't they? What's happened?"

Kaile shook his head as he contemplated the empty cave. The pools still held their turquoise waters, but there were no other signs of life. The baskets that he and Cora had seen the day before were gone. The shelves in the crevices were empty. Not a reed nor conch shell remained. "It does seem like everyone has fled, doesn't it?"

Kaile bent near the largest of the three pools. "They call this the Cradle. This is the healing water, and the place where we…" He stopped short as visions of Ko's transformation flashed across his mind.

"Where you what, Kaile?" Beth spoke softly, her reflection rippling in the pool. She touched his shoulder and knelt next to him. He refused to take his eyes off the image in the water. Her blond hair glistened with shades of red. an aura reflecting over the two of them like shimmering fire.

"…where we change, Beth."

She was so much like his people, like a mermaid. He cupped his palms and scooped the cool liquid into his hands, splashing it on his face. The relief tingled on his flesh and sent waves of healing to his head. He repeated the gesture until there was no more swelling. After he dabbed his face dry with his shirt, he turned to her. Drops of water fell from his lashes and he blinked them out of his eyes. "You see?"

She touched his face, her mouth open in awe. "You're healed? This place is magic?"

"This is where we change."

"Change? I don't understand."

"No. I don't think you could understand."

Beth stood. "This place is sacred to the mers, isn't it? That's why you never tell anyone about it."

"Yes. Someday I'll explain everything to you."

"Why?"

He took her hands in his, spreading Pouraka's water across her palms. Her hands were warm. She had pale fingers with long perfect fingernails painted with stars and crescent moons. The hairs on her arms glistened in the sun. Merpeople have tight, shiny skin even when they take human form. Not like hers which felt softer than the feelers on a sea urchin. He smiled into her blue eyes and hesitated before he spoke. "I want you to know how grateful I am for you."

Even though she shouldn't be here, even though no human eyes were ever supposed to behold the magic of the pools, still this moment was special. He didn't want to lose what he had right now. Never. "Beth, I don't want to change."

"It's okay, Kaile. You don't have to. Not for anyone."

Kaile drew close to her, his lips touched hers gently. He kissed Beth and wrapped his arms around her, pulling her body against his. As he did, all the pain and sorrow he'd experienced these last few months disappeared. He was healed, he was whole.

28. South Shores

Though the water soothed his body during the night, his agony returned in the morning when the rope tugged him through sand and rock. Arnold dragged Tas as if he were an anchor, fast and forceful. Tas rolled on his side and pushed against oyster shells to keep his chest and back from being cut, bearing the damage on his bound hands instead. When the rope fell slack in the shallows, Tas collapsed.

"Get up!"

Arnold gripped the merman's arms and with much effort rolled Tas back into the raft. The obese man fell into the vessel after him and then dug his oar into the grit to shove the rubber boat afloat.

Arnold rowed. The attention he gave Tas was only enough to send an accusing glare. "We'd have been at Ocean Bend by now if we hadn't stopped to spend the night."

There was no sense in arguing, and no reason to make a bad situation worse. Tas hurt. His hands and back were bleeding, his scales raw and peeling. Wet sand plastered his hair to his face, packed his teeth and burned his eyes. At least the tide receded now, and would carry their rubber raft swiftly with it. Ocean Bend was not far away. Once they caught the current, travel was easy, much easier in fact than if they had tried to make the journey the night before. Tas didn't talk but rather watched the clouds from the bottom of the boat as they bobbed along the coast. A moist sea breeze kept dehydration at bay, though Tas drifted in and out of consciousness, waking when Arnold finally rowed into a marina.

Smells of diesel, low tide and fish announced their arrival into a busy port.

"Stay down!" Arnold quickly tied the dinghy to a cleat, set the oars under the bow, and jumped onto the dock.

A musty canvas tarp dropped over Tas, a heavy line fell across his chest over the tarp and was pulled taut and tied. The sound of footsteps tapered into the distance.

Tas was left alone. Humidity crept in quickly. Air became scarce. Tas was certain he would die from suffocation as his body's temperature rose and sweat beaded over his forehead and his chest. Even his hands were sweaty. His only comfort was when he let his mind drift and he visualized Pouraka and its turquoise pools. Tas squeezed his eyes shut and drops of sweat, or tears trickled down his cheeks as he thought of Cora. He could see her silky black hair flowing off her shoulders, her hazel eyes smiling at him, the colors of her scales dancing in the sunlight. He imagined her gentle touch. If he were going to die, Cora's loveliness was the last thing he wanted to see.

29. Aquatic Specimens

Cora didn't tire of walking; physically stronger than a human, life underwater kept her fit. Hiking on the beach was effortless and the basket of water strapped to her back was weightless. She gained even more momentum once she breathed in the salty spray from the sea.

The moon lit her way. No longer were the lights of Barnacle Bay visible, nor were the tiny sparkles of headlights seen on the highway. Whenever Cora climbed a rise along the shore an ominous glow hovered on the horizon to the south- the big city of Ocean Bend that Leni once described as "growing bigger by the day." That was her destination.

The gentle rises gave way to mountainous cliffs that formed coves where the ocean splashed violently against the rocks. When she reached a particularly steep incline Cora decided to stop and rest, and wait until the tide receded so she could maneuver her way through the tide pools.

She set her basket by her side carefully, pausing a moment to reflect on the magical contents inside-the beloved waters of Pouraka. She would miss the cavern and the Cradle before this trip was over. She missed it now, but more than Pouraka she missed Tas. Her heart ached. Pouraka would never be the same without him. Neither would she.

"Bring me to him. Bring your magic to Tas and help us be together again. Let him be safe." There was no way to know if the waters could do something like that, but speaking the words gave her relief.

Though the cove where she rested was remote by land with no visible access other than the shoreline, the ocean harbored more traffic than the coast off Barnacle Bay.

On the horizon were the shipping lanes that Leni talked so much about. She'd soon be at Ocean Bend, perhaps before noon the next day. She'd see new sights, which excited her, but she was also frightened. Danger lay ahead. She'd have to stay keen witted if she were to confront Tas' kidnappers.

Finding him in such a big city would be difficult. If luck was on her side, she'd be able to make contact with Leni's friend, Benson. Perhaps he could help her locate Tas.

Cora let her musings keep her awake until the sun rose. The waters receded leaving a scalloped line of seaweed on the beach. The tide's crest. . When there was enough sand between the cliffs and the foamy surf for her to walk, Cora stood, put the basket on her back and stepped carefully.

Morning light glistened on the wet sand. The anemones, sea stars and crab that inhabited the tide pools reminded her that she too was a sea creature, that her human form was fleeting, that when she and Tas returned to Pouraka, neither of them would be bound to humanity but would return to their natural form as mers.

This whole nightmarish incident was fleeting and soon everything would return to normal.

So involved with meandering through streams of sea water and pools of miniature sea life that Cora didn't notice the wooden dinghy moored nearby. Nor did she see them until their white shirts blazed in the sun in front of her, their tan bodies strong and athletic. Three barefoot men in shorts, sat on the rocks by their boat, and stared at her.

"Well hello there!" The one with cream colored hair smiled, his teeth shone against his bronze skin.

"Hello." Cora's heart skipped a beat. She recognized him.

"Don't I know you?" he asked. He brushed off his shorts and stood, towering well above her.

She had seen him the evening Kaile had jumped from his boat onto the dock; the day Leni got so mad, and the day her brother was murdered. She wasn't sure this man had seen her. But if her assumptions were correct, this was the man that killed Ko, or at least it was his crew that did. He could even be the one that captured Tas. She cleared her throat and answered. "No. I don't think you do."

"You're a long way from home, aren't you?"

"No. Not really." Cora tried to calm her voice so it didn't sound shaky. It'd be dangerous to let him know she was afraid of him. If he knew her fear, he'd attack. Any predator would. If he had Tas hidden somewhere, she had to be clever enough to find out where.

"Aren't you from Barnacle Bay?" he asked.

"Barnacle Bay?" Cora hated lying but if she exposed herself now she'd never find Tas. "No. I'm from Ocean Bend. You must have me mixed up with someone else."

The man didn't stop smiling, nor did he cease to stare at her. He didn't seem to believe her, either. "My mistake, then. The day's young! Can't imagine you walked so far in such a short time. Why, it must be five miles to Ocean Bend from here."

"I enjoy my morning walks."

"A morning walk, is it?" He stumbled over the rocks to get closer to her.

Don't back away, Cora told herself.

"So what's in that seaweed basket of yours?" He turned to the others. The dark haired man raised his brow. Setting a can down on a boulder he came alongside his friend.

Cora grimaced at them. "Sea specimens."

"Oh? Specimens, is it?" The first man nudged the other. "Specimens, Rick! Pat, come see!" The man laughed and waved to Pat. Cora couldn't help but notice how muscular the three of them were. She needed to outwit these guys or she'd be in deep trouble.

"Wonder what kind of specimens, Tom." The man named Pat joined them.

Cora shifted her weight. "Yes. I'm a marine biologist. I work for the University. I'm collecting sea specimens for the lab."

"What kind of specimens do you have?"

His inquiry was intrusive but Cora tried to remember details about the job Beth had at the university.

She kept one protective arm on the strap that held her basket on her back. "Right now all I have are Echinoderms belonging to the Asteroidean class, which are native to these shores and quite abundant, but a particular disorder among the species is being studied by the university and I'm hoping the specimens I bring back will further their research." She also hoped the men would believe her.

"Ah. . .I see. You're collecting sea stars." The man grinned even wider and loosened his collar. When he did Cora gasped and bit her tongue. On a chain around his neck was a piece of rainbow coral. Her eyes darted between the necklace and his sneer. "You should let us give you a ride on my yacht. I can take you back home, back to Ocean Bend." The power he gave the city's name was daunting. He was trying to make a point but Cora wasn't sure what it was. "These shores can be dangerous when the tide comes in."

"The tide's not coming in."

"It will be." He nodded to a boat moored offshore, sparkling in the morning sunlight. "We're going back to Ocean Bend now. And since you have your specimens, well, it's a neighborly thing for us to offer you a ride."

Cora studied Tom, his wicked smirk, his piercing blue eyes and sunburned nose. His intentions couldn't be honorable, but she had an agenda of her own. "I'm not sure if that would be wise on my part."

Tom held out his hands in innocence. "What? What do you think I'd do? I'm trustworthy, aren't I guys?"

The men nodded, their smiles intimidating.

"Well, I don't even know you."

"Sure you do! I'm the guy that dropped your friend off on the old coot's dock the other night."

Cora shook her head, playing innocence. "What friend? What dock?"

Tom winked at Rick, whose dark stare made her even more uneasy than Tom's prodding. Rick might be one of the guys who killed Ko. Maybe he did the bloody work, how was she to know? What if he was on the boat that captured Tas. If so then he knew Tas was a merman.

"Don't be stupid, sweetie. I don't make mistakes. I swear it was you."

"I'm sorry that this mistake breaks your run of good luck, but I have not been in Barnacle Bay since I was a child, and I have no acquaintances in that town."

Tom shrugged, giving no indication that he believed her, still he ceased to argue.

"Your call then, babe. You can walk back to Ocean Bend if you want." He nodded a signal to his friends, who stepped around Tom, their bodies forming a barrier between the beach that led to Ocean Bend and Cora.

Cora felt her temperature rise with anger, but she fought the frown. She was in the human world now and she had to play the part. Around this man's neck could very well be a clue to Tas' location. Only merpeople harvest rainbow coral.

"Actually, it's really kind of you to offer." Cora smiled. "It was a long walk and I'm tired, and I have no concept of time so you're right. The tide could very well be coming in. If you could forget about this silly notion of having met me before, I'll accept your invitation."

He raised his eyebrows. Clearly her response surprised him. She allowed the three men to lead her to their dinghy, help her board, and motor her to the yacht.

30. Lady Rigger

Cora had never been on any other boat besides Leni's Sea Quest. She assumed everyone from Ocean Bend was familiar with yachts so when Tom took her arm and helped her on deck, she pretended not to be impressed.

"Wipe your feet," Tom ordered. "The latrine's down the hall. You might want to wash. Or let me put it this way. The Ransom is clean. I expect you to keep it that way."

Cora glared and followed his eyes when he nodded toward the door. "You need a tour guide?"

"No. I can find it, I'm sure. It's not like this is a humongous luxury liner or anything."

Tom responded with a grunt, and Cora tossed her hair as she made her way to the cabin. The men followed her inside.

If she hadn't seen it floating, Cora would never have guessed she was on a boat.

The interior of the vessel was more like the inside of Beth's beach house, only much more polished and bright, and with more rooms than Pouraka had caves. A well-lit entry led to couches, and a bar. A row of windows opened out over the sea framing purple hills in the distance. The wood on the yacht was polished to a glossy sheen and not even a pillow was out of place.

"There's a bedroom at the end of the hall you can hang out in but take a shower before you sit on any furniture. Shake the sand out of your clothes before you put them on again and there's a broom in the bathroom closet to sweep up your mess. My friends and I have some business to discuss before we take off."

Tom walked to the bar and pulled a bottle off the shelf. The glasses he used were small, the liquid he poured a golden color. He offered his friends a glass and with a sweeping gesture he lifted his crystal into the air and nodded to his friends. "To our little gold mine!" he said. He nodded his head in her direction. They swallowed the contents in one chug and then Tom filled the glasses again.

Cora snickered to herself. She was glad Tom didn't offer her a glass. She wasn't so sure she would accept any food or drink from him. She started down the hall.

"Rick, when are you leaving to run those dolphins?"

Cora stopped short in front of the cabin door when she heard the question.

"The Sealark is iced up and ready to go, but the Dunnabar won't be back until the day after tomorrow. There's a little engine work that needs to be done but she'll be quicker than ever once she's fixed."

"Which pod, d'you think? The fat ones down south?"

"Nope. The spinners up north by Barnacle Bay. Word has it they'll bring more money from the aquariums. They're a little harder to run and not as big, but what we lose in meat we gain in prize money."

Cora studied their heartless faces. Surely they weren't serious.

"We already have several offers for them. Matt says he can off at least five to the tanks."

Cora's face turned cold. She could hardly believe her ears.

"What's the count in that pod?"

"Twelve in all."

"That leaves seven for meat. That will work perfect. We won't need any extra freezers. What about that old fisherman on the wharf? Not that you should be concerned at the moment. We fixed his boat up pretty good. I wondered how you were thinking of dealing with him." Tom offered them each another drink.

"He won't be going anywhere for a long while, you know that, Tom. If by some miracle he fixes his tanks, we'll think of something else. What's he going to do, anyway? Shoot us?"

The men laughed.

"So is everything all set?" Tom downed his drink and wiped his mouth.

"Just say the word!" Rick held up his glass.

"I need your schedule so I can synchronize with Matt. When can you have them down this way? Dates! I need dates."

"It should only take a day or two to run them up the channel into the bay north of here. We'll take the prime specimens aboard the Sealark and then slaughter the rest on site. The Dunnabar has room to ice the meat."

"I'm bringing my little speed boat up there too. It'll make driving those puppies a whole lot easier if we have two boats." Tom said.

Rick caught Cora looking at him.

Tom turned around. "Well? What are you gawking at? You're excused."

She stuttered, completely frozen from what she heard. "I beg your pardon?"

"You can leave us now. We have business to take care of and it's none of yours."

"Oh!"

Cora slipped into the bathroom. Her stomach churned at the thought of their dolphin pod being slaughtered. With shaking hands, she turned the water in the bath on so the men in the other room wouldn't hear her cry.

She wiped her eyes. Cora had seen her reflection before in the clear water of Pouraka and she was familiar with mirrors at Beth's house. She had never seen a mirror like the one here, though.

This mirror was full length, lighted, and showed all her flaws in brilliant reality. Repulsive, her reflection showed every blemish on her face, dirt on her body and her knotted and ratted hair. The walk from Barnacle Bay had taken a toll on Cora's appearance.

Her eyes were swollen red from crying, her hair windblown and dry, and now that she was alone she noticed the smell. She was a wreck. Even the scales on her shimmering tank top were sandy and dull with bits of kelp hanging from them. No wonder the men were laughing at her! The bath would be welcomed.

Cora lost the sense of time as she slid into the tub and under the water, soaking her hair and absorbing every particle of moisture her body would drink. The only thing not comforting about the bath was the tight quarters.

And her thoughts.

How could she feel any comfort knowing Tas was imprisoned by ruthless men, and the dolphins of Barnacle Bay faced a bloody massacre?

Once clean, Cora mopped her hair dry with a towel. Her tank top scales glistened again. Cora swung the basket over her shoulder, opened the door and peeked down the hall to the sitting room. Rick and Pat were gone, but Tom was talking on the phone. Cora stepped back into the bath and listened, peeking out the slit of the door.

"What do you mean it's sick? What happened on the way there?" He was angry, his gestures animated. "You spent the night on the beach? Why? Arnold, don't argue with me. Where is it now?"

Tom stopped talking and walked to the bar. With his free hand shaking, he poured more liquid into his glass.

"Then find a cure." He paced across the room and Cora ducked behind the door. "How should I know? No, don't call a vet. Why? Think about it. All right, all right, I'll come but not until later. Make sure it doesn't die before I get there." Tom peered over his shoulder down the hall, but Cora was quick to shut the door. "And Arnold, keep your mouth shut!"

She slipped quietly into the bedroom and tucked her basket carefully under the bed. When she was certain he had hung up the phone, she strolled out of the room.

"Hungry?" Tom's back was turned to her when she strolled into the room.

Cora shrugged.

"I asked you a question." His tone was bitter, leaving a sour taste in her mouth.

"I'm only hitching a ride to Ocean Bend. I don't need your food and I don't really need you to talk to me like that. I'm ready to go whenever you are."

"Sit down."

He fell on the couch across from the easy chair.

"Why?"

"I have something to ask you."

Cora hesitated for a moment but when he waved for her to sit she did.

"You say you're a marine biologist?"

"Yes."

"Okay, I'll go with that."

"What do you mean, you'll go with that?"

He leaned forward as if he wanted to tell her a secret. "Let's say you're telling me the truth."

"I am telling you the truth. Why don't you believe me?"

He fell back against the couch and stared at her. "I think you know the answer to that."

Though fake, Cora's sneer was timed appropriately. It made her story valid.

"If you are a marine biologist, how good are you at marine medicine?"

"What?"

"Medicine for fish. What do you know?"

She laughed and then it struck her what he might be asking for. "I know something, why?"

"Say there's this fish in captivity that is kind of going, you know, belly up."

Cora paled and tried to recall what Beth had taught her. Nothing came to mind. "Maybe you should find a fish doctor."

"Can't."

"Why not?"

"I'm asking you what you know. You're my fish doctor?"

"I'm not a doctor." Why was he so insistent, unless the fish he was referring to wasn't really a fish? "I'd have to see…it…in person to tell you."

Tom shook his head. "Can't do that."

"Why not?"

"It's a government tank. You'd have to have clearance."

Cora sat back and watched his eyes, seeking a clue that would indicate how much truth he was telling her. "You'd have to give me more specifics. What kind of fish is it? How big is it? What's it been eating? Does it have light? A good supply of water? Any signs of disease?"

"Haven't seen it. I don't know. I only know what the workers tell me. You think you can help?"

"Without knowing anything?" She shook her head but then thought better of it. "Did you recently catch it?"

"Yesterday."

"I see. Your fish probably is… I don't know, upset."

"Stressed? Yeah, probably."

"It needs some sun and something that reminds it of home."

"Like its mate?" His tongue was in his cheek when Cora squinted up at him.

"Yeah. Something like that. Anything it might be familiar with." Cora said.

"Can't be done without throwing the darn thing back into the sea."

He had her attention.

"Well then why don't you?"

He laughed. "That would cost me too much money. I think I'll go see how bad off it is. I'll be back later."

Her first response was to beg to go along but she controlled herself. Being eager would have validated his suspicions. "Be back? I thought I was going home?"

"Really? Why would you think that?"

"That's what you promised."

Tom rose from the couch, walked to the bar, and helped himself to another glass. "I don't keep promises. Don't have to."

As Cora studied him, a mix of fear and anger stirred. "So why would you keep me here?"

He held up his glass to her and then chugged the drink down, quickly pouring a refill. "Because I believe you're a mermaid."

"What?" Cora's jaw dropped, hoping her dramatic response would be convincing. "You're insane. No one believes in mermaids! And why would you think I'm one even if they were real?"

"Nice try." He returned to the couch, this time with the glass and the bottle. "You see, I saw you with a merman. And if you haven't guessed already, that fish I have in the holding tank is your boyfriend. At least, I'm presuming he's your boyfriend. And yes he is going belly up and no we don't want that to happen because there's a price on his head if we get him to the mainland alive. A big purse! So if you, as a marine biologist..." His laugh was evil. Cora clasped her hands together to avoid slapping him or throwing the nearby vase filled with artificial flowers at him, or pulling his hair out. "...think he needs to be around something he's familiar with, like his mate, then the best solution would be to put you in the tank with him."

Cora flushed and opened her mouth to speak.

"Yes I know you aren't in mermaid form. Which is why I don't have you in my nets. Believe me, I would if I could. As it is, we'd be pretty sleazy if we threw a pretty young lady in one of our holding tanks. No doubt you'd drown. So I'm giving you a choice. You figure out a way to be a mermaid again and join your lover, or nothing gets done about his condition."

Cora had nothing to say. Schemes flew through her mind, scenarios of what she could do to get Tas and herself out of this situation, but none of them seemed feasible at the moment. She could transform now by splashing herself with the magic waters in her basket but it would be a fool thing to do. It might save Tas' life, it might not, but it would put her in a holding tank with him, and what good would two merpeople in a tank do for Pouraka, or a pod of dolphins about to get slaughtered, or the world for that matter?

"So! What do you think?" His piercing eyes made Cora all the more sick.

"I think you're drinking too much of that gold liquid."

He spit out a laugh. "You aquatic fools are so dumb. It's called whiskey."

"Your whiskey is proving you the fool and I need to go home."

Tom wiped his face with his hand and set the bottle down rather clumsily.

"Go. Swim!"

"I've had enough of your insults, sir. You can't prove anything. And it all sounds rather ludicrous. I don't know what kind of fish you think you have in your holding tank but I assure you the chances of it being a merman are highly improbable. And to accuse a complete stranger!" Cora laughed this time. The look on his face was comical. "I wonder if you'll remember this when you wake up tomorrow."

"I'm not drunk, little lady."

"And I'm not a mermaid."

"So you care nothing for this fellow?"

"I care nothing for your fish!"

He shrugged and Cora walked to the bedroom and shut the door. Her heart raced so rapidly that she nearly blacked out. She sat on the bed and took deep breaths. "We can do this. We can help Tas and save the pod and get these devils out of our waters." She rested her eyes on the basket and a peace came over her. She had a portion of Pouraka with her, all she needed to do was get the magic water to Tas and they could both walk away from Tom and return to their people. Tas would know how to save the dolphins.

Cora pulled the basket from under the bed and strapped it over her shoulder. A glance in the mirror gave her the confidence she needed. Cora the mermaid faced her. Strong, determined, loyal and in love. Her attributes were mightier than any darkness trying to destroy her. With a determined pull on the door she stepped into the hall and walked into the room where Tom had been. She breathed a sigh and stepped outside.

The engine started. Tom was at the helm with his two friends as the motor rumbled and the Ransom made wake moving swiftly through the busy waters of Ocean Bend.

31. The Holding Tank

Cora presumed the unfamiliar tower that the yacht was headed toward was the oil rig that both Leni and Tas had talked about. From far away it appeared harmless, but as they approached, the rumble that emanated from the motionless platform made her shudder. Why had men built such a puzzling and mysterious object? The size alone left her in awe. She jumped when a shrill whistle wailed from the platform above her. The yacht slowed as a man on the oil rig leaned over a railing and called out.

"Tom, call your dad! There's been an emergency. He needs a diver!"

"I don't have any divers! They've all been laid off."

"Your dad wants to talk to you. Call him."

Tom waved to the man and put his cell phone to his ear. The Ransom came to an abrupt halt causing the yacht to rock violently as the boat met its own wake. She hadn't realized how noisy the engines of the Ransom were until they were shut down, although the monotonous sound of the oil rig kept on.

Tom kept his so voice low that Cora couldn't hear him. The conversation escalated and soon he was shouting. Even his friends dropped their mooring lines.

"How am I supposed to do that? They all went home? It's too deep for those guys, Dad. It would take three weeks to get a Saturation Diver ready."

There was a pause as he listened, though it was apparent he didn't like the way the conversation progressed. "Do you know how much that would cost me?"

Tom pulled the phone away from his ear and shook his head at Rick. When he did speak into his cell he was much more reserved. "Okay, okay I'll find someone. Only I'm not spending a fortune. Don't worry it'll get done right."

Whatever the conversation with his father was about, it wasn't pleasant. As soon as Tom hung up he swore, waved Rick to the ship's wheel and went inside the cabin. Cora ducked out of view and hid in the shadows. Finally the engines started again and the yacht rolled across the waters to the harbor.

The crew coasted into a slip and secured the Ransom to the dock,

"Come with me, Rick. I need your help at the tanks. Let's go see that fish that Arnold's been talking about." Tom brushed Cora's shoulder and jumped from the boat to the pier without saying one word to her.

Surprised that she was free to leave, she followed Tom and his friends. If this fish was who she thought it was, there was a good chance Tom would lead her directly where she wanted to go. With her basket secured on her back she strolled behind the three, keeping her distance. Rick looked over his shoulder immediately before the men turned into an alley but he didn't seem to see her, nor did they slow down.

Daylight had faded but darkness wouldn't fall for another hour. For that she was thankful as she'd be lost in this city at night. Tall gray buildings lined the streets; at their doors were an array of windows and awnings and flashing neon signs. Cora had never been in a city like Ocean Bend before. A harbor town for the wealthy, the busyness made her head swim. So many people rushed along the roadways, bustling about to untold destinations.

Aside from the day Radcliff mistreated Tas' clan, Cora never witnessed merpeople treating each other so coldly. She couldn't imagine swimming around Pouraka and not talking to anyone. Here in Ocean Bend Cora was witnessing a part of mankind she'd never seen before, and which she found repulsive.

She followed Tom and his friends past a street market where merchants had stacked fresh seafood behind glass cases on piles of ice, the same sort of display she'd seen in the deli at Barnacle Bay. The difference being, these aisles were crowded with people pushing their way to the front. Greedy, selfish shoppers, taking care of themselves with no thought for anyone else.

The smells seeping from the vendors were delectable, but there were too many choices, Cora thought. Humans were not at all like merpeople who scavenged for food, who would find a clam here, a crawfish there and eat little bits at a time until they had their fill. And when they weren't hungry anymore, they shared their abundance. What they stored from their forage expeditions was shared later with everyone.

Here the shoppers were so numerous and frantic that she was engulfed by hordes of people. Shoved through the crowd, she panicked when she lost sight of Tom and his friends. Luckily Rick's shirt was bright enough to spot.

The three men meandered away from the congestion of the port, through an alley and finally up a street lined with another row of grey buildings. When Cora turned down the alley, Tom and his friends were nowhere to be seen.

No signs of life rustled on this narrow lane. The structures facing the alleyway were peculiar to Cora. They had no shop fronts or windows, but seemed abandoned and haunting like the sunken ship Tas had taken her to. An unfamiliar stench seeped along the ground, an odor of decay.

She walked cautiously until her pursuit ended at a fence. Beyond the chain link stretched an empty yard of concrete, pavement and dust. No sign of Tom, Rick or Pat existed. She doubted they would have climbed over the barrier, as a prickly roll of barbed wire above it threatened any trespassers.

The men must have entered one of these buildings but there were no entryways except for one ominous dark gray edifice which was sealed shut by two metal doors. At least she assumed they were doors as there were no handles. She dared not knock on them even though that was her first inclination.

After catching her breath, and taking a moment to calm her thoughts, she surveyed the walls carefully and found a button next to the two metal panels.

She pressed the button and a light came on. After a few seconds a door opened into a small enclosure. She stepped inside and the door closed. Afraid she had walked into a trap, she gasped and banged on the wall. Another light came on and the box she was in moved. Cora gasped again, the sensation of falling acute. Her fear lasted only a moment when the door opened and she stumbled out of the box into a dark hallway.

This was it! Cora immediately smelled water. The walkway meandered through cold, grey walls that towered over her head. A senseless labyrinth, yet the moisture in the air gave her hope. Condensation seeped from the partitions, staining the concrete. Perhaps this was the tank that Tom had talked about. Not until she saw rays of light bounce off the wall to her right did her hope return. She knew that kind of light ray. They were the same sort of beams that rippled across the ocean floor. Cora hurried up the ramp toward them and stopped when she came to a thick double paned window.

There she froze in horror. Indeed, the light was coming from above, through the water, and onto the walls behind her. On the other side of the glass lay a dreary subaquatic panorama with cloudy blue liquid, stagnant and dirty. Though the sun rays danced on the surface, their movement was more a funeral march than a ballet. She pressed her face against the pane examining the pool for any sign of life, for any sign of Tas, though she'd be relieved if he weren't here as the tank was so filthy and lifeless.

At first she saw nothing move in the murky water except floating debris of leaves and sticks that must have blown in from a storm. With closer investigation, she eyed a dark object toward the surface. Something did move. Was that a fin stretching out from the shadow or was her imagination playing tricks on her because she was so desperate? Cora followed the walkway to get a better view, and that's when she found the stairwell.

With hurried steps she climbed to a higher level. From there she acknowledged that the object was indeed a fin. She ran up another flight of stairs and burst through a doorway that opened to the outside. Thick concrete walls surrounded the pool preventing any sunlight from hitting the sides of the tank. She shivered with remorse when she saw him.

Tas. There was no mistaking the merman, and, to her distress, he didn't move. She ran, holding her hand over her mouth to keep from gagging or crying out, but she couldn't hold back the tears.

To see him in such a condition was scandalous. He lay afloat on his back, his eyes closed, his face pale, his body up against the side of the tank as though he had drifted there like a log that had fallen in a storm. His hair swirled aimlessly in the little bit of current that stirred the water. His once glistening scales were dark and pasty.

Cora knelt at the edge of the pool and reached for his arm, pulling him closer. With one hand under his neck she lifted his head above water.

"Tas." She felt his cheeks. There was some warmth left, though not much. Cora released him long enough to let her basket slide off her shoulders. She unfastened the tightly woven lid and filled it. Resting the cup at her knees, she lifted his head again and slowly dribbled the magic water of Pouraka onto his lips, leaning over to kiss him after every drop. Her tears met his cheeks, so cold and lifeless. "Tas, please wake up."

For merpeople, Pouraka offered eternal gifts: solace, healing, comfort, and life. No matter how far from the cavern the mers traveled, if their hearts were set on home, the gifts were with them. Cora brought that nourishment to Tas and Tas received it. His eyes opened, though glassy. His body was weak and weary, but he gained consciousness and finally responded to Cora's care.

"Is this a dream?" It was a whisper, but he was alive.

"Tas? Oh Tas!"

"Cora? Is this really you?"

"Drink more of this. It's from Pouraka. The waters will heal you. Drink."

She put the cup to his mouth and he swallowed. With each sip his color returned. Soon, much of his strength was restored and he didn't have to rely on her to hold him, though he was still disoriented. Well enough to tread water, Tas wiped his hair away from his face and grimaced. "Where am I?"

"You're in Tom's holding tank."

"How did you get here?"

"It's a long story but simple enough to say I followed Tom here. What happened to you? How did you get so ill?"

"I was dehydrated for a very long time. When I was on the raft I was wrapped in a hot tarp and then I passed out. That's all I remember aside from waking once or twice and being very alone."

"Those men are brutal."

"You followed Tom? That means he's here!"

"Somewhere. I'm not sure where. We need to get out of here."

"How?"

"I have enough water from Pouraka to change your form. Come sit up here and let me splash it on you and then you and I can walk away."

"Shh!" Tas' eyes widened when he looked over her shoulder and he covered his lips with his finger. He reached by her and seized the lid to the basket, fastening it tightly. "Don't say a word."

"What are you doing?"

Their eyes met. "Slip the basket back on your shoulders as quickly as you can. Now."

She did what he requested, but his actions confused her. "Tas!"

"Shh."

"Tas, we have to get you out of here."

She flinched when Tom came up from behind her and spoke. "We can't let you do that, babe. Sorry. It would be a huge financial loss for us."

Cora spun around to find Tom standing over her.

"What do you want from us?" Tas asked.

"The little lady has already given me what I want: you healthy! From you? I need you to earn your keep. The coral girl can do whatever she wants now. I'm no kidnapper, solely a dealer in marine mammals."

"What do you mean 'earn his keep'?" Cora stood.

Tom nodded toward the door as Rick, Pat and several other men rolled a dolly with a metal cylinder secured to it through swinging double doors. Once at the poolside they laid a blanket on the ground and opened the lid to the cylinder.

Tas dove into the depths of the pool.

"Thanks for helping out." Tom smiled at Cora. "I love how you fish-folk chase after bait, hook, line and sinker. You make it so easy for us!"

Cora was speechless.

Tom laughed. "You don't get it, do you? I planned for you to follow us here. I figured you had a cure for the aquatic man. Love always finds a way, doesn't it? I was right! My, how cooperative you are!"

"Haven't you done enough damage? You nearly killed him."

"True, Arnold was a little rough on the dude but we learned our lesson. Don't fret. There's a little job for him on the rig before Arnold's uncle comes. You can volunteer to help too, but not dressed like that. I'm afraid you'll need scales for this assignment. I can be patient. You'll find your fins sooner than later."

Rick and Pat positioned themselves on both ends of the pool, a net weighted by anchors stretched between the two. They dropped the weights into the water, forming a wall of mesh.

Though Cora couldn't see him she knew Tas would be trapped.

She burned with anger. "You're evil!" She threw her fists into Tom's chest and beat on him. A spasm of pain shot through her hand and up her arm as he stood untouched. Cora screamed at him. "Leave him alone! Let him go!"

Tom clasped her wrists and twisted them behind her back. He turned her to face the pool. "Watch."

The net shook and twisted. The merman battled under the water against the ropes. Rick and Pat struggled to keep the net steady but it was a game to them. They laughed.

After a fierce struggle, Pat maneuvered his end to Rick. They heaved the ends of the net to a motorized pulley and flipped a switch. The machine took over, hoisting an entangled Tas to the surface and out of the pool where the men rolled him flat on his back. Pat held his arms and Rick injected a hypodermic needle into Tas' neck while the other four men untangled him.

Cora watched with horror as the men moved Tas onto a spongy material that was spread over the blanket. The whole bundle was lifted by two poles on either side of the sling and the sling lowered into the cylinder. They shut and clamped it tight.

Cora's stomach turned. "Stop! Please let him go. Please don't do this!"

"Look, honey, if you want your lover back, this is your opportunity to join him."

Cora jerked her arms free from Tom. She was tempted to pull the basket of magical waters off her back and shower herself right in front of all of them, but what good would it have done? Would Tom really keep a promise?

"Calm down. He's not hurt. We drugged him so he won't even know he's in there. This is the most humane way to transport a mammal. It's exactly how we transport dolphins and we do it all the time. Very rarely do we have a casualty."

"Transport him where?"

"If you want to know, put on your mermaid suit and I'll show you."

He winked at her with a malicious scoff. If he were alone she'd jump on him and pull every hair out of his head. She'd claw his eyeballs out and feed them to the Mako.

Cora followed the men and their cylinder out the door though she kept her distance and held tightly to her basket.

32. Change for the Better

Cora stepped into the alley in time to see a long black van pull away from the building. There were no windows in the vehicle but she knew the van's cargo. As she watched the wheels roll through the dusty alley kicking pebbles into the air, smelling the stink of diesel emitted from its tail pipe, hope vanished. She'd been so close to freeing Tas. His escape had been at her fingertips and she let it slide. She should have been more intuitive and known that Tom had set her up. Now she may never have another chance to rescue Tas.

And there he went. Confined in a cold hard box, unable to move and barely able to breathe, destined to be a slave to a heartless race of beings. Everything Tas had ever said about mankind was accurate. She was a fool to have argued with him. She was a fool to have believed that she could change the world. Even Leni let her down. Even Beth was nowhere to help.

Cora paid little attention to the fading commotion of the city as she wandered. No trace of the van could be seen as darkness prepared to swallow the earth. Cars became dark shapes with headlights that left spots in her eyes. Shop owners hung their closed signs on their doors as the sun fell to the horizon and the sky turned pink. It would have been a beautiful twilight save for the heaviness in her heart. How often she and Tas had admired a setting sun like this one. Hand in hand they would sit on the hillside above Pouraka.

She wiped her eyes.

Maybe she should give in. Accept Tom's offer. Change into a mermaid and let him take her. If she did join Tas in his captivity at least they would be together, even if they were in a filthy tank. Even if their lives were cut short in a prison. Wasn't it Tas who said, "What difference does it make what form we're in, if we're together?"

She reached the marina and followed the shoreline north, but not to go home. She wouldn't leave Ocean Bend, not as long as Tas was here.

The sand was cool, the shells sharp and prickly, making her toes itch.

She strolled to the wet sand where the foam still bubbled into clam holes and the remnants of waves frothed over her feet. Seagulls clustered, pecking at shellfish and welcoming the end of day. Farther out the ocean throbbed, constant and carefree.

Ever faithful, the sea rocked back and forth over the earth as it harbored its creatures, protecting them from the sun's vicious heat, feeding them, nourishing them and cradling them. Cora should be in its belly, accepting its nurturing. She was the oceans' charge and yet here she was, walking the land as though she were human. She'd been denying her heritage all this time.

A surge of shame swept over her. Why did she even want to be human? Merpeople were so much kinder to each other, and to the animals they lived among. Why did she ever doubt that she should live as a mermaid?

Cora took the basket off of her back and unfastened the lid. The water inside was so clear she could see the interior weave of kelp even in the fading sunlight. Scooting closer to the surf so that the waves rolled over her, she held the basket above her head.

Pouraka's water dripped over her hair, onto her shoulders and her face. She lifted her chin and let it run down her neck, her chest, her belly. Cora poured the water over her hips, her legs, and her toes as the sea rumbled and came to her, a white roll of salt water rushing to immerse her. Cora leaned back and let the ocean swallow her human body. The sea wanted her home, grabbing her form and pulling her far away from shore. She tumbled in the breakers until she was saturated and far from land. Cora came to the surface and viewed the vanishing shoreline one last time. Sunset shined its face on her scales as golden fragments of evening glitter. She hadn't felt so alive in a long time. She felt good, and somehow she would bring this freedom to Tas. She had to.

Cora was not accustomed to night travel. Tradition held that merpeople rested in caves or caverns when the world grew dark. There they would be safe from predators. But no rocky cliffs surrounded the shoreline of Ocean Bend, only gently sloping beaches that sunk into underwater valleys. These were lined with gravel, silt and the oily residue from the frequent freighter transports.

She moved on, exploring the coastline and harbors of Ocean Bend. She had no desire to sleep. If Tas was taken to a vessel, she was determined to find out which one.

Night had fallen, melting land and sky into one dark bowl glimmering with stars. Lights flickered everywhere, on shore, on boats as they floated by, and on the water from reflections of the heavens. On the horizon the oil rig reflected a bright orange. The constant hum could be heard all the way to shore. How did mankind ever get any rest? Traffic in the harbor was heavy, Cora had to maneuver around propellers, fishing lines, nets and other clutter.

Cora swam quietly around the outskirts of the marina, surfacing often in hopes to see Tom's yacht, or perhaps his fishing boat or the boat he had called the Sealark. There were way too many watercraft. Perhaps if she swam nearer, in between the docks she would see better..

Only a few people walked the wooden floats. A group of fishermen shone flashlights at the water and bobbed fishing poles methodically in an attempt to lure squid. Cora dove deep when she passed them in an attempt to avoid the artificial light that rippled through the water.

The night deepened and life on the docks stilled after the fishermen left. Quiet settled in the harbor though the gentle splashing of water against hulls, the creaking of the docks, and the smell of creosote remained. Cora swam through the slips searching for anything familiar until a certain yacht caught her attention. Two people were on the deck talking low, a lamp between them. She listened but she couldn't understand what they were saying. She dared to swim closer, to reach her head a little farther above water when something splashed at her side, startling her. A mussel?

"Hey!" A voice called quietly.

Cora prepared to dive but the voice sounded familiar.

"Over here."

A man in a fishing boat leaned over his rail.

"Is that you, Cora?"

Cora swam nearer, tossing the water from her face as she emerged. "Benson? Yes, it's me."

"I thought I saw a mermaid! What in Neptune's Army are you doing in Ocean Bend? What if someone sees you swimming around here?"

"I'm looking for a boat."

"Well, there are quite a few here, take your pick." His smile glowed under the starlight. Benson was a handsome man, tall and well built, his blond hair neatly combed and tucked under a baseball cap. He was a welcome sight for mereyes, being especially kindhearted to her species. "Seriously, Cora, why would you need a boat?"

"There's a certain boat that belongs to Tom the oil rigger's son."

"Shh."

Benson stood up straight, signaling for Cora to dive. She sunk under the water quietly as the people on the yacht opposite them walked down the pier. Another shell dropped into the water, a signal that all was clear. The dock was quiet now, all lights were out.

"Are you talking about Tom Weatherford?"

"I don't know his last name. All I know is that he captured Tas and has tortured him horribly. They're planning on selling him and sending him away to live in some kind of tank. I can't bear it!"

"That's right. Tom Weatherford deals in marine mammals. He has Tas?"

Cora wiped the tears away. She was so close to breaking into pieces. "Yes."

"Leni told me Tom came snooping around the Sea Quest one night and put sand down the engine. Your friend Kaile just happened to be on the beach at the same time. I guess they beat him up."

"Tom beat up Kaile? Is Kaile all right?"

"He's fine now, he's staying with Beth. So Tom has Tas in his holding tank?"

"He almost killed him, and now he has him in transport in a tiny box and he said he's going to make him do some kind of work on his dad's oil rig. After that he's going to sell him to someone's uncle to put in an aquarium. Plus I overheard him talking with his buddy Rick. They're heading north and they're going to herd our dolphins into a trap and kill them."

"Dolphin running?"

"I guess. They're going to choose a couple for the tanks and slaughter the rest. I have to stop them!"

"Cora, how are you going to do that all by yourself?"

"I don't know." She bit her lip holding back the flood that was welling inside. "I have to though. Someone has to and there's no one else to help me."

"Hey slow down, little lady, you have friends."

Despite her efforts to hold them back, the tears burst forth. "I've asked everyone for help, even Leni, and no one is willing."

"Whoa, sis, that's not quite true. Leni called and told me about Tas, but he didn't have any details. When he spoke with you the night you left, he thought you wanted him to go gun down Tom. As it is Leni has put in a police report for destruction of property. I doubt that's enough to stop the rascal though, but dolphin running requires permits. As for rescuing Tas, that might be more difficult. You say Tom has him working for his dad?"

"On the rig or something."

"Really? Diving?

What a sleaze. He's probably going to get a few thousand dollars' worth of work for free."

"No he won't. I won't let him."

"Be careful and don't let anyone see you. The more folks know about you merpeople, the harder it's going to be to keep you safe. It's only natural for the world to put you on display. Mermaids have been a legend for hundreds of years but there was never any proof you existed aside from a few sightings."

"I don't care about what happens to me. I simply want to free Tas."

"I understand but we don't want any harm to come to either of you."

Cora wiped her eyes.

"Sweetheart, if Tom gets away with selling Tas to this aquarium, people from all over the world will be coming here trying to catch mermaids. Leni and I will do everything we can to prevent that. If we find Tas and manage to free him, than the two of you need to hightail it out of here, and out of Barnacle Bay too. I mean no one but no one should see another mermaid ever again. Do you understand that?"

Those were hard words, but they were true. Leaving Barnacle Bay meant she'd lose her friends. Life would change so drastically for everyone. "I know."

"Okay. Then you do what you can to locate Tas and don't get caught. I'll give Leni a call and have him get his tail down here. You're not alone. We'll see you through this the best we can."

"Thank you."

"Now get away from here before you're seen. I'll check the marina log and see if Tom or any of his crew is registered in this harbor. You get under the water. Now!"

33. They Answered

Kaile wasn't really that beat up, not like Beth and Sasha seemed to think. Their sympathy overflowed far more than needed, but he wasn't going to argue against having breakfast in bed, a foot massage and wildflowers arranged in a vase next to his side.

"Thank you for the bouquet, Sasha! I can't think of when I was treated so lavishly."

Beth took his cup and set it on the dresser. "Then you deserve it all the more. I wouldn't want you to tell the merpeople how ruthless we humans are."

"I would never do that. I defend you!"

Beth gave him an inquiring eye. "You've had to defend us?"

"Unfortunately, yes. Some merpeople are suspicious of mankind."

"Understandable considering what you went through last night, which is why Barnacle Bay has sworn to keep your secret. Please let your people know we aren't all bad."

"We love mermaids!" Sasha interrupted, standing at the door in a shiny yellow bathing suit. "And I bet if I swim with you enough times I will turn into one, too!"

Kaile laughed and beckoned her to give him a hug. "Sorry to say, it doesn't quite work that way."

"Well, maybe it does. We can go for a swim now and see. I even have an extra bath towel for you." She shoved a bundle of pink terrycloth into his arms. "Let's go!"

"Where to?"

"The beach. If Cora won't let me see her as a mermaid, than you should let me see you as a merman. Come on. Please?"

"Sasha, stop." Beth lifted the girl gently and sat her on the bed. "You shouldn't ask Kaile or Cora to reveal themselves as merpeople. It could get them hurt. You saw what happened to Kaile last night?"

Sasha frowned and her eyes widened. "Those bad men beat you up because you're a merman?"

"I'm not exactly sure why they beat me up. They might have had some other reasons, or no reason at all."

"So if not, why would it matter if anyone in Barnacle Bay saw you as a merman? It's no secret."

"No, I suppose it isn't. But I don't really have time to go swimming with you today, Sasha. I need to get back to my people." Neither of them could know how much turmoil Pouraka was going through. Would it be fair not to tell her? "Remember when you came to me on the beach and offered a listening ear?"

Beth smiled at him, her blue eyes framed in long black lashes.

Her smile touched him like no one ever had. His heart raced and he felt lightheaded, especially when she took his hand. "Do you want to talk right now?"

Sasha sat on the bed and moved closer to Beth. Ignoring her presence would be impossible, and yet the story of Pouraka's sufferings was nothing for a little girl's ears.

"Let's go for a walk." Beth suggested.

"Good idea."

He handed the towel back to Sasha and ruffled her hair. "We'll swim some other time." Kaile swung his legs over the bed.

"Are you well enough to walk?" Beth asked.

"Yes. I'm fine. The fresh air will feel good. Let's go."

"Hey!" Sasha pouted and followed them to the door, her footsteps unusually heavy.

Beth turned to her. "Stay here, please Sasha? Kaile and I need to be alone for a little while."

"Why do I always have to stay behind? Why do you always get to be with Uncle Kaile and I don't. You ruin everything. We were going to go swimming. I was going to get to see a merman."

"Sasha, it's foggy outside, and cold. You'd catch a chill if you went swimming now. Wait for the sunshine. Please go watch cartoons. We'll be back in a little bit."

Kaile felt Sasha's disappointment as Beth shut the door behind them.

"She'll get over it. She's got a quick temper but it never lasts long." Beth assured him.

"As much as I enjoy being with her, I think we need to talk alone."

"That was my thought."

There was a misty breeze. The morning was young the sun was barely visible above the horizon. Kaile led Beth past the back door of the deli and across the empty street toward his favorite hill.

"Remember when I told you I didn't want to change?"

"I do. I wondered what you meant. People are forever changing, so you had me puzzled. Were you referring to something metaphorical?"

"I suppose I was." The urge to tell Beth everything pressed on his heart, but describing how merpeople transformed into dolphins didn't seem right.

He scrutinized her as they walked; her head was partially covered and bowed. Strands of blond hair that were not tucked under her hood danced wildly in the wind.

"Never mind."

Her laugh was sweet. "No, Kaile, please tell me what you meant. You can trust me with a merperson secret."

A gust of cold wind from the sea hit them, prompting Kaile to zip his sweatshirt.
"Maybe...maybe it's that I don't really want to be a merman."

That would certainly sum up his feelings, but did he really confess it aloud? He stopped to see how she would take his humble denial of his species, but instead, Beth had turned around.

"Sasha, I told you to stay home!" Sasha was so near her heels that Beth nearly tripped on her. The girl froze but didn't speak. "Go back home. We won't be gone long."

Sasha shivered. She had pulled a sweater over her shoulders but it was not enough protection from the wind to keep her body warm. Her cheeks were blue as her teeth chattered. Tears rolled from the corners of her eyes.

"Sasha, you're freezing. Go home." Relieved that his recent confession had been ignored, Kaile spoke gently to Sasha, mindful of how excited the girl was around merpeople.

"I'm always in trouble no matter what I do!"

"No, Sasha, you're not in trouble. You shouldn't be out in this weather." He knelt to her height and buttoned her sweater.

"You're going to that big cave, aren't you?" The wind blew the girl's hair across her face as she picked up her chin and squinted at them. "I know you are and you never bring me."

Kaile gawked at the child. What more did Sasha know about Pouraka?

"No." Beth said after a moment's pause. "We're going to sit at the top of the hill."

"That's what you told me last time. But you didn't. You disappeared and I know where you went."

"You do?" Kaile brushed Sasha's hair out of her eyes. "What do you know about the cave?"

"It's a mermaid sanctuary. I've seen the pools."

"Did you go inside?"

Sasha shook her head. "Not all the way."

"Did you see any mermaids?"

"I saw the tail of one but she swam away. I thought it was Cora but I think Cora would have come back to talk to me."

This was not good news. It was bad enough that a six-year-old had been in the cave. Worse, that the merpeople knew she had been there.

"Don't ever go inside again. Do you understand?"

Sasha nodded.

"Do you know why you shouldn't go inside?"

Sasha shook her head.

"Because if you do and the merpeople see you, they may never return. It's like a mother bird leaving her eggs in a nest touched by humans."

"But you took Bethie into the cave. Does that mean there won't be any more mermaids? Does that mean Cora won't ever come home?"

Kaile studied the girl's eyes. He couldn't lie to the child. "I don't know, Sasha. They may have left because I brought Beth in there or because some other strangers went in there even before I took your sister. But we have to be careful. We can't let it happen again because they could be watching and waiting to see if anyone else comes in."

"So I'll never get to see them?"

"I can't answer that."

Sasha stood bravely before them, holding back tears, her rosy cheeks brilliant against the gray skies.

"There are other dangers in sea caves too." Kaile explained. "There's the danger of flooding during a storm. We need to make a pact. None of us should go in again. Not as humans."

Sasha's eyes filled with tears and Kaile wiped a droplet away with his thumb. The girl looked up at her sister, and at Kaile again.

"I only wanted to see. That's all."

She bit her lip and then without another word took off running down the hill. Kaile watched as the child crossed the street and ran through the alley, skipped up the porch stairs and disappeared into the house.

"I'm sorry, Kaile."

"Don't be. It's my fault. If I hadn't brought you to Pouraka, Sasha would never have known about the cavern."

"That makes me doubly sorry."

"It's not your fault." He took her hand. "Don't regret anything that we've done together. Regardless of whether you or Sasha stepped into Pouraka, there's every indication that the Cradle had already been abandoned."

"What about the mermaid that Sasha saw?"

"A kindermer, perhaps, as curious as Sasha. Mothers of the young mers wouldn't leave their home until the elders found a safer cavern. Then again, the cavern might not have been abandoned and mers are lingering in the shadows simply as a precaution. If the mers leave permanently, I'm not sure what will happen to them. We need the magic pools to survive."

"How so?"

"They cleanse, and heal, and provide our bodies with the oxygen we need to stay under water for extended periods of time. Not to mention that they help us to change."

They exchanged a glance.

"Change? Change into what?"

"Human beings." Kaile recovered the slip of his tongue. He wouldn't tell her the other. She didn't need to know about the dolphins. "And back again."

"I think I'm beginning to understand now."

Did she?

The peace was gone. His stomach churned and there was a hollow feeling inside.

"You're worried about Cora and Tas, aren't you, Kaile?"

They sat down in the grass on the crest of the hill where they could see the entire inlet. The wind had already blown away the fog. The sun's glare bounced off the choppy waters and rolled across the beach atop the surf.

"I'm worried about Pouraka, too."

"You said you didn't want to be a merman."

"I said that, yes. Life has become difficult for the merpeople, and in such a short time. I'm not sure we can recover. It seems so much easier to be human now."

"Easier? That's the reason you don't want to change back? Let me clue you in, it's not so easy being human either."

"I didn't mean I wanted an easy way out. Merpeople have certain rituals that they perform in life-threatening situations and I don't really care to be a part of those ceremonies."

Beth could have pressed for more information, but she didn't. He almost wished she had. Kaile's recollection of Ko's transformation boiled in his mind. Beth most likely let the matter drop because she could see his pain. He sat in silence, his eyes on the sea while she took her cell phone from her pocket. White caps dappled the ocean and if he hadn't had his gaze fixed so intently, he wouldn't have noticed the fishing boat. "It's still there."

Beth shaded her eyes. "Yes, it is."

"They're up to no good, I can feel it. Can you call your father?"

"I sent him a text. Dad just now got his engine going again. He's getting ready to take the Sea Quest out."

"Does your father have any idea whose boat that is? Did he say?"

"He said it might be Tom's father's fishing boat, but he doesn't think it is."

"I'm going with him." Kaile jumped up and brushed the grass off his pants. "Would you text him and tell him to wait up?"

"Kaile!"

"We can't let your dad confront those people by himself. Not after what Tom did."

"What if it isn't anyone associated with Tom?"

"Then there'll be no problem."

"I'm coming with you too, then."

Kaile prevented a protest from escaping his lips. Her defiant blue eyes caught his. Nothing he was going to say would stop her. They were of one mind.

"Let's go, then," When he turned, she pulled him back. When he stopped she stood on her toes and kissed him. He released her hand, held her face and sealed his lips on hers. Their breaths moved between them, warm and savory. After a moment, she broke away from the embrace.

"I'm never going to let you out of my sight, Kaile. Never. I want to be with you every moment of every day whether there's danger or not, I don't care. I love you."

"How can that be possible? We're two different species."

"I don't care."

"If there were a way to live out my dream of never changing form again, I would. I'd stay here on land with you forever. I can be as much of a man as anyone. But I don't know if it's even possible. I have friends..."

"And they're in trouble. Come on, let's go help them!" Beth made a quick phone call to Jamie to arrange a babysitter for Sasha. Once the answer was affirmative, she texted her father.

"We can do this!" She took Kaile's hand and together they jogged down the trail toward the wharf. Kaile's heart raced with a new life. Something happened on the hill above Pouraka at that moment. Something more magical than the pools could conjure. Their love was confirmed. Even though their union, two different species, two completely different worlds, might end in heartbreak, Kaile swore to stay by Beth regardless.

When they reached the Sea Quest the engines were already revved and Leni was moving about on deck preparing to leave.

"This is getting out of hand." Leni flipped his buoys into the boat, jumped onto the dock and untied the lines. He hopped back into the Sea Quest as it drifted away from the pier.

"Did you hear any more news?" Beth tucked her phone in her pocket and helped her father coil the bowline.

"Benson called again this morning. That's one of Tom's boats out there, sure enough. He spotted another headed this way. I guess the devil and his cronies plan on having a little dolphin drive." Leni steered the fishing boat toward open waters.

"Dolphin drive?"

Leni shook his head, his lips curled into a scowl. "You wouldn't have any way of knowing what's going on in our world, would you? But being as you asked to work with us let me clue you in. Dolphins are a business in these parts. Not many get a license for these waters, but that leaves the market wide open for rogues like Tom. The other islands witness this practice on a regular basis, but up until now the folks at Barnacle Bay have kept our inlet safe. Times are changing, I guess."

"What? What's happening?" Kaile urged him to explain.

"Dolphins are a commodity, like rock cod and barracuda, Kaile. And this fellow Tom is reaping in what he thinks is his share of the profit."

"You mean they fish for dolphin?"

"Yeah. I guess you could call it fishing. Except that fishing is more humane."

"Not from what I've seen of gillnets."

Leni snickered. "Gillnets are merciful compared to dolphin running. Tom will get in his little speed boat up here and drive the pod. That means he'll race them against the current full speed pounding on drums and whatever other noise makers he can conjure up until the poor creatures heads burst in pain and they get confused and panic. He'll drive them into a shallow cove and then start killing them except for the fat ones. Those they save for their aquariums. In short, Tom is getting ready to slaughter or capture every member of your pod."

"You know that for sure?"

Leni nodded. His eyes remained fixed on the lone boat in the distance bouncing atop the whitecaps. "Yes I do. I know it firsthand. Benson ran into Cora in Ocean Bend."

Kaile's heart skipped a beat. "That's good news! She's okay then? Is she with Benson?"

"She's in mermaid form."

Kaile grew somber when he heard that. He had seen her fill the basket of magical waters. She would not have used it unless she had to. "Any news of Tas?"

Leni didn't answer. The wind beat against his face as they bounded over the swells. Kaile clutched a rail to keep his balance.

"Pops, any word about Tas?" Beth caught her father's eyes and from the expression that Leni gave her, Kaile sensed bad news.

"What's happened to Tas?" Kaile insisted.

"We don't know."

"So what are we going to do?"

"Right now we're going to see if Tom is on that boat out there."

"And if he is?" Kaile walked portside and kept his eyes peeled on the intruding vessel.

"Binoculars are in the cabin. See if you can catch a name on the stern."

Beth disappeared inside for a brief moment and returned with the glasses. The wind had strengthened; whitecaps became surges of churning water. The Sea Quest picked up speed, puffing clouds of black smoke as it revved out across the water and sprung over the waves. "What if Tom is on that boat? What will you do?" Kaile fell onto the seat.

"I'm not sure. Call the cops I guess. Or get out my trusty old rifle."

"You think the police would do anything to him? I mean he hasn't really done anything illegal has he?"

There was a bite to Leni's words and daggers in his eyes. "You've forgotten what they did to you already? Assault and battery? That's illegal, not to mention climbing aboard a private boat and vandalizing it. We have a police report already, son."

It had never occurred to Kaile that Tom might be in trouble for what he did to him. Mers had no crime. Everyone treated everyone else respectfully and no one stole anything because merpeople didn't really own anything to steal.

Beth took a place next to Kaile and held the binoculars to her eyes. "That boat has a name. Dunnabar."

"Not familiar with that name." Leni took the binoculars from his daughter and with one hand on the helm, the other on the glasses, he squinted through the lens. "It's a fishing boat all right. Seems there are some motor boats floating alongside of it. Benson was right."

"Don't let them kill the dolphins, Pops!" Beth shuddered. Kaile put his arm around her.

"I'll do what I can to prevent it, you can bet on that." Leni handed the binoculars back to her.

The Sea Quest slowed; the sound of the engine died as they came alongside the Dunnabar. The man who stepped starboard to greet them sported a salt and pepper beard, ruddy face, and broad smile.

Leni nodded a return greeting but did not smile; nor did he give a cordial hello. "We're not used to strangers in these parts," he said, pulling a bag of snuff from his pocket, still holding the wheel with one hand.

"Protected waters?"

"Of sorts."

"That's not a straight answer. Protected or not?"

"I protect it."

"Then pretty much anyone can come here."

Leni pinched a wad of tobacco from the pouch and tucked it under his tongue. "At their own risk."

The man raised a brow.

After examining the face of the man intending to massacre a dozen dolphins, Kaile turned his attention to a rack behind the man's head, filled with harpoons polished and ready for a kill. The crew of three worked steadily, removing the weapons from the rack and stowing them in the speedboats.

"You come from Ocean Bend?" as Leni chewed his tobacco, his mouth turned to a frown. He gave Kaile a concern glance.

"I do."

"I'm looking for someone. I was wondering if you'd seen him." He pushed the snuff against his cheek and spat.

"Got a picture?"

"No picture. A name. Tom."

The man laughed. "There're more Toms in the world than there are turkeys. Got a last name?"

"Weatherford. Young guy, blond hair, athletic build."

Kaile watched the fellow's eyes. Suspicion rose when the man's smile turned downward.

"Why would you be looking for someone like that on my boat? Nope. Don't know any Weatherfords. Ain't it a Weatherford that owns the oil rigs?"

"So I've been told."

The man laughed.

"Ain't no Weatherford befriending the likes of me!"

Leni surprised Kaile when he laughed with the man. "Yeah, I guess not. What're you fishing for?"

The man changed the subject. "Barnacle Bay your home town?"

"What're you fishing for?" Leni asked.

"You the old man on the wharf I heard about? The Billy Goat Gruff?"

Kaile's eyes widened. These were Tom's friends. How else would he have known about that confrontation on the wharf? He sized up the crew getting into the speedboats. Big guys, all of them. One had dark hair, Rick. Kaile shifted his weight when she squeezed his hand. "What?"

"You okay?" Her eyes were full of fear.

"Yeah." Kaile answered but it was a lie. He felt pain in his stomach all over again when he made eye contact with Tom's thug.

"This your crew? Four of you?" Leni asked.

"You got a search warrant?"

"Not yet."

"Then you'd better mind your own business. Stop asking so many questions."

"These waters are my business. And everything in them."

"We'll see about that, buddy." The man nodded to his crew as Leni threw the Sea Quest's throttle in reverse. They backed away.

"Kaile!" Beth said as they made distance from the Dunnabar.

"What?"

"You're hurting me." She pulled her hand away from his.

"I'm sorry!" He kissed her fingers. "Really. It was really tense there for a moment. I didn't mean to squeeze so hard."

"Did you recognize any of those men?" Leni asked.

"One. His name's Rick."

"So we know that is one of Tom's boats now. I'm giving Benson a call. Kaile, take the helm and head for Ocean Bend."

34. The Foreman

When the lid to the cylinder was finally removed, Tas took a deep breath. His arms were still pinned with straps, numb from being confined. The cooling and hydration system was worthless but the air was now much more refreshing than the stale oxygen they fed him in the tank.

"Wow!" A young man hovered over him. His sandy hair fell loosely over his glasses and his mouth hung open. He wore starched white scrubs, rubber gloves, and had a clipboard in his hand.

Though weary from the confinement Tas found the young man's expression humorous. He cleared his throat. "Let me guess, you've never seen a merman."

The boy shook his head; his face grew paler. "You can talk our language even? You're like a person only...except for you're..."

"My fins? Yes, I talk. I've learned your language from your people. And this is not my natural habitat. Would you happen to know where any water is?"

"Of course. There's a pool."

Tas could hardly believe what he was hearing. "A pool? So can you get me out of this iron box and put me in your pool? It would be much appreciated."

"That's what I'm here for. Sorry I'm gawking." The young man laughed nervously as he unhinged the lid to the cylinder and rearranged the straps to the sling that held Tas in his cushioned bed. "They didn't tell me what was in this chamber when they brought it here. I thought you were a dolphin. That's what we usually transport."

"Where am I?" Tas shivered from being exposed to the outside air, since the heater in the cubicle was no longer keeping his body a stable temperature.

"Oh, you're on the Sealark. A transporter ship. I'm supposed to get you ready for release." He pulled his latex gloves on and fastened a rubber bib and apron around his body. "Hang in there I'll get you in some warmer water in one moment. We'll adjust your temperature to match the ocean gradually once you're in the pool."

"Release? They're letting me go?"

"They're putting you back in the ocean, that's as much as I know. They won't tell me anything else." The boy stepped away for a moment. "Let me get these doors open so I can wheel you outside." When the worker returned he gave Tas a hearty smile. "All ready to go!"

"Well this is a pleasant turn of events. I think." Tas voice rattled with the rolling of the wheels as he watched the ceiling spin by. "What's your name?"

"Jesse. I assume you have a name too, being as you talk and seem to have some intelligence."

Tas laughed at the remark. "My name is Tas. If I were really intelligent I wouldn't have gotten caught."

"How did they get you? A net?"

"Yes. I was in the process of trying to rescue a dolphin."

"How were you doing that?"

"I was trying to saw through their net."

"I don't suppose they were very happy about that."

Tas couldn't see Jesse; the boy was still wheeling the cubicle down the aisle, but he wondered about the boy's reaction.

"I don't much care what they were happy about. It was bad enough to see the other fish suffer. I would have released all of their catch if I could have."

"I see." Jesse peered into the cubicle again and smiled. "You'd have been a hero among your kind, it seems, if you had been successful."

"Some of them got away."

Jesse busied himself with the straps from the sling, attaching them to a mechanism Tas was unfamiliar with. "Well I can't say that I blame you. But don't tell the bosses I said so."

"Not a word."

"If there are any more of your kind out there, they'll be treated as adversaries should word spread that you go around cutting nets."

"We aren't already thought of as adversaries?"

"Right now you're being treated as a curiosity."

"Which means?"

"I can't say for sure what their plan for you is, but since you're on the Sealark, I'm pretty sure they aren't going to kill you."

"Well, that's encouraging. And how many other people know about me?"

"Only a few, sir. We're under strict confidence."

"We?" Tas grew worried. The more people who knew that merfolk existed, the more dangerous it would be for Pouraka. "Don't tell me there are a lot of you that know about me."

"Only a small number of crew members and the fishermen that pulled you out of the water. They'll be spreading rumors like wildfire. I'm going to hook your sling to the pulleys over the pool and then lift you up for a moment. Don't be afraid. Once I have you above the pool I'll lower you and have you out of the sling in no time." Jesse rolled Tas chamber through a set of double doors onto the deck of the ship. The fresh air was life to him and he breathed deeply. The sky welcomed him.

"Salt water?" Tas asked, afraid to hope.

"Yes, sir. You're supposed to be getting some exercise."

Jesse pulled a crane over Tas' container and attached the sides of his sling to the pulleys.

"We're on a ship?"

"Yes, sir." With the flip of a switch, Tas was lifted into the air, swung to the side and let down carefully into the water. "There you go." Jesse released the tension and loosened the sling from around Tas.

The merman slid out of the drape and with one push of his tail fin he gravitated to the cement floor of the pool.

He lay motionless for a moment. Gratitude swelled inside of him. He had been certain that he would never swim again. What turn of fate had allowed him this pleasure? Perhaps this young man Jesse, could tell him more. Tas surfaced and wiped the water from his face.

"And don't worry about me telling anyone what I've seen today." Jesse kneeled by the poolside and spoke quietly as he removed his gloves and wiped his hands on a towel. "When I took on this job I swore to confidentiality. It's one of the reasons they hired me, because I can keep my mouth shut. These oil tycoons keep their business secrets under high security."

"Will these oil tycoons tell me what they want from me?"

"They will. In fact I think the reason I'm bringing you here now, besides making sure you're comfortable and getting your body adjusted to ocean temperature again, is that you'll be having a visit from the foreman."

"The foreman?"

"Are you hungry?"

"Famished. I've not eaten since I was trapped. How long ago was that?"

"You've been sedated for a couple of days. I'll be back in a minute." Jesse left the room.

After Tas worked the kinks out of his muscles, he dove underwater and stayed there, suspended in liquid space, allowing every pore of his body to soak life substance from its surroundings. Cool, wet, and nourishing, for once he was comforted.

"Excuse me, sir?" Jesse asked when Tas surfaced again. Jesse was by the poolside with a platter of raw fish. "Does this work? I mean, it's what we keep for the other mammals we transport. I wasn't exactly sure about the menu for a merperson."

"Fish will do, yes."

Jesse set the tray on the walkway where Tas could reach it at will. Tas was so hungry and ate so fast that the boy pulled another tray from the refrigerator and placed it next to the empty one.

"They should have given you a reprieve from that chamber to feed you before this. Between you and me, some of the things they do here aren't humane. I mean, you don't just cage an animal without taking care of it." Jesse's eyes met his, his face turned red. "I'm sorry. I didn't mean to refer to you as an animal."

"It's okay. I've been called worse."

"I don't agree with them on a lot of their practices. If I could, I would have been right there with you, saving that dolphin."

"Oh? Then what are you doing here?"

"Working my way through college. This is an apprenticeship. From here I'm going on to better things."

"Better things?"

"I'm pursuing a degree in Environmental Science. I really don't like being a part of an organization that puts animals on display."

"What do you mean by 'on display'?"

"Aquariums."

"You mean holding tanks like the one I was in?"

"Cleaner, but worse. Amusement parks. I think ultimately that's where you're headed. You'll be in a tank with glass windows, where people can watch you. You'll probably never get to go back where you came from. I'm sorry."

Jesse was indeed apologetic but his sympathy wasn't going to benefit Tas' situation.

"Can't you help me get out of here?"

"I wouldn't know how."

"Put me back in that sling, reel it over the deck and release it."

Jess shrugged.

"Why not?"

"I'd get arrested."

Tas finished the last of his dinner, wiped his face and dove back under the water, stretching and tumbling and spinning. He'd been confined way too long. His muscles pined for movement and though this pool was small, it was large enough to do a few merman calisthenics. Once when he lunged out of the water, spun in the air, and returned with a splash he heard Jesse laugh and came up for air to laugh with him.

"You're really amazing. Awesome!"

Time passed and when the initial joy of being free, or at least free from the cubicle he had been in wore off, Tas fought homesickness. He would never feel free until he was in the ocean.

"Tell me, Jesse."

The boy was sitting on a lounge chair watching Tas and sipping on liquid from a glass.

"Are you sure they're going to sell me?"

"They don't tell me everything but that's usually what they do with the sea mammals they bring on this ship. I hope they don't. They should leave you, and anyone like you, alone. Return you to the wild. Let you live free."

The door opened and a man in a hard hat walked in, gave an acknowledging nod to Jesse and stepped up to the pool. He stood there for a moment staring at Tas, his hands on his hips and a frown on his face. He didn't demonstrate the same awe that Jesse had when the boy first saw Tas, but the man's expression wasn't unpleasant either. "Thanks, Jess. You can go about your chores now. I'll need to spend a little time alone with this thing."

Jesse's brow furrowed. "Yes sir. But he's a…"

The man turned sharply to him.

"He's not a thing, sir. He's a…"

"A what, Jesse?"

"A merman, sir."

"I see that. You're excused."

The boy gave Tas a sympathetic eye before he turned and left the room. The foreman pulled up a chair and scooted it close to the pool.

"My name is Bret Garland. I'm the Project manager for divers on the Weatherford Rig. There's been an emergency and we need someone to go deep immediately. Most of the crew have gone home, including our Saturated Divers. Tom's hands have been tied…"

Tas scoffed at the statement. He'd like to see Tom's hands tied.

"I'll be right up front with you. Our rig is at risk in more ways than one. There's a leak."

"A leak?"

"One of our pipes is cracked but we don't know what kind of leak it is. It could be oil but it might be gas. It's deep and we can't prepare a diver soon enough. It needs to be plugged immediately if not before. Getting someone down there would take at least a week of preparation and we don't have that kind of time. I've got one question for you before I go on."

"That is?"

"How deep can you dive?"

Tas laughed. "How deep?"

"Yeah, how far can you go down?"

"I never really thought about how far I can dive. I know I can't go beyond the green waters. I can't go past light. Or into the abyss."

"We need you a little over 300 meters down."

"I'm not sure how far your meters are."

"You've seen a swordfish?"

"Yes."

"Their habitat is approximately 300 meters. A diver can see down there, but not well. Can you go down that far?"

"I believe I can." Tas had been as deep as Garland spoke of in the past, though no merperson made it a practice. There were more predators in those waters, and the pressure slowed their swimming and used up oxygen more quickly. "The pipes that need fixing will be barely visible to you unless you have a different sensory system than we have?"

Tas stared at the man, blankly. How well do humans see?

"I'm going to assume you don't, just to play it safe. You'll be equipped with a headlamp and other tools you need. You'll carry them on a belt strapped around your waist."

"Exactly what do you want me to do?"

"Our robot cameras have shots of the split. We'll have you bolt a valve with a compression fitting on it and turn it off after the fitting is tight."

At that point the door opened and Tom strolled into the room. Tas' blood turned cold. He'd had hoped he'd never see the man again.

Bret continued talking without acknowledging Tom's presence, however Tas didn't take his eyes off of the intruder. "After you fix the leak, we need you to swim along the pipe for about a mile to locate any other cracks. It's all pretty simple, really, except for the deep sea diving."

"Diving is simple for me. What is the risk if this leak doesn't get sealed?"

"At the minimum there'd be an environmental risk of spilled oil, something our company can't really afford, especially if the environmentalists catch wind. At the max, there could be an underwater explosion that could cause considerable damage and take some lives."

Tas raised his eyebrows, his eyes widened.

"An explosion?"

"If it's a vapor leak, yes. Hence the emergency."

"There's another risk, too." Tom stepped closer. "If you don't help us, that is."

"What's that? I get sold to an aquarium?"

"That's going to happen anyway. It's going to be a little tougher on you if we don't get this leak fixed. I won't have time to arrange the sale right away like I was planning, so you'll go back into that holding tank until my job is done. That could take two or three more weeks if we have to hire a saturation diver. Then I'll have to make up for the cost and the only way I can do that is to capture a couple more mermaids." He pulled his cap off his head, brushed his hair back and returned the cap, pushing his tongue against his cheek. "I've got my eye on one in particular. Pretty little thing. I think you know who. So it will all work out in the end, regardless of whether you help or not. Especially if we trap some young dolphins, too."

That stung. If Tom ever put his hands on Cora, Tas would find a way to kill him. He turned his attention to Bret and refused to give Tom any reaction.

"Teach me what I need to do to fix your leak." Tom's blackmail was not the deciding factor. Tas offered his services because he was concerned for the other inhabitants of the sea. He may never escape. His own welfare didn't matter. He would cooperate. Tom and his crew were too well organized, and Tas had few resources to defend himself. He was, after all, a sea mammal and at their mercy, or lack of mercy.

Bret nodded. "Thanks, Tas. Tom, Jesse and I will be in the motor boat and we'll have you attached by cable so we can maintain control and pull you out of danger if we need to. We'll stay in constant contact. You'll have a tracking device around your wrist that will be in sync with our GPS. It should detect the leak, and will beep when you're near the fault so you'll know to watch for anything unusual with the pipe. You know, bubbles, oils, any splits in the line. You'll have a camera strapped to your headlamp. The camera will be monitored on our computers so we can advise you. We use this technology with our robots, which we don't have for this particular job or we'd use one of those. Technically we'll be swimming with you. We can see everything you can. We'll communicate by earphones, so you'll get step-by-step instructions as you work. It'll be pretty simple on your part. We'll be the mind, you'll be our hands." He chuckled a bit after giving Tas a once-over. "And our fins. This might prove a valuable experience for both of us." He turned to Tom before he walked out the door. "You're a fool to sell him."

Tom smirked at Tas before he followed Bret.

35 Pipeline

Had he not been weighted down with a shoulder harness, and a chain wrapped around his caudal fin, Tas would have rejoiced that he was in the sea again. His urge to spin was overpowering, yet the consequences would be fatal. The cable would kill him. Tas had a mission and a master.

Bret helped him overboard. As soon as he hit the water the shackle fell and sunk quickly to the bottom of the sea, forcing Tas downward, tailfin first, past the tower and the abundant sea life living under the rig. Schools of barracuda hovered in between the pillars, rainbow runners darted in perfect formation around his head. Sardines flashed by and spiraled as one body, their numbers impossible to determine. Jellies colored the sea with their iridescent pinks and pearly whites, shielding tiny silver fish from predators. Coral, barnacles and mussels clung to the tower and sea anemones swayed gently in the current. Tas caught only a glimpse of them.

Once at the bottom, the sudden tug on his fin reminded him of who was watching. If Tas removed any of the rigging that was strapped to him, Tom would fish him out of the sea in an instant and the trip would not be pleasant. Tas was tired of Tom's abuse, but still there was little he could do to prevent it.

He had always been a strong swimmer and now his strength was tested. The weight of the fetter pulling from behind in a dense environment made movement unusually hard, yet Tas refused to succumb.

The pipeline ran downhill into deeper, darker waters, an environmental condition that made Tas nervous. Merpeople didn't enter dark waters except in emergencies. Tales of sea monsters lurking in the abyss were a part of their folklore, and had never been disproven.

Tas scorned those legends. If a mother really wanted to scare her children, she should tell tales of the monsters that live on land! This unfamiliar territory and abnormal predicament that men had thrust him into kept Tas' heart racing.

Sea monsters kill and eat their prey, ending the prey's life. Men imprison, torture and prolong the pain leaving their prey begging for death. Regardless of the cruelty of his captors, Tas would keep his promise even if he did get sent to the abyss. He'd fix the pipe quickly and then return.

Return to what? An iron tube with a wet sponge for a bed?

"Stop thinking, Tas," he said aloud. That was the best advice to follow. Reality was fearful enough. He needn't use his imagination to make things worse.

Tas moved slowly over the metal tube, his headlamp cast a beam onto the sickly green pipe half buried under bottom silt. Though the sea was dark and murky here, enough light seeped in from above to cast shadows.

He froze.

A dark shape hovered directly above him blocking what little luminance there was.

If this shadow was that of a shark he didn't stand a chance of escape. Bret had mentioned pulling him to the surface should there be danger, but he couldn't have meant a predator. That escape plan would mean certain death. Hooked onto this chain and yanked to the surface he would be nothing more than bait on a fishing line. Could it be that his captors hadn't even considered sharks as a threat to him? Or were they even worried about his life at all? The fear passed through his mind more than once. In nature, and as a merman, his defense was agility. He had no defense.

Slowly he turned his head. The dark mysterious figure was not at a shark, but a dolphin. Not a spinner dolphin like the ones from Pouraka. This dolphin was larger with a long pointed nose and curious eyes. It lingered near, suspended and immobile save for its eyes that watched every move Tas made.

"You're safe." A voice in his ears spoke through static. It sounded very much like Jesse. "It's a dolphin."

"I see that." Tas replied. "What if it weren't?"

As Tas inched along, the dolphin followed.

"I hear dolphins can ward off sharks." Jesse replied.

"They can."

"Someone's watching out for you. I'm glad." Jesse's voice faded with static, but Tas appreciated the young man's concern.

He was also mindful and thankful for the dolphin's presence. Tas followed the line until his scope of vision diminished and he could see no further than his hands. He used his fingers as feelers to follow the cold metal of the pipe.

When the cloudy water grew even darker, Tas regarded the chain stretching toward the surface and the innocent dolphin hovering so close to man's shackle.

"Go home." Tas used his merlanguage to speak to the dolphin. "It's not safe here. If they catch you, they'll imprison you, too."

The dolphin turned and left but his departure was slow as though he was reluctant to abandon Tas.

"Keep to your task." A voice in his earphone, a different voice this time. The men had promised that he would not be entering the abyss, and yet the murky waters were dark and the meter on his wrist remained silent, detecting no leaks. Had they lied to him?

"This is not what you promised," Tas said into his mic. "You said I wouldn't have to go any farther than 300 meters."

There was no answer.

He could head in the other direction but if he did, they'd pull him out of the water. If he fought them they would punish him and there would be nothing he could do to defend himself.

If they asked him to go much deeper he'd have to hold them to their word and refuse. No matter the assignment, as a merman, the abyss was forbidden.

Tas aimed the lamp at the half buried pipe and suddenly the meter began clicking. Black bubbles seeped from the ground. Relieved that his search was over, he dug through the silt to uncover the leak.

"That's it!" This time the voice in Tas' ear was Bret's. "It's an oil leak. Good job, Tas. You found it!"

The praise surprised him.

Bret talked him through the process of repair, setting the clamp over the leak and securing it. It didn't take long and the task was not laborious. The tools Bret had given him were efficient. After he clenched the valve as tight as he could, Tas returned the wrench and wire cutters to the tool bag on his shoulder, pleased that bubbles no longer seeped from the line. That fragment of his job was complete.

"Now follow that pipe back the way you came while we check the pressure." Bret's voice was lost in the mix of static so Tas adjusted the weight on his shoulder harness, pulled some slack from the chain that attached the cable to his tail fin, and began swimming along the pipe back to the rig. When the waters were clearer he heard a sound that he hadn't heard for a long time. Merlanguage rippled in the current, calling his name.

"Tas?"

A school of barracuda flash by.

"Tas!"

The sound came from his left and he turned to identify it. An angel of light out of the blue waters, a mermaid appeared.

"Cora!" His heart pounded with joy. The chain stiffened and yanked him back.

The camera! Tas spun around and turned his back to her.

"Cora, don't come any closer. Swim away!"

"What do you mean?" she asked, but the vibration was drowned out by the sound in his ear.

"Turn back around Tazzy boy. Let me see. Face her, Tas." Tom needled him and then his voice lowered. He had turned from the mic to someone else in the room but Tas heard clearly and panicked. "Get a reading on her location."

"Cora, swim away, quickly! Don't come any nearer. They can see you."

"No, Tas," she answered.

"Tazzy, turn around or I'll drag you back here so hard and fast you'll be pulp by the time you reach my boat."

No way in creation was Tas going to succumb to Tom's cruelty. "Drag me, then!" He refused to aim the camera lens at Cora. "Go away, Cora!"

"I've cooperated with you all I'm going to." Tas sent his mer warning through the depths. "Cora go. They'll imprison and torture you. Save yourself, Sea Rose."

The cable jerked and lurched forward, hauling Tas upside down and through the depths at an alarming speed.

36. Sea Rose

Cora halted mid swim, her wake swept her forward as she watched Tas in horror. Chained by his tail, leather straps across his chest and strange gear on his head, he ordered her to stop and she heeded his command, yet she didn't flee like he'd told her to. Her intent was to rescue him, no matter the cost. When the chain was suddenly pulled taut, yanking Tas backward, and silt stirred from the ocean floor as he reached for something to hang on to, she feared his tail fin would be ripped from his body. But when it towed him against the current with such force that he spun like a fisherman's lure, Cora bolted forward in a race to intercede.

His dark hair twirled around his face as he tore the gear off his head. Cora dodged the object that broke free. With a sweeping push of her fin, she gained velocity and raced alongside Tas, then ahead of him. When she caught the metal links, the cable sucked her into its current and slammed her against Tas' tail. The force spun her in a vicious cycle. She gripped the shackle and inched her way toward his chest, hugging his body lest she be flung away into the depths. With a tight hold on Tas' torso, she rotated to face the same direction.

The metal that was tied around his tail rubbed his scales raw. His eyes rolled in agony from being stretched by the current in one direction and the boat dragging him in another. How he was still conscious, she didn't know. He tried to speak but no sound came out. Tas tried to push her away but she resisted and clung to him tighter.

"I'm not leaving you until you're free, Tas."

How could he hear over the engine noise and the rushing waters?

The closer to the boat they came, the more turbulent the ride. The wake churned and bubbled directly overhead; sucking their heads above the surface and spitting them back under again. Cora saw the hull of the ship and the propeller. A man pointed at them. Time drew near when they'd be hauled up. Cora pushed Tas' hair from his face and when their eyes met he wrapped one arm around her and pulled something from his shoulder harness. Some sort of tool.

She'd never seen a wire cutter before, but she had seen scissors and these weren't much different. She understood. She took the tool and flipped her body upside down along his. Tas held onto her tail as she struggled against the force of the tow. When she reached the chain she positioned the cutter. The push of the water would have forced her to let go of her tool if she hadn't fought against it, and if Tas hadn't held her securely. Cora fit the pinchers of the snipers around a link of the chain and as she was about to cut, the boat slowed and stopped.

The cable fell. Gravity sucked them down so quickly that Cora's stomach lurched. With teeth clenched, Cora gripped both Tas and the cutters with all her strength.

A sudden jolt and everything stopped. Suspended in the ocean, Tas hung upside down and Cora hugged his tail fearing they'd suddenly be towed again.

Now was not the time to give up. She gathered her spirits and shifted her weight, put the cutters to the chain and pushed the pinchers together as hard as she could. The blade made little impact on the thick metal. Tas tried to bend upward. He would have offered her his strength if he could, but he fell back, unable to bend. On the third try he took the handle of the wire cutters and squeezed them, stripping the metal to a shine, but still the link didn't break.

They heard a loud splash above them. The end of the cable plummeted. A stream of bubbles from above followed the shackle as it dropped. When the cable passed them it flipped Tas upright and wrenched him downward. Tas and Cora and the chain plunged to the depths. Past schools of rock cod, jellies, and a rocky reef. A curious white shark turned abruptly and watched.

"Tas!" Cora cried when his hold on her wavered. Afraid Tas had lost his strength and his will to survive, she snatched the wire cutters from his hand and scooted down to the chain.

If she were going to save them both, now was her only chance. She caught the worn link between the pinchers and twisted.

The shark circled over them and the abyss pulled from below. They had only seconds left to save themselves.

Cora pushed the cutter handles together using every ounce of energy and willpower left in her. The link snapped. She dropped the tool and unwrapped the chain from Tas' fin. The cable disappeared, swirling into the deep.

"You're free!" She spoke in their native tongue, sweet sound waves echoing like a symphony across the waves. With a swoop of his body, Tas grabbed Cora and fled to the reef before the shark could catch them.

37. Intervention

A few miles from Ocean Bend the two fishermen made their rendezvous. The mid-afternoon seas were rough; the wind whistled and to the south dark clouds formed. There'd no doubt be a storm soon, but so often in these waters it was never quite certain where the rains would hit or if they would hit at all. The sky might be completely clear by evening.

Leni killed the motor and waved at the man in the dinghy. Kaile raced portside to catch Benson's bowline and pull the boat closer, tying it to the Sea Quest.

"Good to see you. Glad you came along." Benson said to Kaile after boarding. Kaile shook his hand, anxious for word of his friends.

"We heard you talked with Cora. Where is she now?" Kaile asked. A breeze had picked up and with it a chill. Kaile blew in his hands and rubbed them together to stay warm.

Benson shook his head and nodded toward the oil rig. "I'm not sure. Cora told me she was going to find Tas. She thinks he might be near the rigs but in this weather, I can only hope she's safe."

"You said Tom was holding Tas prisoner."

"He is. But that's only part of the story. I wasn't able to tell Leni everything over the phone."

Benson shook Leni's hand as he and Beth approached. Beth handed Benson a cup of coffee. "What's the word?" Leni asked.

The man shivered and held the cup to his face to warm his cheeks. After he took a drink, Benson spoke. "You see that boat out there? That's the Sealark."

Benson pointed toward a large white vessel moored near the oil rigs. "Since I talked to you, I did some research at the marina. It belongs to the Weatherfords. They use it as a transport boat."

"What does it transport?"

"Sea mammals usually. Orcas, dolphin, porpoise. Sea lions and otters. They contract with several aquariums and theme parks on the mainland. Take a look at that deck."

Benson pulled a pair of binoculars from his coat pocket and handed them to Kaile. "There's a huge salt water pool on deck out front. Inside the cabin are refrigerators and cubicles for moving live cargo."

Kaile whistled through his teeth as he scanned the ship through the binoculars. The size of the boat was grand indeed, but not as spectacular as the sleek and shiny design.

Kaile had never seen anything like it. The pool wasn't visible, but he saw men walking on the deck, and he saw a crane.

"You think Tas is on that boat?" Beth asked.

"It's possible. Cora could be there too."

"Cora?" Kaile's eyes widened. "You said you saw Cora at the marina."

"I did. But Tom knows Cora's a mermaid and he's been targeting her. She was pretty close to getting captured once. I hope she's free but there's a chance she isn't." Benson put his hand on Kaile's shoulder. "Cora doesn't have a lot of defense against Tom. None of you merfolk do. You're limited to swimming in the water. Your best defense is to swim fast and hide. It's useless for you to fight. I'm telling you this because I care for you. Merpeople don't have any more defenses against people like Tom Weatherford than do your dolphin friends."

Kaile drew in a deep breath. Though Benson's words were true, there remained one ultimate resolution. How he longed to tell Beth.

"What's wrong, Kaile? You keep staring at me."

He couldn't take his eyes off of her. Ever. He couldn't leave her.

"Benson," Leni had taken the binoculars from Kaile and focused on the oil rig. "What's that smaller boat next to the Sealark? Looks like the Dunnabar."

"If it's like the Dunnabar, it's probably a dolphin driver. You say it's next to the Sealark?"

"Right up against it."

"Could be one of Tom's rigs. If it heads for Barnacle Bay and meets up with the Dunnabar, it means trouble. My suggestion is we intercept it before it heads north."

"And then what?" Kaile asked, but Leni wasted no time skipping to the helm and revving the engines.

"We'll figure that out when we get there."

The Sea Quest fought the whitecaps and skated over its own wakes. Kaile and Beth took a seat near the wheel and hung on. Their hair blew wildly in the wind and sea salt sprayed into their faces as the Sea Quest bumped through the choppy sea.

As Leni's boat neared, the speedboat gunned its motor and screamed around the oil rig.

"You think he saw us?" Kaile asked, his voice raised above the sound of the wind.

"I'm sure he did." Leni answered.

After several loops, the boat spun off into the distance away from the Sealark and into open waters. Leni slowed the Sea Quest.

"What's he doing?" Beth asked.

"Driving like a mad man," Kaile answered.

"Why?"

"I'm not sure." It didn't make sense to Kaile, for the boat was not only doing circles, but crazy eights, flying over its wake.

"We'll find out soon enough." Leni said.

"Pops, can the Sea Quest outrun that guy?"

"We'll find that out, too." Leni kicked the throttle into full speed and raced toward Tom's wake. Kaile held the glasses as steady as he could, straining to see any activity on the speed boat.

Surprisingly, the boat slowed, giving Leni an opportunity to close in and Kaile to observe more accurately.

"It's Tom all right."

"Well at least they stopped." Beth breathed a sigh of relief.

"Some kind of scuffle, and someone working a pulley at the stern. They're reeling it in."

"Fishing at the speed they were going?"

"Seems crazy." Kaile kept his eyes against the lens hoping to see their catch.

"That's a motorized pulley all right." Leni confirmed.

"Whoa!" Kaile gasped. "That's exactly what he did to me!"

"What happened?"

Kaile handed Beth the binoculars. "The person at the pulley threw something overboard. Tom punched him, pulled him up by his shirt collar and hit him again."

"Oh my God!" Beth cried out. "He's got him up against the rail. Pops, do something!"

"What can I do, Beth? Let me see those." Beth handed her father the binoculars. "Damn!" Leni raced to the helm and started the engine. "Man overboard!" he shouted. "Benson, grab the ring buoy and toss it when I tell you."

"What happened, Pops? Did Tom throw the poor soul off his boat?"

"No. The poor soul jumped to get away from Tom. No matter how it happened, he's in the water now."

"I'll get him." Kaile pulled off his shirt and before anyone could stop him he plunged into the sea, his mer strength kicking in. He swam to the drowning victim in seconds. The man had stopped struggling; his mouth was too full of water to cry out. Kaile took hold of his chest and lifted his head above the water. Once Kaile had a hold of the man with one arm, he gripped the ring buoy that bounced by his head.

The victim spat out water and opened his eyes. He was young, more a teenager than a man. His head was bleeding where he'd been hit and he gasped for air. He grappled at Kaile in panic.

"Let go, I've got you." Kaile peeled away from the boy's grasp as the line tightened and pulled the two of them toward the Sea Quest. They didn't have far to go; the hull of the Sea Quest was near enough to touch when Kaile heard an engine rev and saw the bow of Tom's speedboat rear up and spin around toward them.

"Kaile!" Beth cried out.

Kaile held his breath as the attacking vessel fired past the swimmers, swamping them with a rooster tail of water. Before an impending collision with Leni's fishing rig, the speedboat swiveled sharply, splashing another barrage of water into the Sea Quest.

After Tom and his boat sped off into the distance, Kaile swam to the boat ladder where Benson and Leni waited. The two helped Kaile pull the injured man on board.

Kaile's teeth clattered and his body shook uncontrollably, but having saved a man's life was worth the discomfort. Beth wrapped her father's leather jacket around him as they watched Leni dry the young man with a towel. Wet and pale blue from the cold, the boy's lips quivered, and his hands shook but he sat and drank hot coffee from a cup that Benson gave him.

"I'm all right. I'll be fine," the boy said, avoiding their stares.

"I'll take the helm. You talk to him Leni." Benson patted Leni on the back and hopped to the wheel turning the Sea Quest north.

"That's quite the bruise. What happened, son?" Leni kneeled next to the boy and rubbed his shoulder. "How'd you end up in the water?"

"I couldn't take it any longer. I had to stop the insanity."

"What insanity?"

The boy shook his head, his brilliant blue eyes darted from Kaile's to Beth's to Leni's, and then he shook his head again. "You wouldn't believe me if I told you. Besides I've been sworn to secrecy."

"Secrecy about what?" Beth interjected. "We saved you from certain death! I think you could trust us with your secret."

"What's your name?" Leni waved Beth quiet. "Where are you from?"

"Jesse. I'm doing an apprenticeship with Weatherford's firm on their transporter ship, the Sealark. But I wasn't expecting anything like this. I was supposed to be handling dolphins, not..." He looked up.

"Not what? Merpeople?" Kaile blurted. Everyone turned his way. He laughed nervously. "Well? We all know it."

"We do?" Jesse's mouth fell open. "No one else was supposed to know about him."

"Tas?"

"Oh man!" Jesse covered his face and Kaile thought he might be crying.

"It's all right, son, we've got you covered. We'll keep your secret. Nothing's going to happen to you." Leni said.

"It's not me. It's him."

"Who?"

"Tas." He squinted up at Beth for a moment. "You know his name. How'd you know him?"

"It's a long story. Where is he now? Where's Tas?"

The boy's lips quivered again. He had something to say but it wasn't coming easy.

"Tell us. Please?" Beth pleaded.

"Tom had him chained to the boat because the merman was working for the Weatherfords. Don't ask me how that happened. I don't know. All I know is I opened the transport tank and there he was."

"What kind of work?" Leni gave him a dry blanket and wrung out the towel.

"Tas was doing some diving for the old man. It was all pretty legit. No one meant him any harm. They were monitoring Tas from the Sealark, and Tom had a monitor set up on the speedboat, too. Everything was fine. Tas got the job done and was checking the line. But then the mermaid showed up on Tas' cam and suddenly Tom went nuts on us. He revved up that motorboat and started dragging Tas around like a trout on a spinner." The boy gagged.

Leni rubbed his back.

"Cora's alive then?"

Kaile turned to her. That was good news!

"That poor guy. I had to do it. I had to cut him loose."

Kaile scratched his head. It didn't make sense. Why did this kid feel so bad if he cut Tas free?

Beth broke the silence. "He's free?"

Jesse muttered and gagged again. "Free from Tom. But he's still attached to a few hundred pounds of chain and cable."

"No!" Beth gasped.

Kaile stood frozen and stared in shock. A merman in chains at the bottom of the ocean would not last long. If ever there was a time Kaile wished he were a mer, now was the time. He would dive into the water to save his friend.

Leni swore, jumped up, and mumbled as he passed Kaile and walked to the stern of the boat. "If he doesn't drown, he'll be shark bait."

The sloshing of whitecaps against the hull broke the silence. Rain blew against their faces. Thunder sounded in the distance.

There were no words to speak, no questions that could be answered.

38. The Dolphins

Never had Cora's heart pounded so hard with such a wave of emotion than the moment the chain broke and their fall ended. Exhausted from the plunge, Cora was thrilled that Tas was free and relieved that they had escaped the jaws of a shark and the clutches of man. Excited to be in his arms again, she let him swim her to safety. He spun her into a crevice where he curled on a ledge and drew her to him. She laid her head on his shoulder and leaned with him against the rocky reef. He put his head against the rocks and closed his eyes. She felt his body tremble against hers, but she was warm in his arms. The silence between them was sacred.

Tas finally spoke, his voice low and strained. "You can't imagine how thankful I am for you, Sea Rose. I have never felt such pain, terror and despair. I honestly thought I was dead. I had given up on life, being able to escape or ever seeing you again as a free merman."

Cora clung to him. His embrace tightened. His lips touched her hair and she nestled into his chest. Nothing could have been more comforting than being in his arms again, hidden away in the deep blue waters of the crevice, encircled by the black rocks that calmed the sea around them and the intimacy of the space they occupied. For Cora, no other living beings but she and Tas existed in that moment, nor in the world.

"You are my life. I was lost without you." The words seemed less than what she wanted to say.

"You risked your life for me. It seems you've been doing that a lot lately." He laughed softly. "You'd think I'd be able to take care of myself a little better."

"You risked your life for the dolphins, Tas. Your capture had nothing to do with not being able to take care of yourself. We're all so vulnerable. So fragile."

She felt him exhale before she heard his sigh. The last thing she wanted was for him to blame himself for what had happened.

"Unfortunately you're right. When I was in that tank I realized how powerless I am against men."

"You did escape though. That's something."

"And you avoided capture. That's something as well."

"Tas, if I hadn't been able to cut that chain around your tail, then I was going to let them take me prisoner too."

"I wouldn't have let that happen."

"You couldn't have stopped it. I missed you so."

When Tas took her head in his hands their lips met. Hidden from the world, her body melted into his, suspended in the liquid space of time.

Nothing mattered to Cora except being in his arms. The trauma that she had experienced melted away with his gentleness. The touch of his body was warm and soothing, his caresses comforting.

He knew every nerve that needed stroking as though they were his own. She held his face and pressed her lips against his. He swept her into deeper waters and there they remained bonded together, floating and rolling with the current. One warm and pulsating body lost in tenderness.

Eternity passed before Tas pulled away and kissed her forehead.

"I would take you as my own right now. Seal our love forever, but I can't. Now is not the time. Not with the world the way it is for us."

Cora moved away from him. Before this all happened, those words may have hurt, but today she understood.

"It has nothing to do with you, or me or our relationship. As much as I love you and want to seal our union, we can't bring another merperson into our world until we know our world is safe."

"You're right. I agree, Tas." His love was enough. Being with him satisfied her longing. She snuggled into his arms and when the beat of their hearts settled, Tas kissed her neck and returned to the ledge where he fell back against the rocks again, drawing her to him. "You saved my life, but we're not done fighting. Tom and his men made a lot of threats. I don't know which ones he intends to carry out but we need to prepare ourselves."

"An evil man indeed if he can interrupt our time alone without even being here."

"Could we enjoy one more moment together before we talk about him and his rotten plans?"

"Do we have a moment?"

"I hope so." Cora pinched his cheeks and kissed him. He laughed and took hold of her waist, spun her around and then he tickled her.

"Stop, Tas, I can't stand it!" Tears of happiness rolled down her cheeks and he kissed them away, his breath warm against her flesh.

"Enough?" he asked in between his love bites.

"I'm good." Cora caught her breath and met his smiling eyes. He brushed her hair from her face.

"We really can't waste time, Cora. Though, if I'm spending it with you, time would never be wasted."

"You're right. We have work to do. I overheard Tom's plans." Cora stroked his shoulder, sorry their time together had to end. "He's going to round up our pod and slaughter whichever dolphins he doesn't want to sell. They're going to use one of his motorboats and also the Dunnabar. I think the Dunnabar left yesterday for Barnacle Bay."

"The man is sick. He has no thought for any other living being except himself."

"What can we do?" Cora laid her head against his chest again. "I'm exhausted, Tas. I don't know if I can go on like this facing one calamity after another. When will it end? How can merpeople fight something so overwhelming?"

"There a way, Cora." He stroked her hair. "But you've sworn against it."

Cora closed her eyes. Of course Tas would be thinking like that. What did she expect? "Changing into a dolphin didn't save Ko."

"As long as merpeople still linger near the magic pools, the dolphins are at risk. You know that. They linger along the coast for our sake."

"Then everyone has to change."

"Yes."

He affirmed her statement with such resolve she shuddered. "And how are you going to convince all the merpeople of Pouraka to transform into dolphins?"

"I don't know. But it's the only lasting solution I can think of."

"Even if you're right, what do we do now? What practical advice do you have for us?"

"Right now we need to get back to our people. I doubt the two of us can do anything about Tom and his dolphin hunters by ourselves. Let's swim to Pouraka and enlist the help of everyone." Tas pushed off from the ledge.

***

Cora was in deeper water than she had ever been before. Dark, green murk barred their vision. The isolated pillar and its crevice they had taken refuge in had no attachment to any other rock formation nor to a shoreline. Had she been alone, Cora would have headed for the shallows or perhaps she'd even surface to see how far south they had come. Tas held her back and proceeded cautiously. Whenever he spoke, he did so quietly. Perhaps he knew of dangers she didn't.

"I have no idea where we are." Cora murmured, in hope Tas would respond with an answer. He didn't though. They traveled deep for a long while. There was nothing in view to indicate their whereabouts, nor which direction to proceed. Tas ascended. As they swam toward the surface, a sudden drop in temperature, mixed with random and confusing currents suggested a storm. "There should be some kind of landmark soon. I believe the boat was dragging us to the north side of the rig before it stopped."

"Why would Tom drop the chain? I mean if they really wanted you so badly, why did they try to kill you?"

"I don't know. I'm not sure if they even intended for the chain to drop. From the way Tom talked he was going to sell me for a great deal of human coin."

"How horrid that would have been. I'm thankful we spoiled his plans!"

Tas took her hand. "Me, too!"

His touch made being lost in a dangerous sea less frightening. That is until she saw the grey shape in the distance and then her heart stopped and she pulled on Tas' arm. He froze next to her, only the soft ends of their tailfins moved in the spiraling current. Cora wished there was some kelp or something nearby to hide in. The creature approached slowly. More of his kind lingered in the distance.

"Cora, don't be afraid. It's a dolphin."

The tension in her body relaxed. "I've never seen a dolphin like him before."

"I saw this guy earlier when I was working on the pipeline. He's a curious sort. He watched me for the longest time and then he swam away."

"What do you think he wants?"

Cora watched his movements as the dolphin slowly circled around them.

"He's just like Ko with his antics," she said, laughing.

"I think he wants us to follow him."

With that, the dolphin nodded and led Tas and Cora in the opposite direction from where they were headed. It didn't seem possible they could be that lost. "Where is he taking us?"

The murky green turned blue again, though the waters still moved erratically. The dolphin led the two merpeople through powerful currents that were so strong she had to hold on to his fins to keep up.

"I'm giving this guy a name!" Tas said.

"What's that?" Cora asked.

"Bandit. He's stealing us away!"

With that, Bandit lunged forward, carrying Tas and Cora through an ocean forest of kelp, a silvery tunnel of cod, in and out of rock formations, and into even more turbulent waters. Still he never faltered.

"Hang on, Cora! I think this guy knows what he's doing!"

They traveled a long time without seeing another creature until the smells and sounds were familiar. Once the dark form of a reef appeared, Bandit slowed and shook them off his fin. He darted back the way he had come.

"Just like that, you're leaving?" Cora asked as they watched his figure vanish. "Tas, do you think Bandit knows mermaids? Do you think his pod has its own Pouraka?"

"Interesting thought, Cora. One your brother would have taken the time to investigate."

"I would like to know."

"And maybe you will, someday. Come this way. I think we're very near home."

39. Buried Treasure

"Look! The wrecked ship. Now I know where we're at!" Cora laughed with joy when she recognized the familiar waters. Finally she was home, alive and healthy, with the one she loved. Only yesterday she had feared she'd never be so triumphant.

The sunken vessel lay tattered, half buried in the silt. Green moss melted into the rusty rails; broken boards that swayed in the stormy current hung on their frame by threads. The hull which had been split in two protruded out of the sand at both ends giving the appearance of a much larger ship. Cora remembered this skeleton from not too long ago when she and Tas had been chased by a Mako. She searched the shadows for the hungry beasts.

"Are we safe?"

Tas took her hand and pulled her to him, revolving around in the water with Cora in his arms. "Do you feel safe?"

She did. After all that had happened, nothing felt safer than being held by Tas.

"We're almost home, Cora."

"I know. What a journey. But it's not over. The dolphins are still in danger."

"We can't do anything to save them. Not alone. That's why we're going back to Pouraka. The mers have a lot of strength as one body. With our kinfolk, and Pouraka's magic, we may be able to stop the slaughter."

"Then we should hurry."

Tas held her back. "Shh. Listen."

Cora stilled, attentive to the sounds that were carried in the current. At first the hum of water moving in and among the broken boards of the wreckage was all she heard, but when it increased in volume the harmonious chords rippled a familiar tone.

"Music!" There was no mistaking the haunting incantation as that of the mers. "It's a chant."

"And it's being sung by more than one merperson. I think it's coming from inside the ship." Tas nodded to a door at the mouth of a dark passage that led into the wreckage.

Cora followed him through the narrow crack of the ship. A wall of decomposing wood tunneled them, kelp and coral cluttered the hall. The temperature in the sunken vessel was cooler, the passage deeper than what Cora had guessed.

The music grew louder. A low hum resonated through the alley way, not a ringing of bells like those she heard on buoys above the surface, nor the whistle that whispers among the pilings on the wharf. This was definitely a mersong and Cora wondered if there was a connection between the chant and the violent storm that was raging above.

Tas led her past a slab of wood rocking on a still-shiny hinge, holding the weight of a heavy wooden door by its own strength, the other hinge had rusted and bent free from the constant undertow.

The room was very large and open. Many of mankind's articles were tossed and scattered across the sandy bottom. Broken chards from long ago lay heaped in piles vying for space and light. Anemones and barnacles clung to their surfaces. Sea stars and mussels clung to the walls. Kelp, pale and pining for the sun spiraled in circles reaching across the room with ghostly hands.

But the most ominous sight was the congregation of merpeople lining the manmade hall, resting on ledges and overturned chairs and tables that once adorned the ancient ship.

The singing stopped when Tas and Cora entered. All eyes were on them. Cora perused the throng. Most everyone from Pouraka was there. Peara was. Kaile was not.

Peara's eyes met hers.

"Tas!" Radcliff met them in the center of the assembly. His greeting sounded warm and welcoming until he saw Cora and then his smile turned sour. "We're elated to hear you're free."

"What aren't you glad about?"

"Your company."

"What are you talking about, Radcliff? Cora's your cousin."

"Blood relation or not, our family is distinguished by loyalty, not birth."

Shock spun through Cora like a lightning bolt. Why was Radcliff so hostile toward her so suddenly?

"Explain yourself." Tas demanded.

Radcliff lifted his chin to Tas, a reminder that his authority was higher than Tas'. "Events have occurred since you were captured that have incriminated both Cora and Kaile."

Cora gasped. She had no idea what he was talking about and here they were with an audience of the entire clan. She tried to speak but no words came. Tas took her hand, wrapped his fingers between hers and spoke for her.

"What are you talking about? What events?"

"The invasion of humans at Pouraka can be attributed to both Cora and Kaile. They are responsible for Pouraka having been compromised. It's because of her our people have been so apprehensive they felt the only recourse was to leave."

"You've abandoned Pouraka? What are you talking about?"

"I'm surprised she hasn't told you."

Cora's heart beat wildly. She hadn't had time to tell Tas about the humans that followed her and Kaile home.

"I see she didn't have the courage to inform you of what had happened, so let me elaborate. The day you were taken captive, Cora and Kaile appeared in Pouraka and soon after four strangers climbed into the cavern. The humans handled our baskets, laid eyes on the Cradle, and when they saw Cora and Kaile in a cave..." Radcliff's sneer cut into Cora's heart. She had no idea any of the merpeople saw her and Kaile that day. "In a passionate embrace I might add, lips pressed against each other, arms wrapped around one another, well ...the humans left and took with them our safekeeping."

Tas swallowed and lifted his head, avoiding Cora's eyes.

"Tas. . ."

He squeezed her hand.

"You don't know what happened after that, Cora." Radcliff's green eyes reflected fury in the water around them as he turned sharply to face her. "Kaile came again with one of his friends. A blond girl."

"Beth."

"You know her, then?" Radcliff asked.

"Beth is Leni's daughter. She's a friend of Cora's." Tas interrupted.

"Honest, Radcliffe, I had no idea she went into Pouraka. I was gone. I walked to Ocean Bend to try and save Tas." Tears welled in Cora's eyes. "I didn't know Beth knew anything about Pouraka."

Radcliffe remained unyielding. "Beth watched Kaile while he bathed in the pool."

Cora struggled for the breath that Radcliffe's words were taking from her.

"No one is quite sure why Kaile splashed magic water on his face only. He was in human form. Those of us who watched did so from afar. Granted, he had that right. What he did after that was sacrilege, though, Cora. Kaile took water from the magic pool and sprinkled it on this woman. Beth. Our sacred water tainted by a human. There is no worse abomination than that."

Cora boiled inside from shame and embarrassment.

"What Kaile did is none of Cora's doing." Tas defended her, though she could tell his fortitude had weakened after hearing the story of her kissing Kaile.

Radcliff ignored Tas, touched Cora's chin and gazed into her eyes. "You're my cousin. My father's brother's daughter. I would not have thought it possible that you could betray our secret. The very first day you allowed yourself to be seen by humans on the beach I worried about the repercussions. You continued to go to their village and let your identity be known to the entire town. You and Kaile. Tas mingled with them too, but Tas is not of our clan. He's a stranger to our traditions. He's not at fault. You are. Every time you transformed from mermaid to human in our sacred pool, did you ever wonder why none of us followed your example? Didn't you ever consider why we stayed in the shadows? You leave us no choice, Cora. Pouraka has been violated. It's tainted now. Our magic waters will never be the same. Pouraka will never bring us back the life as we knew it."

Cora pulled away from Tas. Surely there was a crevice nearby in which to curl up and die alone away from these condemning eyes.

With a quick tug Tas brought her back to his side.

"Cora saved my life, Radcliff. Leave her alone. If she hadn't sacrificed for me, I'd be in a prison tank, or on a ship to another land to do who knows what. We'll clear up any miscommunication about this human invasion into Pouraka through peaceful talks. I'm sure whatever involvement Cora had in this will be justified. We honestly don't have time to be fighting amongst ourselves. We're in grave danger and not because of anything Cora or Kaile have done."

Radcliff straightened. "What additional danger are you talking about?"

"Men. There are two boats headed this way that are going to be rounding up our pod with the intention of capture and slaughter. Even the people at Barnacle Bay are in danger because of us. Kaile was assaulted by the same men that captured me. I doubt Kaile has any ill intentions against Pouraka."

Radcliff eyed Cora before he moved toward the congregation of merpeople. Someone in the shadows began to hum again and others joined in.

"Radcliff, wait! Listen to me!" Tas spoke angrily but it didn't seem to persuade Radcliff. "What are you doing? What is this song you're chanting? You're calling on magic?" Tas gestured to the crowd. "For what purpose?"

"Can you think of a better way to protect ourselves? We have no other choice, Tas. You know that. I suggest you join us. I suggest Cora join us. If what you say is true then our storm will be even more beneficial."

With that Radcliff took the chorus to another level, louder and in a higher key. He held his arms up and threw his head back. Other mermen came forward in harmony with Radcliff's intonation.

"Tas!" Cora cried out over the song. "What does he mean? What are they doing? This isn't what I think it is, is it?"

Tas had no reaction that she could read, not to her protest, nor to the siren song. He swam to the door, still holding her hand, took a look at everyone in the room and then pulled her outside. When they found a sheltered ledge on the exterior of the sunken vessel, Tas let go of her hand.

"Tas, I can explain everything."

"Can you?"

She was stunned by the wrath in his eyes.

"I am indebted to you for saving my life, Cora. But I'm also confused. How do you think I feel when the woman I love shows devotion to me, risks her life for me, and yet when I'm not around, she kisses another man?"

"Tas, please let me explain."

He gave her the opportunity to explain yet the droning of the sirens confused her thoughts.

"I don't know who those people were who followed us into Pouraka. The only way I could think of to distract them from touching the pools was to...well...to kiss Kaile. A dumb idea, I know. It was the only thing that made any sense at the time."

Tas stared at her. His face reddened even more.

"Tas!"

"Really? You expect me to believe that?"

"Do you honestly think I have feelings for Kaile? After walking all the way to Ocean Bend by myself in the dark with nothing but a basket of water on my back? Do you think it was easy contending with Tom and his thugs for your sake? You think that I am not sincerely devoted to you?"

He bowed his head.

"Not to mention willing to sacrifice my freedom for you?"

"I'm sorry, Cora. It hurt that Radcliff had to make a public denouncement like that. And it frightens me that you might not be included in what's happening here." He nodded toward the door, indicating the sound that now shook the very ledge they sat on. "Kaile's not in there, you noticed?"

"I noticed."

"You know what that means, don't you?"

Cora watched the motion of the door as it swayed to and fro. One hinge had already broken apart since they arrived. Bits of shell and seaweed soared by, spiraling in an increasingly agitated current.

"They're calling on magic?"

Tas didn't answer. He didn't have to.

"An incantation? Are they going to...?" She didn't want to say it. If the merpeople were going to change as a whole, she'd have to make a choice. She'd have to go with them, or move to land because if she stayed behind as a mermaid, the dolphins would die. She'd destroy any hope of survival for any of them.

Tears welled in her eyes and she met Tas' stare, his expression full of worry.

The song grew to such deafening volume that Cora plugged her ears. When she did, Tas moved away from her and joined with the singers, meeting the host of merpeople at the swinging door, and taking the lead with Radcliff.

"No." Cora mouthed but her words were powerless. No one listened to her.

The ocean swelled. Inside the broken ship the water rumbled. The sides of the sunken boat swayed, barnacles were loosed from rocks, sea stars floated from the ledges. Man-made objects that had been buried for a hundred years rolled from their graves.

Cora still curled in the shadows and watched as her people schooled past, with Tas now well out of sight. Her friends scrutinized at her as they drifted by. Their faces were tear-filled; some were as wide-eyed and anxious as she. Peara paused and reached out her hand. Cora bit her lip and shook her head, but because her friend waited, Cora uncurled and floated slowly out where Peara could reach her. Immediately Peara wrapped her arm around Cora and the two fell into formation with the others. The merpeople left the sunken ship taking their song and the ocean swells with them.

Once out in the open, the clan moved faster as the waves that had been created by their voices rushed them forward. Cora was swept along with the school. Shimmering bodies flashed through the sea as brilliant as lightning in a dark and terrible storm. Above them the ocean surged, rumbled and foamed. Underwater funnels snaked along ahead of them, tornados stirring up silt and shells.

The tides rushed them far up the coast where Cora could see the bottoms of Tom's boats bouncing. She heard the angry engines ripping through the storm, recoiling wildly on the swells. First the large black hull of the Dunnabar and then another smaller and faster boat. Propellers whirled through the water, spitting bubbles as the beat of the breakers pounded on the hulls.

To her dread, ahead of Tom's vessels were the dolphins spinning frantically in the waves, racing for their lives. Cora's heart broke. The creatures were terrified. The men in the boats made a horrible racket, beating on drums above the water, confusing their prey in an attempt to drive them to their bloody deaths. The dolphins cried out in panic, their screams deafening.

Fueled by the moans of the dolphins, the school of merpeople quickened. Coming from behind the pod, Tas and Radcliff whistled so loudly the sound broke over the noise. Several dolphins turned. When the mermen whistled again the pod slowed and circled. Another shrill whistle and the mermen dove opposite the direction of Tom's boats. Mertails flashed silver, catching the pod's attention. In an instant, the dolphins followed.

With somersaults and spins, Tas and Radcliff piloted both the mers and the dolphins to agitate the waters into an enormous and violent wave.

Above Cora, the hulls of the boats thrashed against the surf. Powerless against the mighty tempest, one final crash and the larger vessel broke apart. Fragments of hull, deck, and cabin splintered into pieces and dropped into the sea around her. Men screamed as their bodies tumbled through the surge, tossed with the remnants of their craft. Cora saw Tom hit the water in a cloud of bubbles and then the storm swept him away. Remnants of the Dunnabar tumbled to the bottom of the sea

The dolphin run was over.

Cora was swept along, the force of the tide so great she could not have avoided the phenomenon if she wanted to. When the wave was fully formed, the song at its greatest crescendo, dolphin pod and merpeople were carried in one final sweep to Pouraka.

40. Come home

Kaile slipped from the Sea Quest and wrapped the bowline around the cleat on the dock at Barnacle Bay, while Beth and Leni tossed buoys over the side.

"You make sure those lines are secured nice and tight," Leni called to Kaile over the pounding rain as he secured the cabin door.

Water poured from the hood of Kaile's poncho onto his nose and down his chin. He wiped his face with his hand, and then checked the loop, giving the line an extra tug.

"Tom's boats are still out there!" Beth's voice was hardly audible over the sound of the violent downpour. Leni waved a gesture of disgust.

"They aren't going to drive any dolphins today. They'll be lucky to keep their boats afloat. Come on, let's go home and get dry."

"Are you sure about that?" Kaile asked as Leni gave Beth a hand onto the dock. The Dunnabar was clearly tossing in the storm, and Tom's motorboat disappeared sporadically into a surge.

"Would you want to be out there in this storm?" Leni asked.

Ever since they dropped Jesse off at the marina in Ocean Bend, the weather had become increasingly turbulent. Wet and cold from the long and rocky haul, Kaile looked forward to a hot shower and a warm cup of cocoa.

Whatever Tom was doing in this weather would be his own demise. Kaile wiped his nose and pushed away the hair that dripped over his eyes. He trailed behind Leni and Beth, glancing over his shoulder at the torrential rain pounding on the sea. The dolphin hunters didn't appear to be quitting, but he'd trust Leni on this one. A clap of thunder and a bolt of lightning caught him off guard. He hunched over, rain pounding on his back, and ran to the end of the pier where Leni's truck waited.

Though the ride from the wharf to Barnacle Bay was less than a mile, Leni drove slowly, avoiding the puddles that flooded the streets. The wipers on the old pickup barely kept up with the battering rain and Leni had to clear the steam on the inside of the windshield with his sleeve. Once they pulled into the driveway Kaile was the first one out of the truck. He gave Beth a hand and escorted her to the porch where Jamie greeted them, pushing her umbrella open.

"Leaving so soon?" Beth asked.

"Sasha's gone."

"What?"

"The storm came up so fast. She was playing outside and I didn't realize it was raining until I heard thunder. I called for her, searched the yard, the neighbors. No one has seen her since it started raining."

"Jamie!" Beth gasped.

"Where would she go in a storm?" Kaile directed his question to Beth as he stomped the mud off his shoes.

"I'll check at the Deli." Leni hopped in his truck again and started the engine, mud spinning from his tires as he drove off.

"I've been looking, believe me, Beth. I decided I'd better put my boots on, grab a coat and get my umbrella. My clothes are soaked. Five minutes in this torrent and you could drown. I was headed for Paulette's. Her dog had puppies and Sasha was asking about them." Jamie opened her umbrella. "I'm really sorry about this, Beth. One minute she was there and the next minute poof! We'll find her."

Kaile and Beth exchanged glances. Odd, but he swore they were both thinking the same thing. Neither one of them said a word, but after Jamie left, the two jogged down the alley and crossed the highway.

"Sasha!" Beth called, but Kaile had doubts the girl could hear in the storm and they'd be much less likely to hear her answer. The trail to Pouraka was no longer mud, but a creek rushing down the hillside, so Kaile walked in the grass to keep his shoes from getting drenched. He jumped at the next clap of thunder. Lightning flashed directly overhead.

"If Sasha is running around in this weather she's probably terrified." Beth closed the collar of her jacket and fastened it around her neck.

Dark clouds hovered over the coast. Rain and surf roared in unison as water covered the shore, spitting salty foam over the guardrail. If the water was raging that hard on the beach, it would be flooding the cavern. If Sasha had gone there exploring she could very well be trapped. Ignoring the slippery hillside, Kaile broke into a run.

"Kaile, wait!"

Kaile slipped, skidded in the mud and bruised his knee on a rock. Beth plodded up the hill behind him, her drenched hair peeking out from the hood of her coat, her eyes were red and rain dripped from her nose. Mud caked her jeans cuffs and she shivered. Kaile managed to get up before she reached him and he laughed nervously at his own clumsiness. When their eyes met, the expression on her face broke his heart. She was terrified. He had to find Sasha and he hoped beyond all hope that she wasn't in Pouraka.

"Beth, you should go home and get out of this weather. Let me climb down into the cavern alone. It'll be treacherous in there. The rocks will be slippery, and the cave may well be filled with water."

Beth paled. Whether she had considered the dangers that an ocean cave like Pouraka could present, he didn't know. He hadn't. Merpeople didn't think about what happened on shore during a storm, either.

"Go home, and wonder if either of you are coming back? I can't, Kaile. I'll wait up here."

Kaile's teeth clattered and so did hers as they stared at each other wondering what to do.

"I'll wait for you. I doubt I could make it down the ledge, I'm shaking so much. Besides, it's not right for a human to be in Pouraka. Call me superstitious, but I don't think going down there would be a good idea."

It was a rotten place to leave her, though. On top of a hill in a thunderstorm. Kaile took his poncho off and slipped it over her head. "Is that better?"

She nodded. "If it gets too freaky, I'll go home."

Kaile scrambled to the crest of the knoll where the grass met the black rocks of the cavern. With a deep breath, he took the first step down the ledge. Indeed, it was slick.

"Be careful," she said.

Never had Kaile descended this ridge so slowly. Never had he been in such a storm in the form of a man. The rain, the mud, the thunder and lightning were new experiences for him. Merpeople hid in underwater caves and crevices during bad weather so they weren't aware of what happened in man's world when a tempest brewed.

As Kaile lowered himself into Pouraka he was surprised by how calm it was inside the cavern. Though the step-way was wet, and rain still dropped down through the mouth, he could see the pools quite vividly, turquoise as always. He had suspected the surge would have filled the cave here, but it hadn't.

He heard the soft melodic voice of a child and as he stepped out of the rain he saw Sasha near the Cradle. Who she was talking to he couldn't tell but something in the little girl's voice compelled him to listen.

"Please come back to your home. We aren't going to hurt you. We didn't mean anything by being here and I promise you just let me see you once and I will never ask to see you again."

When he first saw her, Kaile wanted to grab Sasha and carry her up out of this dangerous cave, out of the rain, and back to her home. But if he had he would have interrupted something he knew was very important to her. He waited and watched.

"Oh my goodness! How beautiful you are!"

Kaile saw her too, one of the kindermers. He recognized her lovely red hair, but wasn't sure of her name. She swam in the shallows and behind her were other kindermers. Kaile smiled at the way Sasha's sandy curls bounced when she jumped up and clapped her hands and giggled. "Oh thank you! Thank you for letting me see you! Thank you for letting me into your world!"

The hand clapping may have scared them, or the sounds coming from the tunnel. The kindermers scattered suddenly.

The sound of many voices entered the cavern like the whistle of a tornado. Kaile knew those voices, and he knew that incantation. He rushed for Sasha as the chant increased in volume. A loud whistle was accompanied with a rushing thunder. Sea spray and foam flew in his face, blinding him. He stumbled, no longer able to see Sasha. The wave crashed into Pouraka and slammed into its beach.

Sasha's scream ended abruptly.

41. Cleansed

The wave came to the crown of its fury, its journey's end. Cora surfed in formation with the other mermaids, rising with the curl of the surf, viewing the sky, the cliffs, and the rocks.

When the tsunami met the cavern, the surf triumphed with raging force. Sea and rock collided. Cora spun as the ocean released its wrath. Angry rolls of salty brine, foam, and kelp gushed through the tunnel. Pillars of salt water splashed up and out of the skylight and rained down again in a torrent. The waters shook viciously at first and finally settled to a gentle rock, releasing the merpeople and the dolphins from its pull.

The end had come.

As the waters calmed, the Mers congregated in the hollow, exhausted. At last they were home. The dolphins that had battled the surge with the merpeople now coasted around them offering their thanks. Cora lingered in deeper waters. She shook her hair from her face and pinched the salt from her eyes. Laughter and conversation echoed in the cave, but something in the shadows distracted Cora from the celebration.

A man was in Pouraka! A human frantically swam toward the stairs that were now submerged. When he reached a dry ledge he lifted something out of the water and rested the object against his chest. He was so insignificant compared to what was happening in the pools that no one else seemed to see him. Cora watched as he leaned over his burden and when he looked up, she recognized him.

Kaile. Wet and worn and so human-looking, as he wept over the bundle on his lap, leaning over again and again to touch his face to it. When he raised the bundle to his shoulder Cora realized it was a child. When she saw the petite figure, pale and limp, her heart stopped. The bundle was Beth's little sister, Sasha.

"No!" She cried out and would have raced to the two but the cave was crowded with mers and dolphins and fish that had been washed along with them. There was no passage up to the niche where he sat.

"Cora!" Tas called. With his chin above the water he waved for her to join him. He too was beyond reach, though. The music began anew. Tas sang with the others. The waters churned, agitated again by the incantation, this time rolling the sea back away from the rocks until the turquoise Cradle lay open and bubbling. Cora was sucked away from the pool by the receding tide among the crowd of other mers.

Peara startled Cora when she took her arm and coaxed her even farther into the tunnel.

"The men are going first," she whispered. "One at a time. We'll follow after."

"What? Go where?"

Peara didn't answer.

"Go where, Peara?"

There was a subtle smile on her friend's face. "Home. Where we belong," she said.

"Home?"

Peara nodded toward the dolphins.

"No!" Cora gasped. This can't be happening. "Didn't we save the dolphins without changing? Aren't things better now? We're already home."

"Cora, we've made the choice. Mers are of one mind. I've gotten over my fear. You should too."

With her pulse racing and feeling lightheaded, Cora pushed away from Peara toward the ocean, away from Pouraka, away from the pools that were swallowing her friends. As hard as she struggled, she got nowhere, lost in a tide of sparkling fins and swirling hair all pushing her back toward the cavern while that resounding incantation rang in her ears.

The music grew in intensity. Even the mermaids that surrounded her moved in rhythm. Their voices rang in harmony together as they parted to make way for the mermen's procession.

No one hesitated as one by one the men lifted themselves onto the ledge with the rise of the surf and dove into the pool. The song continued. One by one they lay in the water as spray broke over them, transforming their shiny scales to dark grey flesh. And one by faithful one the dolphins spun from the Cradle and splashed into the stirring sea.

Cora watched, aghast. She should have expected this.

Radcliff had, after all, affirmed that the merpeople had only one resolution for Pouraka's troubles.

Still this ceremony was so final, so eternal, so encompassing. Today was the end of merdom and she too would have to decide how she wanted to live the rest of her life. Kaile still trembled near the stairs holding on to the lifeless body, observing the throng from the shadows with Sasha next to his chest. Dolphin after dolphin jumped from the Cradle into the sea. So many mermen were gone now as the dolphin pod grew larger in number. Cora counted them. Twenty-two already.

Before the next merman slipped into the pool, Kaile waded through the flood into the light. His arms were wrapped tightly around Sasha. He made no qualms about being seen.

So surprised were the singers that the music ceased and an odd silence penetrated the cave. Kaile's gaze found Tas in the assembly, and then Cora.

Ritual dictated that no human should ever touch Pouraka's pools. Contamination was forbidden. Yet Kaile marched to the Cradle's edge, stepped into the water and submerged the drowned child.

Boldly, daring anyone to stop him. time stood still. The entire congregation watched as Kaile blatantly defied tradition. His face reddened with compassion as he gazed on the child's face. He lifted Sasha out of the water and held her, his hands cradled her head, and he kissed her.

Cora swore she saw the child move. He glared at the throng before he left the pool and walked to the stairwell. When he turned back around, Sasha stirred. She wiped her eyes with both of her hands and then met the stare of all the merpeople in Pouraka. She pointed at them. "Oh! Uncle Kaile. How beautiful!" She coughed. Kaile patted her gently on the back.

Someone started singing again and the others joined in. Oddly the song sounded triumphant as if the miracle they had witnessed meant more than a child's life, but rather a renewal of all their lives.

If Sasha were to have seen the merpeople transform into dolphins, her little heart would have been broken. She would have been terrified. Cora had been horrified the first time she witnessed the ceremony. Kaile was sensitive enough to know the trauma that a changing could have on the little human girl, so he let Sasha enjoy a moment in Pouraka, but no longer. In that moment Kaile had given fulfillment to Sasha's dream of seeing the mermaids. A moment was enough.

Kaile walked to the stairway and peered back at the merpeople one last time. If he felt remorse for leaving the clan it didn't show on his face. There was a sureness in Kaile's countenance the moment before he ascended into the world of man. He had chosen.

The merpeople delayed their ceremony until Kaile had carried the child up the stairway. Cora's heart broke a little when he disappeared. She wiped the tears from her eyes. In a way he had been a brother, and Sasha, a little sister. Farewells are difficult the moment before eternity.

She could follow him if she really wanted to. She still had time to make that choice.

The chant resumed and that's when reality robbed her peace. Tas slid into the pool.

Cora struggled for breath as her pulse raced and faintness returned. This was her most dreaded fear. Every day of her life since she had fallen in love with him, Cora had struggled with the notion that Tas might decide to change. The constant pull of his desires against hers was the only cause of friction in their relationship. That's why they had argued so much. She bit her lip as he lowered himself into the pool, too horrified to even watch. Tas stood in the Cradle while the merpeople chanted their incantation. The sea stirred and Cora willed with all her might that the magic would stop working. Witnessing her beautiful Tas turn into a dolphin was her worse fear. But here he was, right in front of her, crushing every hope for a family and a happy life. Her insides screamed.

Before he lowered himself their gazes locked onto one another's and Cora refused to let go. She refused to let her heart release him. His eyes spoke of love for her, yet they also spoke of doubt, pain, and remorse.

And then it struck her that he wasn't dreading these moments because of his decision. He anguished because of her. She was the cause of his pain. Never once had she indicated to Tas that she would join him in his new life.

Tas stood there, alone, despondent. For all he knew, this would be the end of their love and that alone tore her heart into shreds. Tears rolled down her cheeks. Now, not so much because Tas was going to dive into the pool but because he was convinced that she wouldn't.

"No, Tas," she cried out. His final transformation couldn't happen this way, not after all they'd been through. Not after the love and devotion they had shared or the sacrifice they had offered to each other. She pushed past the mermaids that massed together in front of her. She snaked through the mermen that congregated in formation below the ledge.

"Tas! Wait!" Cora cried out to him. He turned again, this time in surprise. She pulled herself onto the ledge of the Cradle and slid into the water. "If there's an ocean calling for you then there's a sea calling for me." She took his hands, the warmth of his palms satisfying. "I've already felt the emptiness of living without you. I couldn't live in that void."

"Nor could I," he echoed. Tas took her head in his hands, leaned over and gave her the last kiss she would ever receive from him. She would never forget how it felt. No matter what form her body took, his kiss would flavor her lips forever. Chants from the merpeople filled the cave and with it the grey ocean. Cora held Tas and he wrapped his arms around her. She closed her eyes and together they went under the water.

Her body tingled next to his. Foaming sea water crashed over her. Grayness fizzled into a world of color, greens and purples and blues, sparkling with light. Instead of the hues that had embellished her scales, those were the colors she could see with, the colors of her world shimmering and beautiful. Tas released her but his body stayed near to hers. She sensed his heartbeat and his warmth.

Never had she felt so exuberant.

Their joy quaked the pool. She heard him laugh and she laughed; and with that laughter she found herself spinning energetically, like the spinner dolphins that played in the sunlight off the shore of Barnacle Bay. Her body rotated wildly until she spun out of the pool, Tas spinning alongside of her. They splashed out of the cradle and into the shallows where the pod waited for them.

When all the mermaids joined them and only dolphins lingered in Pouraka, the pod swam through the tunnel and out to sea.

Cora whirled with the others, laughing, catching glimpses of the sunlight that sparkled on the ocean as they broke the surface and swam west.

The pod stopped. Suspended in the salty ocean, they turned around, their noses faced east, toward Pouraka. The whole world paused with them. Clouds crept in front of the sun, darkening the sky, deepening it to purple until it seemed as night. The water turned cold and still. Even the wind fell silent.

Cora felt herself being pulled. First gently, and then there was no mistaking the current that forced the pod backwards, west in the direction of the horizon. The sucking pull ceased when a giant surge lifted her higher than she ever felt the ocean swell, a valley of water between her and the shore. It lowered her gently. She watched the wave move on as it rumbled east, gaining momentum as it traveled, rolling faster and faster toward land.

When it hit Pouraka, the sound of the impact rumbled through the water like thunder. The earth shook. Rocks spewed into the air atop the salty spray, falling in pellets and splashing back. Again and again, boulders crashed from the shoreline into the sea.

Amid the ocean's newfound fury, the sky let loose. Lightning struck, cracking into the cliffs. Rocks fell and slammed against each other. Mud slid from the crest of the hill. Rain and sleet poured so heavily from the heavens and bounced on the salty surface of the sea that any sight of Pouraka's remains were blotted from her vision.

Cora watched in silence. The memory of the hill she once stood on faded as her dolphin vision grew stronger. Tas nudged her and she turned. The pod moved west again together, diving deep and swimming far away from the troubled coastline.

Epilogue

A year had gone by since Pouraka had caved in, destroyed during the worst storm on record for the northwestern shore of Talbatha Island. Kaile tried not to think about the cavern that had once been his home; the memories were still painful. But he never once regretted his decision to remain human. He married Beth that year and Leni hired him as a fisherman. Someday, Leni promised, Kaile would have a boat of his own. Kaile swore he would do whatever he could to protect the coastline and its inhabitants.

No one had ever told Sasha what happened to Cora or the other mermaids after Pouraka caved in, though often Sasha would talk about merpeople and dolphins in the same sentence. Kaile had a suspicion that she remembered seeing more in the cave on that stormy day than she admitted.

One summer evening the three took a walk up the grassy hill to their favorite hillside.

"Careful, Sasha. Don't go near the edge."

"I won't," the girl answered, and in obedience, slowed her steps. "I simply want to see the sunset."

"You have time." Kaile took Beth's hand and squeezed it tight, grateful for their new life together.

"One year ago today," Beth said.

"It's been a long year." Kaile sighed and viewed Sasha's silhouette against the setting sun as the little girl sat down on the grass above what was once the mouth of the magical cavern. It was now nothing more than the remnants of a landslide, a concave, broken cliff eroded by pounding waves during high tide, and a new trail to lively tide pools during low.

Kaile fell on the ground between Sasha and Beth. The spray from the ocean still had the same fragrance here. Perhaps it was the scent of the wildflowers mingling with the sea air that reminded him of Pouraka. Whatever reason, Kaile would never lose the nostalgia he felt while sitting on this hill watching the sunset.

Sasha chewed on a blade of grass and smiled at him. The gold of the sunset shone in her eyes, dissipating any homesickness still churning in his gut. She made his decision worth it. Pouraka had saved her life, and to him that alone made up for the cavern's destruction.

The sun sank lower and sent them a chilling breeze. Beth moved closer and Kaile wrapped an arm around her.

The pinks and golds that shimmered on the ocean were mesmerizing. Kaile gazed in quietude.

"Umm..." Sasha began as she drew in her breath. Kaile anticipated a mermaid question would be coming.

"Yes?" This was the time of day for her to ask. He lay back in the grass, waiting for the inquisition with a smile on his face.

"I was wondering why so many colors glitter on the ocean at sunset," Sasha blurted.

Surprised with that inquiry, Kaile wondered how to answer her. When no one spoke, Sasha glanced over her shoulder at him.

"Okay. Let me try." Kaile said. "The sky turns color at sunset. And a big body of water like the ocean reflects the colors in the sky. So...maybe?" He never claimed to know science, not like Beth did anyway.

Sasha shook her head. "Nope, that's not why."

Kaile gave her a defeated smile.

"It's a bit complicated, but I would say that it's because the ocean scatters the colors from the sun." Beth sat up and tucked a curl behind Sasha's ear.

"Not even close," Sasha argued. Clearly she had her own reasoning in mind.

Kaile chuckled. "Okay, then why do so many colors sparkle on the ocean at sunset?"

Sasha let go of her knees, sat cross-legged and flipped her ponytail back over her shoulders. She sighed, her gaze on the horizon as she paused.

The constant hum of the breakers below, a sea gull's call as it swooped down to the beach to harvest a clam, and the wind as it whispered in the grass were all that broke the stillness.

"I'll tell you since you don't know. At sunset, mermaids turn into dolphins. When they do they scatter all their colorful scales behind them like flower girls tossing rose petals at a wedding, as a final goodbye to the people they love."

Pouraka

I hope you enjoyed Pouraka. Please visit my website often and subscribe to my newsletters for updates to this series, free short stories that go with it, and for more news. Also, please visit Pouraka on Facebook!

Other works by this author

- Sasha: The Secret of Barnacle Bay *Prologue to Pouraka*
- Deception Peak Book I The Ian's Realm Saga
- Dragon Shield Book II The Ian's Realm Saga
- Rubies and Robbers Book III The Ian's Realm Saga
- Diary of a Conjurer Book IV The Ian's Realm Saga
- Cassandra's Castle Book V The Ian's Realm Saga
- Altered

ABOUT THE AUTHOR

With a passion for teens, Dianne Lynn Gardner dives into their world with her young adult fantasy novels. She is both a best-selling author and an award winning illustrator who lives in the Pacific Northwest, USA. Mother of seven and grandmother of 16, Dianne wants to make sure that the teens she knows have wholesome and healthy books that ignite imaginations, strengthen friendships, spur courage and applaud honor. Though she targets her stories for young adults, her books are enjoyed by all ages.